Pr

LENORA BELL

"Lenora Bell is a true delight to read."
Lorraine Heath, *New York Times*
bestselling author

"A debut that reads like an instant classic.
Message to my readers: You'll love Lenora
Bell!"

Eloisa James, *New York Times*
bestselling author

"Trust me . . . you've been waiting for Lenora
Bell."

Sophie Jordan, *New York Times*
bestselling author

"Fresh, flirty, and fabulous! Lenora Bell is
the new Belle of Historical Romance!"
Kerrelyn Sparks, *New York Times*
bestselling author

By Lenora Bell

IF I ONLY HAD A DUKE
HOW THE DUKE WAS WON

Coming Soon

BLAME IT ON THE DUKE

LENORA BELL

If I Only Had a Duke

⊡ The Disgraceful Dukes ⊡

AVONBOOKS

An Imprint of HarperCollinsPublishers

IF I ONLY HAD A DUKE. Copyright © 2016 by Lenora Bell. All rights reserved. Printed in the United States of America. No part of this book may be used or reproduced in any manner whatsoever without written permission except in the case of brief quotations embodied in critical articles and reviews. For information, address HarperCollins Publishers, 195 Broadway, New York, NY 10007.

First Avon Books mass market printing: September 2016

ISBN 978-0-06-239774-4

Avon Trademark Reg. U.S. Pat. Off. and in Other Countries, Marca Registrada, Hecho en U.S.A.
Avon, Avon Books, and the Avon logo are trademarks of HarperCollins Publishers.
HarperCollins® is a registered trademark of HarperCollins Publishers.

16 17 18 19 20 QGM 10 9 8 7 6 5 4 3 2 1

For all the girls who doubt themselves.
Let your light shine.

Acknowledgments

Everlasting thanks to Amanda Bergeron, Alexandra Machinist, Elle Keck, Pam Jaffee, Jessie Edwards, Angela Craft, and Tom Egner for their expert guidance and assistance. Huge love to my husband, family, and friends for riding the roller coaster and holding my hand.

I'm so grateful for the generous support and mentorship from so many of my writing idols, especially: Sarah MacLean, Eloisa James, Lorraine Heath, Kerrelyn Sparks, Sophie Jordan, Meredith Duran, Courtney Milan, Tessa Dare, Meljean Brook, and Eva Devon. The 2014 GH Dreamweaver community of writers inspires and uplifts me every day.

To the booksellers, librarians, reviewers, bloggers, critique groups, and, most of all, the readers . . . thank you for being passionate about romance!

Prologue

County Cork, Ireland, 1818

Dear Duke of Osborne,

I hope you will forgive my impertinence in writing to you without a formal introduction, as I am temporarily your neighbor. My aunt's Ballybrack Cottage overlooks the park of your Balfry House. Yesterday your housekeeper kindly offered me a tour.

Such a rare collection of old masters you possess! I haven't seen their equal since I toured the museums of Italy. As a student of art I recognized works from the hands of Caravaggio, Raphael, and Titian.

Your housekeeper tells me you haven't visited Ireland in over a decade. I wonder if you can be aware of the significance of your ancestral collection?

In curiosity,
Lady Dorothea Beaumont

London

Dear Lady Dorothea Beaumont,
  Can there be two Lady Dorothea Beaumonts? I find it difficult to believe the lady I'm thinking of would write to me, given her involvement in the strange and scandalous circumstances surrounding my friend the Duke of Harland's marriage last autumn.

In puzzlement,
The Duke of Osborne

County Cork, Ireland

Dear Duke of Osborne,
  I fear there is only one me.
  The events to which you allude are the reason I'm hidden away here in the Irish countryside like your ancient masterpieces.
  I confess that I continued my tour of Balfry only to discover an attic room filled floor to ceiling with mysterious painting-sized parcels. How I longed to unwrap them. Perhaps you would benefit from a catalogue of your collection?
  My services would be gladly rendered.
Lady Dorothea Beaumont

London

Dear Lady Dorothea Beaumont,

His Grace forwarded us your petition concerning the collection of stored artworks at Balfry House. Please be aware that the matter has been assigned a number and will hereafter be known as MCCCXXVIII.

While His Grace makes every attempt to answer such queries swiftly, delay is often unavoidable and usually prolonged.

Your humble servants,
Stallwell and Bafflemore, Solicitors

County Cork, Ireland

Dear Messrs. Stallwell and Bafflemore,

Please inform His Grace that I'm not so easily dissuaded.

I may have unwrapped a portion of one painting and found it to be an important lost work by Artemisia Gentileschi, a female Italian Renaissance artist whose work greatly interests me.

Her Sleeping Venus reposes on turquoise velvet while Cupid fans her with peacock feathers. While she may be a little old for the duke's taste (nearly two hundred) she's a diamond of the first water and deserves to be admired by an adoring public.

I implore His Grace to allow more unveiling.

Lady Dorothea Beaumont

London

Dear Scheherazade,

There will be no unveiling.

My late father was the art collector; not I. Dusty old paintings leave me cold. I'm strictly a connoisseur of the warm and living variety of Venus.

Allow me to assure you that Balfry House, and all its contents, is closed for good reason, and will remain so.

Firmly,
The Duke of Osborne

County Cork, Ireland

Dear Duke,

You cannot be so flint-hearted as to forbid the uncovering of what is quite possibly the finest assemblage of paintings by a female Renaissance artist in the world (yes, there are more lost works by Artemisia in your late father's collection!).

You deny the public, and the student of art, great edification and pleasure.

If you would only come and see the paintings for yourself, your heart could not remain unaffected.

The undeterred,
Lady Dorothea

London, Autumn 1818

Dear Determined Lady,
You seem to be spending quite a lot of time at my house. Should I be charging you rent? I trust you have other pursuits? Cow pastures in which to gambol . . . country squires to enthrall.
If you will forgive me, important and urgent business calls.

The flint-hearted,
Duke of Osborne

County Cork, Ireland, Autumn 1818

Dear Duke,
If by important and urgent business you refer to leaping from the balcony of Mrs. Renwick only to be spied scaling the rose trellis of Mrs. Beckham-Cross the very same evening (I read such a thrilling account in a broadsheet) one wonders if all this leaping about can be good for a gentleman's health?
Allow me to prescribe a peaceful rest in the Irish countryside and a quiet contemplation of seventeenth-century artworks.

The rusticating,
Lady Dorothea

London

Dear Rusticating Lady,
 Please don't trouble yourself. I'm in the prime of vigor, virility, and health. Just ask Mrs. Renwick.

A beast of Town,
The Duke of Osborne

And just how was she supposed to respond to *that?*

Thea dipped her quill into ink.

Dear Duke, she began. But he really wasn't a dear. He was an arrogant rake who ignored a lady's sincere petition.

Thea scrunched the sheet of foolscap into a ball and placed a fresh sheet on her sloped writing desk.

Dear Beastly Duke.

Satisfying, but probably ill advised.

A gentleman thrives upon flattery. There was her mother's voice again. Even after a year of exile in Ireland, Thea hadn't been successful in banishing that imperious internal monologue and its constant instructions.

Find something to praise. Anything. Compliment the sheen of his boots. Commend the bloodlines of his stables. Then ask him a question about himself. Gentlemen never tire of the subject.

Right, then. Flattery. Questions.

Dear Virile Duke, how do you manage to satisfy so many widows when there are only twenty-four hours in one day?

And yet another discarded ball of foolscap hit the basket by her feet.

Thea propped her elbows on her desk and stared out at the window. There was Aunt Emma, a plump figure in a white gauze-draped bonnet, tending her beloved woven basket beehives.

Behind her, the sparkling green waters of Balfry Bay caressed rocky cliffs and beaches strewn with the rosy fossilized algae known as *maërl*, which the local farmers crushed and sprinkled over their fields.

Hundreds of years from now archaeologists would find Thea buried beneath a drift of crumpled paper.

Slow death by inarticulateness.

She was an expert on the subject. Just ask her mother, the Countess of Desmond.

Poor Lady Desmond. She'd had such plans for her daughter. Thea couldn't remember a time when she hadn't known she was meant for Great Things.

A triumphant come out, a dozen marriage proposals to closely follow, selection of the most eligible duke, and a long, unchallenged reign as England's most envied duchess.

The plan even possessed a motto: Propriety. Elegance. Refinement.

A code of conduct formed from the first three letters of the word perfect—because nothing less than perfection would suffice.

Thea conversed in Italian and French by age eleven. Read Ovid in the original Latin epigrams by twelve. Mastered all of Mozart's concertos on the pianoforte by thirteen.

Her dance steps were light, her watercolors captivating, and her posture impeccable.

Mr. Debrett could have consulted her for corrections to his guide to the peerage, as she knew more about each peer's prospects than they did themselves.

While she practiced the proper method of pouring real tea from actual Wedgwood's creamware for her pretend future duke, other children shouted with laughter in the square outside their town house in St. James's.

But Thea was meant for Great Things. Not grass stains.

Her only adventures occurred within the confines of the mythological paintings on the walls of the schoolroom. In those misty, verdant forests dotted with silver pools she wandered—a laughing wood nymph, frolicking with her woodnymph friends, and winning the heart of a handsome Apollo who would never scold her if a drop of tea splashed over a rim.

Of course accomplished, elegant young ladies never rambled in woodlands and *never* held trysts with handsome deities.

In fact, they never stepped outside the house without a lady's maid, two footmen, and a sharpeyed mother.

And so it was that when Thea reached seventeen years of age, the countess finally judged her elegant and refined daughter ready to conquer society.

The countess had made only one slight miscalculation.

Thea had been so cloistered, so sequestered and silent, that she'd never actually conversed with a real live eligible gentleman, let alone a duke.

Her interactions with the male of the species had been limited to brief glimpses of her two brothers who were much older than she and away at school during her childhood. On the rare occasions her father was at home and not out dallying with paramours, his entire conversation consisted of grunts, and quotes from the financial section of the papers.

And the pretend duke at Thea's tea parties had always been portrayed by an old stuffed cloth doll with painted-on eyes.

Not very intimidating, the Duke of Stuffing.

He'd never said a word to fluster her, or made comments so inane as to render her entire education the premise of some monstrous joke.

At her debut, when presented with precisely such inanity from an elderly duke with violet veins webbing his cheeks and absolutely no chin to speak of, Thea opened her mouth to make an elegant, refined reply . . . and nothing emerged.

She was terrified to speak because she might say something wrong.

And if she said something wrong, she wouldn't be perfect.

And if she weren't perfect . . . her life thus far would be rendered meaningless.

At times during that interminable evening, Thea managed monosyllabic responses. Or a high-pitched giggle.

The giggle was simply the worst. It erupted like lava from the volcano of self-sabotage bubbling inside her chest.

To quench the errant giggle, Thea desperately gulped several cups of sugary ratafia punch, which, unfortunately, also erupted . . . all over the gown of a horrified baroness in the lady's retiring room.

Obviously, after a coming out such as that, nothing else went according to schedule.

After two disastrous seasons marred by painfully awkward social interactions, Thea was sent abroad with her grandmother, the formidable, forbidding Dowager Countess of Desmond.

A summer's sojourn amid the dignified British society of Rome and Florence was to have imparted a Continental polish and cured Thea of nervous giggles forever.

Somehow her mother's best-laid plans never quite seemed to work out.

The only polish Thea acquired in Italy came from the waxed marble floors of as many museums and galleries as she could induce her grandmother to visit.

For Thea, the art in Italy was a revelation.

Here she could escape into new worlds, unhampered by her mother's constant rules.

She discovered the female Renaissance painters and fell in love with their fearlessness. She stood in front of Artemisia Gentileschi's *Judith Slaying Holofernes* in a gallery in Florence for a full hour, stunned by the luminous skill and unflinching honesty of the brutal scene.

A woman painted that.

She couldn't have articulated why, but the painting moved her in a profound way. She scoured art history books for a mention of Artemisia, but found only a few lines focused on colorful details of her personal life, with only brief mentions of her skill and oeuvre.

From which Thea determined that this powerful, masterful painter had been overlooked and brushed over simply because she was a woman. Her achievements forgotten. Her talents overshadowed by scandal.

For some reason, this discovery sparked a rebellious thought in Thea's mind.

Perhaps she didn't *want* to marry a duke and immediately bear his chinless progeny and be relegated to the role of ornament and broodmare.

Perhaps she could use all of that education for something more than merely capturing a duke—a husband who would no doubt expect her to remain silent while he betrayed her with every courtesan in London, as her own father had shown her was the expected way of things.

She began to make plans that did not involve propriety, elegance, or refinement. But when she arrived back in London she'd found that any choice in the matter had been stolen from her. There'd been a hasty wedding to arrange.

Her wedding.

To a duke she'd never even met.

Worse still, a duke who'd been won by her nearly identical half sister Charlene, one of her father's many unacknowledged offspring. Which made perfect sense, in a way, because Thea was never going to procure a duke on her own, so her mother had taken matters into her own hands.

Thea knew she never should have gone to the church that day, never should have agreed to marry a stranger.

But the tidal wave of filial obligation had proven too strong. It had swept her into the church and deposited her next to the tall, handsome, and very intimidating Duke of Harland.

Luckily, halfway through the ceremony she'd finally found her courage.

She sent the duke away to find his true love, Charlene, the woman who'd stolen his heart.

In retribution for her honesty, Thea had been exiled to live with her eccentric aunt Emma in a rustic cottage in the south of Ireland to contemplate her errors, repent her rebellion, and return to her senses.

Except that what was meant as a punishment quickly began to feel like the first glimpse of freedom Thea had ever known.

She blossomed in her aunt's nurturing warmth, feeling useful and genuinely happy as she helped research and implement new and more humane methods of beekeeping so that instead of smoking out all the bees, the honey could be removed while leaving most of the colony intact.

And when Thea found the painting by Artemisia in the Duke of Osborne's attic she'd known she was meant to be there to study Artemisia's lost paintings and show the world the extent of her genius and talent.

But the duke stubbornly refused to let Thea unveil more paintings.

It was maddening to know there could even be a self-portrait by Artemisia moldering in his attic, shrouded in linen and forgotten by the world. What harm could it possibly do if she were allowed to unwrap the paintings?

Thea dipped her quill into ink once again, determined to find the right words.

My Lord Duke,

I've been summoned back to London for what is certain to be another failed season. While I can never hope to fulfill my family's expectations, I fully intend to win my campaign to rescue Artemisia's paintings from your attic.

It would truly be a shame if the world, and in particular the governors of the British Institution, remained unaware of these important works.

Sincerely,
Lady Dorothea

Thea dusted the sheet with sand from the tin box on her desk to blot the ink, and folded the paper.

She'd be squarely on the shelf next summer.

All she must do was endure one more disastrous season and secure the duke's permission to study his art collection. And then she could return here to dear old Ballybrack Cottage and dear old Aunt Emma and her bees, where she belonged.

Far from glittering ballrooms.

And far from arrogant dukes.

Chapter 1

London, Spring 1819

Thea had made an error of epic proportions.

A tall, broad-shouldered, duke-sized error.

From the safe distance of her quill and foolscap her courage had been indomitable.

She'd planned to approach the Duke of Osborne at the first ball of the season, scatter his entourage of fluttering females with a quelling stare, and say something brilliantly persuasive and business-like.

Something along the lines of *Your Grace, hiding Artemisia's lost paintings in your attic is akin to General Hutchinson abandoning the Rosetta Stone to Napoleon's forces in Egypt.*

Well, maybe that was a *trifle* dramatic, but it would deliver her point.

Knock over that first ivory domino piece and the rest in the formation always followed. And before she knew it she'd be back in Ireland, free to be imperfect at last.

But that first piece . . .

Of course she'd observed Osborne during her

first two seasons, when he was still the Marquess of Dalton.

But tonight was different.

Tonight she needed something from him.

And he was so large. So very powerful and male.

A lady could feel all that maleness across a cavernous ballroom.

He didn't walk—he strode. He didn't ride—he galloped.

And when he wanted something—it was his for the taking.

He would not be easily toppled.

Even his cravat had a defiant air of carelessness that made the other gentlemen seem garroted by starched linen, while he roamed free.

Candles hissed overhead.

The sugary almond smell of ratafia punch triggered a sloshing of the old familiar panic in her belly, and the weight of the pearls her maid had threaded through her upswept curls sat heavy with the promise of a headache.

"Lady Dorothea, if you please." Lady Desmond snapped her fan shut in front of Thea's nose.

Thea blinked. "Yes, Mother?"

"This constant woolgathering simply won't do. You must at least *try* to appear sufficiently transformed. Must I remind you that this is your final chance to make a good impression?"

No chance of *that*. She was too thoroughly ensconced in the collective mind of the *ton* as Disastrous Dorothea. Which was quite convenient when one wished to remain a wallflower veering into spinster territory.

"Are you listening to me?" Lady Desmond asked, narrowing her pale blue eyes.

"Yes, Mother."

"Now I'm going to leave you on your own soon so the gentlemen won't be . . . *dissuaded* from asking you to dance."

Terrified away from it, more like.

Thea had a bad reputation, but her mother's was atrocious, since half of society suspected the deception to which she'd stooped in her ill-fated attempt to secure a duke for a son-in-law. Although it had never been proven.

"Do try to smile when a gentleman draws near," Lady Desmond urged. "You look as though you're at a funeral."

In a way, she was. The final wake for her mother's dreams . . . and Thea's marital prospects.

To hasten her mother's departure, Thea fastened a bright smile across her face. If she grinned any wider her head would split in half.

"And not one sliver of a giggle tonight, do you hear me? Not one little snort."

"Yes, Mother." Frustration simmered, but Thea refrained from a sharp retort. She needed her mother to leave so that she could find a way to corner the duke. "Of course I hear you. You're standing right next to me."

"Humph," Lady Desmond responded. "And stop staring at the Duke of Osborne. It's most unbecoming."

Thea started guiltily. "I'm not staring at him."

"You're practically salivating, girl." Lady Desmond tapped her fan against her palm. "I'll grant you he's a fine sight, but he's not our target. Foxford will do nicely, I should say." She glanced around the room. "Hasn't arrived yet."

Thea suppressed a shudder. Foxford would *not* do.

Not in a million years.

She'd been dutiful and obedient her entire life. Except for that one time. In the church.

But she had absolutely no intention of marrying a gentleman of her mother's choosing.

The Duke of Osborne now commanded the exact center of Lady Thistlethwaite's ballroom, his long limbs anchored to the marble floor, as if he were a ship's masthead.

Widows in daringly low-cut satin eddied around him like frothing waves, and debutantes glowing with youth and optimism cast blushing glances, while their mamas plotted to entice the duke away from his aversion to marriage.

What had she been thinking? She couldn't march right up to such a notorious rake. Every gaze in the room was fastened upon him.

She'd just have to write him another letter. Yes, that's exactly what she'd do. A nice, safe letter from her desk.

Let's see . . . *Dear Monumental Duke, tonight I didn't speak with you because—*

"Oh, there's Lady Gloucester." The countess peered across the length of her narrow nose.

"I *must* hear the tale of Lady Augusta's marriage. A mere officer. Poor as a church mouse. Can you imagine? I always knew she'd marry beneath her."

Her mother sailed away in search of gossip.

A group of young, beribboned debutantes stared at Thea, giggling and whispering behind their ivory fans. She could just imagine their whispers.

Do you see her? That's Disastrous Dorothea. *Back from exile.*

Really? Let me have a look at her. Why is she so disastrous?

You mean you haven't heard about the jilting?

Thea unclenched her hands and stared up at a copy of Titian's *Perseus and Andromeda* in its gilt frame, awash with stormy gray and flowing scarlet.

If only a fierce demigod would swoop down to rescue Thea from the sea monster of polite society.

Polite? Hardly. Only a thin veneer of civility masked the snide whispers and scrutinizing glances.

Ten years in Ireland wouldn't have been sufficient to make them forget.

She caught sight of the duke disappearing through the glass doors leading to the balcony with Mrs. Renwick on his arm, no doubt headed for an intimate tête-à-*tête*.

Now was her chance to approach him with as few observers as possible.

What's the worst that could happen? He could laugh in her face. Someone could witness her latest humiliation.

They've laughed before. Called you names.

Thea's white slippers tapped across the rose-and-gray patterned marble before she had time to change her mind.

Conversation ebbed and flowed around her.

She kept her head lowered, concentrating on swirling white satin.

When it was absolutely unavoidable, when she could see the heels of the duke's black dress shoes, Thea lifted her eyes.

His back was turned to her. He leaned down to whisper in Mrs. Renwick's perfectly shell-shaped ear.

Dear heavens. From across the ballroom he'd appeared slightly more . . . *manageable.*

He was much, much larger up close.

Monumental.

Thoroughly untoppleable.

This was never going to work. But it was too late to turn back now.

His shoulders stretched far above her head, as wide and tall as an executioner's scaffold.

"Ahem." She cleared her throat in a thoroughly unladylike manner.

He paid her no notice.

She reached up, and then up some more, and tapped his shoulder.

She could have been a fly buzzing around a bull for all the attention she generated.

Mrs. Renwick giggled and swatted the lapel of his black tailcoat with her red silk fan. "You're incorrigible," Thea heard her say.

Thea cleared her throat more loudly this time.

"Your Grace." To Thea's mortification the words emerged as a high-pitched squeak.

He turned.

Good heavens, his eyes were blue. And not a faded blue gray like hers. A ruthless, take-no-prisoners midnight blue.

His forceful gaze held her transfixed. Pinioned to the balcony floor.

Waves of nausea sloshed through her belly.

Had his jaw always been so prominently carved? And that cleft directly in the center of his chin. Had it always been so pronounced?

Dark eyebrows arched.

Thea's palms dampened and her heart raced.

"Ah, there you are, Scheherazade," the duke said with the hint of a smile. "I was wondering when you would make good on your threat."

Not one sliver of a giggle, Thea heard her mother say.

She surreptitiously wiped her palms on her skirts. "Here I am, Your Grace," she said brightly. "And there you are. I'm here . . . and you're . . . well, you're . . . *there* . . ."

She was dithering. Of *course* she was dithering. She hadn't once spoken to a gentleman without turning into a complete and utter ninny.

Mrs. Renwick's violet eyes narrowed. "What sort of threat?"

"Lady Dorothea wishes to rummage about in one of my attics." He didn't sound pleased about it.

Mrs. Renwick closed her fan with a disapproving snap. "Whatever for?"

"To uncover lost paintings," the duke replied.

Thea swallowed.

Right, then. She could do this.

"I never meant to pry into your affairs, Your Grace," she said in a rush, attempting to explain before her nerves got the better of her. "But when I discovered the *Sleeping Venus* in your attic, of all places, I couldn't remain silent. The layers of lapis lazuli Artemisia used to create that particular shade of turquoise must have been very expensive. It was most probably created for a royal patron and is truly a rare example of—"

"Goddesses." A slow, lazy grin quirked up one side of the duke's sensuously molded upper lip. "I'm an admirer of goddesses."

Mrs. Renwick pouted. The duke wasn't paying enough attention to *her* celestial attributes. She swatted him again with her fan. "La, you do say the most outrageous things, Osborne."

The emphasis she placed on the familiar use of the duke's title was clearly meant to serve as a warning to Thea about poaching on other women's territory.

She needn't worry. Thea was no threat.

The duke held out his gloved hand. "Why don't you tell me all about this Venus while we waltz, Lady Dorothea."

What? She hadn't said anything about waltzing.

Mrs. Renwick's gaze turned positively poisonous.

And Thea's hand did a very strange thing. It nestled into the duke's palm.

Because those midnight eyes mesmerized her.

Because that seductive smile was a formidable weapon and she'd been asked to defend Rome against the Visigoths with only a toy sword.

Because the feeling of his large hand cradling hers was more powerful than nerves.

And then, quite suddenly, they were on the dance floor.

He captured her waist, fingers splaying wide, his other hand still engulfing hers.

One swift nod to the orchestra and the first strains of a waltz march spiraled into existence. He swung her in circles until they careened into the center of the floor and the other couples faded into blurs at the edges of her vision like flickering stars in a Michelangelo sky.

It was like waltzing with a windstorm.

The violins sawed faster, forced to skip directly to the Pirouette and then rush straight into the energetic Sauteuse in an attempt to match the duke's punishing tempo.

Orchestras did his bidding.

The entire world danced to his direction. How supremely annoying.

"You're not easily dissuaded, are you, Lady Dorothea?"

"I can't . . . speak . . . if you spin me so fast," she huffed. Which was true, but Thea also needed time to marshal her thoughts to order.

She hadn't expected to make her petition while held in his strong arms.

He slowed his pace, and the violinists breathed sighs of relief.

Thea filled her lungs with air. She wasn't drowned yet. "About those paintings, Your Grace—"

"Yes, tell me more. This Venus . . . is she"—eyelids lowered over dark eyes—"nude?"

Thea blinked. "Uh . . . she has a diaphanous drapery."

"Diaphanous." His hooded gaze flicked down her body, lingering on her bodice. "I like diaphanous."

His hand tightened around hers, pushing her shoulders back until her bosom was almost touching his chest. That almost contact sent awareness tingling through her body.

His wolfish smile told her he knew exactly what effect he had on her.

He danced so well, with such authority. She didn't have to worry about doing anything disastrous. He'd never let her trip over her skirts.

She shivered, feeling out of her depth.

Obviously he wanted her to know he was in control.

And everything inside her wanted to surrender.

Suddenly she wished desperately for the distance of a letter. She wished she had hours to compose the perfect clever response to his scandalous innuendoes.

And she wished most of all that he wouldn't look at her like that. As if she was the only girl in the room.

She mustn't let him distract her. "Will you be serious for one moment, Your Grace? I believe there may be a lost painting in your attic of great importance."

"Oh, come now, you don't care about the art. Let's be honest, shall we?"

"I'm being completely honest. Why else would I have approached you?"

"Why indeed?" The sarcastic edge to the question drew her full attention.

What did he mean by that?

And then it dawned on her. *Of course. How stupid.* He thought this was yet another marriage maneuver.

Thea drew herself up with displeasure. "I assure you, Your Grace, trapping you into marriage is the very last thing on my mind."

Burnished hair glinted in candlelight. His head dipped closer and his nose brushed her cheek. For one mad moment she thought he was going to kiss her, until he changed course and his lips brushed her ear.

"Is that so," he said in a husky whisper.

"Absolutely." She nodded in a businesslike fashion. "I truly believe that if you visit Balfry House and see the paintings for yourself you will realize the significance of your collection."

A shadow stole across his face, leeching the light from his eyes and the curve from his lips. "I'll never see Balfry again, so you can banish that notion from your pretty head."

He thought she had a pretty head? Heat rushed to Thea's cheeks.

"And so you truly have a fixation with the ancient masters? I noticed you staring at that Titian earlier." The duke raised his eyes to the wall. "I never thought it was very good. The kraken's not frightening enough. Snout's too rodentlike."

Thea tried not to smile. "It's not his best work. But I was thinking about the coral Andromeda is standing on. Its significance."

At his quizzical look, she continued. "Medusa's severed head still had the ability to petrify living plants into coral. Poor Medusa. I've always felt a little sorry for her. She had such a terrible reputation."

"Turning men to stone does tend to make a lady unpopular," he teased. "Of course, acknowledging you've read Ovid might have a similar effect."

"Ha! There's nothing wrong with reading Ovid."

"I didn't say there was. Some gentlemen find intelligent ladies quite . . . *stimulating.*"

The way he held her gaze made her heat from the core and melt around the edges like a candle.

His thumb traced circles on the small of her back.

She forgot her mission for one moment.

Forgot every other ball she'd ever attended.

The humiliation. The disasters.

She could have this one waltz.

One perfect waltz.

In the arms of the most handsome man in the room.

And that's when Thea made her second monumental error of the evening.

She closed her eyes . . . and surrendered to the moment.

Such an innocent-looking little lamb.

Only Dalton knew better.

He knew she'd tried to lure his best friend James, the Duke of Harland, into marriage using her half sister Charlene as bait.

It was truly uncanny how much Lady Dorothea resembled Charlene, her father's love child, the one who'd married James and transformed him from an unshaven brute into a nearly respectable member of Parliament, and a doting husband and father.

They had the same roses-and-clotted-cream complexion and golden hair.

Although Lady Dorothea's abundant curls had a bit more copper when one was close enough to see the difference. Orange marmalade on hot buttered scones.

Her eyes were slightly more blue than gray, yet just as wide-set in the same oval face with the same arrow's point of a chin.

She was a tiny thing, the top of her head only reaching Dalton's chin. She made him feel gargantuan and ungainly, as if he might crush the delicate bones of her fingers in his huge paws.

He stroked his thumb across smooth satin over supple flesh, and a deep blush spread from her neck to her face, coalescing into two round, rosy patches high on her cheekbones.

He didn't remember her half sister blushing, but Dalton recognized that maidenly flush and those artfully mussed curls as a carefully constructed façade.

She and her scheming mother had obviously decided Dalton was to be the consolation prize for losing James.

All those letters about his father's paintings. Did she really think he'd fall for that?

She conspired to capture and tame a duke of her own.

Not going to happen.

He never danced with well-bred, unmarried ladies because it gave their mamas hope, and he was a lost cause.

Marriage wasn't in the cards.

What he had to do tonight . . . he'd built his own façade just as carefully, to deflect attention away from his true purpose.

But he couldn't have troublesome wallflowers pursuing him around London, digging up his buried past, so, for this single occasion, he'd been willing to make an exception. Preempt the attack by striking first.

Dance with her.

Make her popular.

And then sit back and enjoy the fireworks, achieving two goals at once.

She'd have no more time to plague him when she was mobbed with suitors.

And the *ton* would be far too busy gossiping about the waltz and its consequences to concern themselves with his exact whereabouts this evening.

She nestled closer and silken curls tickled his chin.

That's right, little lamb, sway into my arms.

She smelled of wild rose petals, feminine and sensual.

If he licked her neck she'd taste creamy, like Madagascar vanilla.

She released a small, breathy sigh that navigated straight to his groin.

Oh, she was good.

But he was better.

"Our dance is nearly over, one and only Lady Dorothea," he whispered.

Thick, black lashes rippled over wide ocean eyes. "So soon?"

"Alas, all good things must end."

The hint of a smile played over her sweetly curved lips. "Must they?"

"I'm afraid so." He kept his voice low and a provocative smile on his lips. He wanted their audience to wonder what endearments he whispered in her ear. "Let me make one thing clear before our waltz ends, my lady."

Watchfulness in her eyes now. A slight tensing of her fine-boned shoulders. "What's that, Your Grace?"

"There will be no more visiting of properties or excavating of attics. I see through your act and I know you're not searching for ancient goddesses. It's a modern-day duke you're after."

She drew a swift breath. "You're entirely mistak—"

"It won't be me," he said abruptly, cutting her protests short. "It won't be me . . . but you'll have your pick of every other eligible peer."

"What . . . what do you mean?" She searched his face with something close to panic in her eyes.

"Look around us. Everyone's watching. The first waltz of the season and I chose you."

Her gaze darted around the room. "No, no. This isn't what I wanted at all." She shook her head and silken curls brushed his jaw.

The music ended. He stepped away.

She hugged her arms against her chest, her eyes flat as etched glass.

He experienced a tiny qualm of something close to guilt. She was a very gifted actress.

"I made you popular." He bowed. "You're welcome."

Cold alertness froze her face. "Nothing can make me popular, Your Grace. Not even *you*."

"Care to place a wager on that?" Dalton was known for his outrageous wagers. The diversion of Lady Dorothea's instant popularity would make excellent fodder for the betting books at White's. Keep all those idle noblemen entertained.

Keep them from suspecting him of being anything other than one of their tribe—a rakehell with too much leisure time and a taste for scandal.

Dalton steered Lady Dorothea back to her mother, Lady Desmond, whom he'd had the distinct displeasure of spending several days with during Harland's bride hunt the previous summer. The countess was as cool and calculating as they came.

"Truly, I'm not after suitors, Your Grace," Lady Dorothea whispered urgently, attempting to slow his progress. "I only wanted to convince you to let me study Artemisia's paintings."

Matrons whispered in huddled knots, gentlemen circled like sharks scenting fresh blood, and young ladies shot envious glances.

"This will ruin *everything*." Her fingers tightened around his arm. "This is . . . this is my idea of *hell*. You must do something to show them you were only toying with me. You can tell your friends you only danced with me because of a wager."

Lady Desmond's light blue eyes blazed with triumph. "Your Grace." She inclined her head regally.

Dalton made a peremptory bow.

He leaned close to Lady Dorothea, steeling himself against the seductive sharp-sweet scent of wild roses.

"Welcome to hell," he whispered.

Chapter 2

The doorway to hell was covered in green baize and always stood at the end of a narrow passage.

Inside, hollow death rattle of dice, scrape of wood raking wool, agonized shouts and keen-edged laughter. The most exclusive club and the lowest hell sounded the same.

There were countless gaming establishments in London. Some folded and others sprang up almost nightly. Dalton knew the location and stakes of every one.

It was his duty to know, as it was his duty to record the names of every patron—aristocrat, churchman, magistrate, or fishmonger—who sought the green door and craved what lay beyond.

As the Duke of Osborne he had access to the exclusive private clubs, where he gambled away his late father's cursed fortune and gathered information in secret.

But tonight he was cloaked in invisibility. Hair dulled with soot. A ragged neck cloth that doubled as a mask if pulled over his chin. Threadbare coat.

He'd learned to hunch his shoulders. Amble with the diffident gait of a dog who'd been kicked as a pup.

If he spoke at all this evening, he'd used the same lilting Irish brogue as his manservant, Conall.

They made a disreputable pair of prowlers, Dalton and Con, lurking in a darkened doorway that commanded an unobstructed view of the Crimson gaming hell in Piccadilly, so they'd be able to see their target, Lord Trent, exit before he saw them.

They waited in silence.

Dalton stamped his feet in the cold air. Winter hadn't quite decided to yield to spring yet.

Con kicked at the doorjamb. "Enjoy yourself at the ball, did you?"

Dalton made a noncommittal noise.

"Saw you dancing with that wisp of a lady. Not your usual sort," Con observed.

No, she wasn't.

Dalton preferred statuesque, worldly widows and disenchanted wives with voluptuous curves made for hard bedding.

Lady Dorothea was petite, innocent, and completely off-limits in the bedding department.

"She's the one who wrote me all those letters about the paintings at Balfry House. The same one who tried to snare Harland. She won't be plaguing me anymore, though."

"And why's that?"

"I very cleverly danced with her in order to make her popular."

Con snorted. "Clever plan, eh? Sure and you didn't just want to have her in your arms?"

"Absolutely not. It *was* a clever plan. She'll be beating away suitors now."

The Duke of Foxford had claimed her for the next dance. The sight of the aged peer touching her had wrenched Dalton's gut with revulsion.

Foxford's grasping fingers were clenched around the throat of some of the most corrupt establishments in London. Gaming hells. Brothels. Gin houses.

Guilt twinged as Dalton remembered the dazed expression on her face as Foxford claimed her hand. She'd appeared genuinely horrified by the stampeding herd of gentlemen.

Not his vexation anymore.

An entry in a betting book, that's all she meant to him now.

The Duke of Osborne wagers five hundred pounds that Lady Dorothea Beaumont will have ten proposals of marriage within the fortnight.

Con's boot thudded against rotting wood. "So you didn't enjoy dancing with the little lady, then?"

The scent of roses and the memory of soft sighs flooded Dalton's mind. "No enjoyment whatsoever," he lied. "A diversion tactic, nothing more."

"Huh." Truly a talent how Con was able to convey such disbelief and sarcasm with just one small syllable. "I used to save my dances for only one girl once upon a time. Not that you've ever asked."

In all the years they'd been employer and employee, Dalton had never once heard Con mention his past. He hadn't wanted to pry. He'd figured there was a reason the older man never spoke of Ireland, or his family there.

Con was . . . *Con*. Always there, like the rain and the wind. The man his father hired to protect him when he was a boy and later, when it became clear Dalton needed no protection, his only man-servant, the only person Dalton trusted.

"Had eyes the color of freshly plowed sod, did Bronagh. Made a man consider becoming an honest farmer. Only one snag. She was promised to my elder brother Seamus." He spat into the street. "Not even the tide would take him out, the cursed bastard."

Dalton couldn't see Con's face clearly in the gloom, but he heard the uncharacteristic jag of emotion. "Is that why you accepted my father's offer to leave Ireland?"

"Had to leave, or I would have killed my own brother and gone to the gallows and left Bronagh completely alone." Con lapsed into silence for several minutes.

Dalton waited. He was good at waiting. Silence made people talk. He'd learned that trick from Con.

"Never did have the chance to say goodbye to brown-eyed Bronagh." Con leaned back against the sidewall, staring across the street at the Crimson. "Heard Seamus died a year back," he muttered.

"You should go home for a visit." Dalton was careful to betray no emotion. He knew it would make Con uncomfortable.

"Ah, *no*." Con tugged at his long gray-and-red-streaked beard. "Bronagh wouldn't see me. Not after all these years. She thinks I abandoned her. Just look at me. Gray hair. Bit of a paunch." He snorted. "I'm not the handsome devil who left her that summer's day, nearly twenty years ago."

That may have been the longest collection of sentences Dalton had ever heard Con piece together. The man was given to laconic profanities, not confessions.

Dalton cocked his head. "I've seen prettier, and that's a fact."

"The point is that you're not getting any younger, either."

"You know I can never marry."

There was always the threat of his secret identity being discovered. If that day came, a wife would become a target.

He jammed a hand through his hair. He had far graver problems on his mind than marriage.

Two young bloods sauntered up the street, inebriated and oblivious to danger. They could have their pockets picked out here on the streets of Piccadilly, or inside the gaming hell. But tonight Dalton couldn't press his steel to their throats, warn them that if they beggared their families they'd not only answer to God, they'd answer to him.

The swells disappeared around the corner where Trent's carriage was waiting. Only a matter of yards, but the coachman couldn't see the entrance, he was huddled in his wool greatcoat, fast asleep.

Most nights, Dalton came to the gaming hells to save men from making mistakes that would devastate their families.

The gaming hell and gambling club owners hated him for it, seeking to unmask him and planting lies about him in the papers.

The penny papers and Grub Street scribblers had dubbed him the Hellhound. Writing fanciful stories of a marauding Irishman, come to London to avenge himself on the noblemen who stole his lands back in Ireland.

The broadsheets got one detail right, at least. He did hunt revenge and exact justice.

Revenge on the man who'd murdered his younger brother, Alec.

And justice for the powerless victims of the hypocrites and fiends who ruled the gambling world.

Pitiless, wealth-obsessed men like his own father, who'd owned a controlling interest in an exclusive gaming club. His father and his partners had ruined countless lives, stealing inheritances, leaving broken lives and destitute families in the wake of their endless thirst for power and wealth.

Alec had been killed to punish their father's sins. He'd been pushed from a stone cliff in Ireland to his death in the ocean after Dalton left him there, unattended for only five minutes, when Dalton was ten and Alec only five.

His mother had been devastated by the death of her favorite son, her Irish Alec, with her auburn hair and leaf-green eyes, while Dalton had the bronze hair and blue-black eyes of her hated husband.

Until he turned eighteen, Dalton had thought his younger brother's death was a tragic accident. That he'd slipped and fallen off that cliff. At Cambridge, Dalton had been the tragic poet, haunted by his brother's fingers slipping from his grasp as he had pulled away.

Go back to the house, Alec. Don't follow me.

Indulging in bad wine and even worse rhyming couplets.

His father put an abrupt end to that, spilling the dark secret one night when he was reeling from drink. *Your brother didn't fall into the bay, so you can stop writing that sentimental rot. Someone pushed him to spite me.*

The words slurred by drink but the meaning clear as a funeral bell's tolling. Then the old duke had shoved a list into Dalton's hands. A list of the names of every corrupt, ruthless man the old duke had ever stolen wealth from, double-crossed, or betrayed.

So many names.

Lord Douglas Trent.

Circled twice.

"Taking his time, Trent," Con muttered. "I'd like to be in bed right about now, with the covers turned up."

"Not going soft on me, are you?"

Con sighed heavily. "I'm getting too old for this."

Dalton had never heard him say that before.

"Burns is the last name on the list, Con. If Trent doesn't know where to find Burns, I won't know where to search next."

Anger boiled inside his chest. Ten years. Ten bloody years hunting the killer, crossing names off the list, and he was no closer than the first day.

Trent had successfully evaded Dalton, never staying in one city long enough to leave a warm trail. Dalton had long since ruled Trent out as the murderer . . . but he was also the only person who might possibly know the identity of the last name on the list: Daniel Burns.

Dalton had been searching for years and still hadn't found a Burns who could have been associated with his father.

"Could be the man's not on your father's list," said Con. "We'll have to hammer at it from a different angle, that's all."

The door to the Crimson opened and Con jerked back into the shadows.

Dalton reacted with practiced fluidity, reaching Trent in a few strides and grabbing him by the collar. The baron fought the neck lock but Dalton pinched the bridge of his nose to close his air supply and dragged him toward the alley behind the club.

Con would keep watch on the mouth of the alley to make sure Dalton was undisturbed.

When it was dark and quiet enough, Dalton pushed Trent face-first against a brick wall, twisting his arm behind his back and holding a knife to the back of his neck.

"Who's Daniel Burns?" he asked without pre-
amble, using the broad Irish brogue he'd learned
from Con.

He'd elicit the information and then decide
what to do with the target. Sometimes he stripped
their pockets of the evening's winnings. Sent the
funds back to the family of the desperate soul
who'd gambled it away.

"Who's asking?" Trent replied.

He attempted to twist free but Dalton held him
easily. "None of your concern. Tell me who Burns
is, or I'll slit your throat, slow like."

"Must be a lot of men named Burns," Trent spat.

Dalton pressed his blade harder, the tip drawing a bead of blood.

"Easy now." Trent stilled. "I used to know a
Daniel Burns. Doorman at a brothel in Cheapside.
Dead as a doornail for five years now. One of the
fancy girls shot him with his own pepperbox.
Flossy was her name. Toothsome little tart."

Over the years, Dalton had learned to recognize
the telltale signs when a man was lying. Trent's
words rang with the details of truth. Doorman?
No wonder Dalton hadn't found him. He'd been
searching for someone powerful and wealthy.

His mind went bleak and cold.

The last name on his father's list. Yet another
dead end.

Only his years of training saved him from
Trent's sudden, powerful maneuver.

The hours spent drilling one thing over and
over: hands up, head down.

Trent's elbow caught his wrist and Dalton's knife clattered to the cobblestones.

A flash of warmth. Wetness on his cheek.

Moonlight glinted on metal. Trent had a knife.

Dalton was cut.

Trent backed away. "That's so I'll know you the next time we meet, Hellhound," he spat.

Dalton planted his back foot and exploded forward, his right hand firing a powerful straight punch.

Trent went down heavily, cracking his head on the cobblestones.

Dalton staggered against the wall, breathing heavily, shaken and wounded.

He hadn't underestimated an opponent like that since he was a young pup just learning the rules of combat.

"That'll leave a scar for sure," Con grunted when he and Dalton were a safe distance away and headed home.

"Would have spurted my life out on the cobblestones if I hadn't dodged. He was aiming for my jugular."

Con's huge hands curled into fists. "I should have gone with you."

"This is my battle."

"I'm your hired guard."

"I hope so, because you're a damned sorry excuse for a valet."

Con gave an amused snort. "Ungrateful gobshite."

Dalton grinned, wincing as pain forked across

his jaw. It was one of their little rituals, the gallows humor that kept Dalton from losing his mind.

They melted into the shadows, knowing which lanes to avoid. Changing the route every time. Keeping the pattern unpredictable.

The beasts among beasts.

Slouching and hugging the dark places.

As he sped toward home, Dalton's thoughts turned to Lady Dorothea asleep in her maiden bed. Tomorrow's penny papers would crown her this season's Incomparable, a butterfly forced from her wallflower chrysalis.

He'd done her a favor.

Widened her prospects.

She deserved far better than the likes of him.

Not for him, the marigold silk of her hair.

The sweet summer scent of roses.

His, the cold that snarled and bit like a cornered wolf. Yawning doorways leading to dark gullets of rooms warm with stale breath and spilled gin and dark as the belly of a whale.

One miscalculation and a knife slid home.

Crawl home like a cur. Use the back stairs.

And try not to bleed on the carpet.

Fate had been very clear about one thing—whether lingering, or in one agonizing blow, love died.

Brothers drowned. Mothers faded into wraiths.

And melting blue-gray eyes couldn't dull his pain any better than a bottle of brandy.

Chapter 3

Nothing can make me popular, Your Grace. Not even you.

Care to place a wager on that, Lady Dorothea?

Thea would have lost that wager. It was the morning after the ball and the Desmond town house was overrun with roses.

Great big bunches of hothouse roses. Pink, white, yellow, they clustered on every surface, crowing gleefully that after four seasons she was an overnight success.

All because of one waltz with an arrogant, manipulative duke.

He'd toyed with her as a lion taunted a lamb, rearranging her life to suit his whims. And she, knock-kneed creature, had succumbed to his velvety caress, heedless of the razor-sharp jaws waiting to rip apart her plans.

If only she'd caused a scene. Tripped over her skirts. Stepped on his toes. Done *something* customarily disastrous.

What followed after the waltz had been a nightmare.

The avaricious gleam in the elderly Duke of

Foxford's eyes when he'd asked her to dance had made Thea's skin prickle with foreboding.

Being a failure had its rewards, one of those being that men never looked at you like that. As if you were displayed in a shop window and they were contemplating making a purchase.

The gloves or the girl.

She was *not* for sale.

The aged peer hadn't given her a chance to demur, pulling her into line so fast she'd had to trot to keep pace. The relentless tide of twenty years of good breeding had been the only thing that swept her with him.

"Where shall I put these, my lady?"

There must be a footman somewhere in the hall. Thea could hear him, but she couldn't see him because of all the dratted flowers.

A lady never swears. Never. Not even blast. Or drat. And certainly not bugger. Or blast.

Blast it all! She didn't want to be a lady anymore. And she didn't want all these tokens of intent to purchase. "Don't put them anywhere, John," she called. "I won't accept them."

A startled, youthful face with raised dark eyebrows appeared from behind an enormous bouquet of yellow roses. "Beg pardon, my lady?"

Thea swiped a hand through the air. "Take them all away." She didn't want the roses and she didn't want the success. Really, the flowers should have been sent to the duke, not to Thea, since her sudden popularity was entirely due to him.

Now there was an idea.

"John, I want you to have every single one of these flower arrangements delivered to the Duke of Osborne's residence. I believe he still lives in his bachelor apartments, and not at Osborne Court."

Ha! That would teach him to make her popular. See how he liked *his* home transformed into a flower market.

"Excuse me, my lady, but did you say the Duke of *Osborne?*" John's voice held the awe all young men reserved for their masculine heroes.

"That's right. These roses were meant for him, not for me."

"Are you quite sure, my lady?"

"Quite. Now I don't want to see a single petal left behind."

"Very good, my lady." John hoisted the yellow roses.

"Wait," Thea cried. "Wait a moment. I'll be right back with a note." She snatched a creamy, gilt-edged card from one of the flower arrangements.

As she hurried toward her chambers she was stopped by the sound of an argument emerging from the parlor.

"Foxford!"

"Marwood!"

"I say Foxford. He has *three* castles." Thea recognized the far-from-dulcet tones of the dowager countess and her heart plummeted into her slippers. That never boded well.

If her grandmother was here the situation was dire indeed. The dowager visited them only in times of great upheaval.

When her elder brother Andrew had nearly gambled away his portion but had been saved from ruination at the last possible moment by a sobering encounter with the mysterious Hellhound character the papers made such a fuss about.

When Thea had thrown away her chance to marry the Duke of Harland by telling him the truth during the wedding ceremony.

Or today.

Because Thea had achieved the unthinkable. She'd finally, *finally* taken.

And it was her worst nightmare.

She'd counted on being a failure. One more lackluster season, an unobtrusive exit back to Ireland, and then blessed, blissful freedom.

The duke had ruined *everything*. Perish his seductive smiles.

Thea poked her head into the parlor. Just as she'd thought. It was a war council with the dowager facing off against her daughter-in-law the countess. The names of potential husbands volleyed back and forth between them like canon blasts at Waterloo.

It didn't bother them a bit that Thea wasn't there to express her opinion.

It had always been like this with her family and with society. Everyone moving in rehearsed, choreographed precision, delivering their lines to perfection, while Thea stood, watching from behind the curtain, unconsulted, ignored.

The dowager wore fine black merino unrelieved by even a hint of color, her dark hair scraped back from her forehead and covered with a black turban finished off with waving black ostrich plumes.

She was flanked by her daughter, Thea's spinster aunt Henrietta, or Hen, the earl's youngest sister.

Thea's father, the Earl of Desmond, sat in a chair by the window, his upper body completely obscured by the *London Times*.

"Foxford," the dowager insisted. "He's the better catch."

Thea's mother shook her head. "He's nearly seventy. He has less than a dozen teeth to his name."

"Who needs teeth with three castles?"

Aunt Hen caught sight of Thea in the doorway. "Oh, hello, dear." She waved and the bow of her white lace cap bobbed against her double chin.

Thea reluctantly entered the room.

"Who would you prefer to marry, my dear?" Aunt Hen's kindly gray eyes scrunched up as she smiled. "The Duke of Foxford or the Marquess of Marwood?"

"Neither," Thea replied.

"Desmond," the dowager countess huffed. "Please impress upon your daughter that she'll marry whom we choose."

Silence from behind the newspaper.

"Desmond!"

The paper rustled and lowered a couple of inches. "Er, what was that, Mother?"

"Tell your daughter she's wrong."

"Lady Dorothea, your grandmother is always right." Desmond flipped the paper back open.

And that's what Thea had always received from her father: casual dismissal.

"Thank you." The dowager pursed her thin lips. "Now then. Back to the subject at hand."

"It's early yet," Thea said. "Many of the other ladies are still at their country seats. I'm merely the novelty of the moment." One could always hope.

"Nonsense. You were selected by the Duke of Osborne for the first waltz of the season. You are thoroughly ensconced as a success. Nothing will dethrone you." The dowager narrowed her eyes. "Do you understand me? Nothing."

"We must give her some credit," Lady Desmond said, with uncustomary softness in her voice. "She was the one who secured the dance with the Osborne."

"One of the only intelligent things she's ever done," the dowager sniffed.

"Excuse me," Thea said. "I'm right here, you know. I can speak for myself."

"Absolutely not." Her grandmother frowned disapprovingly. "Speaking for yourself is what caused Harland to run. Or have you forgotten?"

Lady Desmond tensed on the edge of her seat. She didn't like the Duke of Harland's name spoken in her presence. She was still deeply wounded by the fact that Thea had been so close, so very close, to marrying a duke and had thrown her chance away.

"Wait just a moment." Aunt Hen tilted her head. "Are you telling me that our little Thea danced with Osborne? *The* Osborne? He of the deep blue eyes and delicious cleft chin? He of the thousand broken hearts and impeccably tailored coats?"

And shoulders like a Viking.

And wickedly stroking hands.

"All completely beside the point." The dowager's nostrils flared with annoyance. "Osborne is not the opportunity, merely the catalyst. He's in no hurry to marry; he's made that abundantly clear. He's out of Lady Dorothea's sphere, given her tainted reputation. Who knows *why* he danced with her, but he did. And we must capitalize upon this opportunity immediately."

"Such a shame." Aunt Hen made tsking noises and set her lace bow quivering again. "Handsome dukes are *such* rare creatures. Rather like silvery snow leopards, one imagines." She stared out the window dreamily. "Crouching on remote mountaintops, taunting hunters, and then melting into the brush."

"Stay focused, Henrietta," the dowager admonished.

"Yes, Mother." Aunt Hen folded her hands in her lap dutifully, but she gave Thea a small wink of encouragement.

"As I was saying," the dowager continued, "Osborne is not the opportunity. Foxford, however, would be a splendid match."

"I know you want me to marry well, Grandmother," Thea said, striving to keep her voice even and calm. "However, I very much doubt that will ever happen."

"I mean to personally ensure you make a

brilliant match, my girl. And to that end, you're coming to live with me."

"Pardon?" Thea and her mother cried in unison.

"Henrietta, the schedule, if you please."

Aunt Hen startled. "I know it's here somewhere, Mother. Now where did I put that schedule?" she mused, digging through her reticule. "Ah, here it is!" She held up a wrinkled sheet of foolscap. "Oh dear, it seems to have had a losing encounter with a macaroon." She stared at her mother guiltily.

"Really, Henrietta," the dowager huffed.

"Here you are, dear." Aunt Hen handed the paper to Thea.

"'Breakfast at half past six,'" Thea read aloud. "'Deportment from seven to eight. Modiste from—'"

"You'll see that every second of your day is planned. You'll have no time for disasters," the dowager said briskly. "When you lift a spoon, I'll be there to guide it to your mouth. When you appear in public, I'll be by your side. And when you receive a proposal from Foxford, which you will, I'll be there to witness the triumph and ensure the wedding ceremony reaches completion."

Thea shook her head desperately. "I'm not seventeen anymore, Grandmother. I can manage my own opportunities. And if you'll give me a chance to speak—"

"My mind's made up. And as your father has observed so astutely, I'm always right. Pack your things, Lady Dorothea. Leach will collect you at noon tomorrow."

"I really—"

Raising her voice to stop Thea's objections, the dowager rose from her seat. "No arguments. It's all settled."

Lord Desmond leapt to his feet, finally setting aside his paper. "Leaving so soon, Mother?"

"Humph. And what's there to stay for? I've yet to be served a proper cup of tea in this household."

Lady Desmond flinched but didn't say a word; she merely followed her mother-in-law and her husband out of the room with shoulders held as erect as ever.

Aunt Hen turned back before she reached the door. "Oh, I nearly forgot, dearie." She scooped a parcel from a side table. "I missed your birthday while you were in Ireland. Here you are."

Thea accepted the gift. "How kind of you," she said dully, her mind reeling with the sudden turn of events.

She couldn't go live with her grandmother.

"I hope you like them, dearie. I meant to send them to you in Ireland, for mucking about in all those bogs, but I seem to have forgotten."

"I'm sure I'll love whatever it is."

"Don't look so crestfallen, my dear. It's not as bleak as all that." Aunt Hen chucked her under the chin. "I'm sure Foxford's not long for this earth." She leaned closer, her gray eyes twinkling. "We could brew some arsenic tea," she whispered. "I read about it in a horrid novel. There now, that's better. I wanted to see that smile before I left."

"Henrietta," came a stern call from the front entranceway.

Aunt Hen's hands fluttered. "I must go. Please don't be sad, dear. We only want what's best for you."

Thea caught her aunt's hand. "Are you . . . are you lonely? Do you wish you'd married?"

"Why, what a strange question, dear." Aunt Hen blinked. "I never really think of it. You see I've never been a beauty like you."

Thea clenched her hands into fists. "I won't marry Foxford. Or Marwood."

"Henrietta! I'm not waiting a moment longer," the dowager called loudly, because dowager countesses never shouted.

Aunt Hen planted a kiss in the middle of Thea's forehead and hastened away.

Thea sank into a chair and unwrapped the parcel.

Ruby-red leather winked at her. She drew out a pair of red half boots that laced up with jaunty black string.

Supple, yet sturdy, the rich red leather glowed in the morning sunlight.

Thea glanced up at the Gainsborough landscape hung on the parlor wall with its enticing, curving pathway that led into a dense, twisted forest.

These were boots for walking. Rambling across fields and through forests.

Not for sitting at home, following the rules and waiting to accept an offer of marriage from a man she loathed.

She would *not* marry Foxford, or Marwood, or any other pompous windbag who would keep her on a shelf as a mute and decorative ornament.

She was well and truly tired of being a pawn in other peoples' games.

If a lady could become an overnight success, she could become an overnight failure just as easily.

The Duke of Osborne had inflicted this unwelcome popularity on her—and he was just going to have to remedy the situation.

She hurried upstairs to pen the note for sending with the flowers.

First, her note would arrive.

And Thea would follow.

Pert, pink nipples like little strawberries atop meringue cakes.

Golden curls spread over turquoise velvet.

An oval face with a sharp little chin.

A plump cupid fluttering about overhead waving peacock feathers.

It had been a hard day on Mount Olympus. Dalton had been doing . . . godly stuff. Now he was home, and his Venus was waiting, arms outstretched, smelling of sweet spiced roses.

Smelling very strongly of roses, as a matter of fact.

An odor that was not very dreamlike at all . . .

Dalton's eyes flew open. "What the devil?"

He sat bolt upright. His bedchamber was covered in roses.

Great big bunches of overblown, too-cheerful roses. He rubbed his eyes. What the bleeding hell was going on here?

Con entered the room carrying yet more roses, whistling a cheerful Irish tune. "Look here. Another bunch. They just keep coming," he crowed gleefully.

Dalton stared at Con.

His head hurt. That was the brandy.

His jaw hurt. That was the souvenir from Trent.

Damn it, what time was it? He squinted his eyes at the insouciant sunbeam that had snuck uninvited through his curtains. "Why are there flowers filling my chamber?"

"Well now. Need you ask?" Con grinned and deposited his floral burden on the sideboard. "Obviously you've an admirer."

Must have drunk far too much last night because apparently Dalton was still deep in a drunken stupor. This couldn't really be happening.

Con clutched at his chest, near where his grizzled heart beat. "Finally the day has arrived. The day when that special young lady makes her intentions known." He sighed. "I've been waiting for donkey's years."

"Stubble it, Con," Dalton growled. "I'm not in the mood."

Of course Con ignored him, as he always did. "Ah, she's a bold one, your lady suitor. She knows the road to a duke's heart is paved with a thousand roses." He plucked a fat yellow bloom and threw it at Dalton.

Dalton caught the rose and attempted to throw it back. "Hellfire," he cursed through gritted teeth when his throwing shoulder wouldn't cooperate.

It throbbed like the dickens.

"Just tell me who sent all these," he growled. "So I can murder them."

Con plucked a card from the side of a basket. "'Roses are red. Violets are blue,'" he read. "'Lady Dorothea's lips are as red. And her eyes far more blue.'"

Lady Dorothea? He should've guessed she had something to do with this. "Give me that."

Con handed him the card. "You might want to read the other side."

On the back of the card, scrawled in a hand he recognized all too well, was written *Roses are red. Violets are blue. I don't wish to be popular. So I'm coming for you.*

Dalton groaned.

That didn't rhyme.

But then nothing about the lady made any kind of sense.

Why was she so outraged?

Dalton dropped the note and jumped out of bed. "The chit should be thanking me."

Con shrugged. "Maybe she didn't want to be a success."

"What lady doesn't wish for success?" He stalked to the washbasin and splashed water over his face. "She's addled. Completely unhinged. Beautiful . . . but unhinged."

"She'd have to be, to send *you* roses."

"Very funny." He twisted his head to examine his jaw in the glass. The jagged cut began under his right ear and ended at his chin.

Pain sliced through his shoulder and knifed toward his head. He tried to move his right shoulder again and groaned aloud.

"The old injury?" Con asked, sobering.

"Must have aggravated it." Dalton clenched his teeth. "I need another session with Olofsson. She worked wonders last time."

"I'll send for her, then." Con bobbed his scraggly beard at all the roses. "What should I do with this lot?"

"I don't know. Bathe in them for all I care. I'm off for my weekly visit to Osborne Court."

"What if the lady herself comes a-knocking?" Con chuckled. "She did say she was coming for you."

Dalton reached for the brandy bottle.

"If the Devil's Own Wallflower darkens my doorway, send her straight back to the inferno, where she belongs."

Chapter 4

"**G**ood afternoon, Mother." Dalton gave his mother, Abigail, the Dowager Duchess of Osborne, a peck on the cheek and took a seat in her dainty pastel-hued sitting room.

Abigail nodded a greeting, but her pale green eyes didn't truly see him. She didn't even notice the jagged, swollen red welt along his jaw, only continued stroking the flank of the fluffy peach-tinged Persian cat she held in her lap.

He'd considered staying home, but he always visited his mother at Osborne Court on Saturday afternoons when he was in town. He knew she relied on his visits to bring her news of society.

It was only a brief walk through shady back streets to reach the family town house.

"I attended a ball last evening," Dalton said, feeling awkward as hell in the lace-trimmed room, worried the delicately carved legs on the chair might snap under his burden.

Society affairs were usually safe topics that wouldn't set her off into one of her panics.

They called her the Dowager Recluse now. Said she must have contracted the pox from her philandering husband. Must be hideously scarred and unfit to be seen by society.

Dalton knew her scars were all internal.

"And did you have a pleasant time, Duke?"

He wouldn't call it pleasant. "Most pleasant indeed." He kept his voice soft and soothing. "I saw Lady Clyde there. She asked about you."

"And what did you tell her?" Abigail murmured, her face clouding over.

Blunder. Dalton tensed on the pale-green-and-white-striped settee, bracing for an outburst. He wasn't supposed to mention the fact that the outside world still thought about her.

It was just that his head and his shoulder ached so.

"I can't remember," he said carefully. "I drank too much ratafia."

Her face eased. "Oh, you. Always drinking too much. Why don't you move here with me? We could have Cook fill your brandy bottles with apple cider. Why, you'd never even know the difference."

Dalton laughed, relieved that the potential storm had blown over. "I should think I'd be able to tell."

He hadn't moved to Osborne Court after his father died last year, as everyone expected him to, because his secret life had been planned from his nearby bachelor apartments, and there'd be no way to come and go as easily from the ducal house.

Many of the powerful men he'd crossed had the

ear of the Prince Regent himself. They could un-
doubtedly have his title and all that went with it
stripped away for treason.

Which would devastate his mother.

Her quiet, secluded life in the comfort and fa-
miliarity of her home was all she had left.

Taking that away from her, forcing her to leave
her sanctuary would be unthinkably cruel. He
would never let that happen. Not until she found
the will to leave on her own.

And so he continued his quest to bring the murderer to justice. Maybe then his mother would feel
safe enough to reenter the world.

And he continued righting the wrongs of his
father, but he did so carefully.

So very carefully. Keeping his two worlds entirely separate.

Never betraying weakness.

Fear and love.

The emotions that made a man weak.

He'd learned to control his fear, sculpting his
body and disciplining his mind for vengeance.
And he'd methodically eliminated the need to
love, or be loved.

When the judgment day came and he finally
faced his enemy, he would be ready.

Ruthless and in control.

No fear. No weakness.

He did worry about his mother, though, even
if she had dozens of servants. Ten years ago, she'd
retreated into her apartments at Osborne Court
and never left again.

She called it her cloister, as if she were a nun. As if she'd taken a vow of pious seclusion.

Nothing could induce her to leave. Not her husband's enraged accusations, nor Dalton's increasing concern.

Later, they realized that her self-imposed seclusion had been a gradual thing. She'd started leaving the house less, sending the servants out to do all her errands. She'd begun eating in her apartments, instead of the dining room.

She'd added more and more distance between herself and outside world, refusing invitations, not even allowing her own mother to come for a visit.

A small army of physicians concluded that she suffered from mental anxieties of the most severe kind. They said this fear of leaving the house sometimes manifested itself in females, particularly in females who'd experienced traumatic events.

The week of Alec's death they'd been visiting Balfry House, the country estate the duke had purchased for his Irish Protestant bride, one of the famously beautiful Kerry sisters.

Sometimes, when Dalton closed his eyes, he saw sunlight glinting on the green waters of Balfry Bay. Felt a chubby little hand clasped in his. And then not clasped.

Never again.

He should have been watching Alec more closely.

Some of his clothing had washed up onshore, though his wee body had been carried out to sea. A forlorn tweed cap, waterlogged and torn.

Dalton squeezed his eyes shut.

The cut on his jaw stung; his right fist and shoulder ached.

His mind ached as well, sitting with his mother, unable to tell her the agonizing truth.

He'd reached the end of his father's list last night and was no closer to finding the murderer.

She'd confided to Dalton that she thought the murderer was in London. She was sure he was waiting for her out there. Waiting to end her life, as he'd ended the life of her darling son.

The old duke had threatened to send her away to an asylum, but Dalton had fought with all his might, and his mother had remained at Osborne Court.

"Cook made a rather fine pheasant pie yesterday," Abigail observed, stroking the fluffy cat until he purred. "Wasn't it delicious, my darling? Didn't you lick your wee little paws?"

Dalton had lost count of how many cats had taken up residence at Osborne Court. They were all enormously rotund, with round moon faces and worried, wrinkled expressions.

One of them rubbed against his Hessians. He gave its chin an obligatory scratch and it flopped onto its back, all four paws raised like some enormous fluffy capsized insect.

Shameless hussy, he thought. But he couldn't resist the siren call of that soft fur. When he rubbed its ample belly, the cat purred so loudly his hand vibrated.

"Buttercup, sweetling," remonstrated his mother. "Don't you know dukes never pet kitties?"

The old duke certainly never had. He'd always been bellowing about the Persian Menace, as he called the cats. Threatening to stuff them all in a sack and drown them in the Thames.

Dalton hadn't thought to become the duke for many years to come. He'd even thought he might die before inheriting the title since he was reckless with his body, plunging into perilous situations that would have killed a weaker man.

He'd never even considered his father might go before him.

The old duke had seemed healthy as a horse. He drank excessively, bedded a different woman every night, and gambled into the wee hours with his crooked friends.

But one morning, at the breakfast table, he'd apparently clutched at his chest, turned blue about the lips, and fallen face-first into a pile of fried lamb's kidneys.

Dalton had never told his father how much he hated him, but he'd shown it, gambling away his father's money and playing the rake, the wastrel. Becoming the Hellhound and wreaking justice on his father's corrupt set.

There'd been one day, six months after the old duke's death, when Dalton and his mother had looked at each other over a glass of sherry and he'd seen it reflected in her eyes.

The macabre sense of relief.

"I think I shall have Cook make a gooseberry

tart tomorrow," Abigail mused, scratching the cat's tufted chin.

"That would be nice," he said in a neutral tone. If she wanted to say more she would.

His mother glanced up, her face brightening. "Oh, I nearly forgot to tell you. I had a letter today. From Ginny." She waved a pale hand through the air. "She wrote about the old times, when we were famous beauties. My, how many beaux we had between the three of us sisters."

Dalton smiled. "Tell me about one of your suitors." It seemed everyone wished to chat about former loves lately. Even gruff old Con.

"Well, let's see . . ." she mused. "There was the Earl of Kilkenny, of course, he was a great favorite, not as rich as your father, though. And there was one . . . Mr. O'Roarke, Patrick was his given name." She stared into the flickering flames in the grate. "I haven't thought of him in years."

"Merely a mister?" Dalton teased. "Doesn't sound suitable for one of the Kerry sisters."

"And he was poor as a pauper as well. A lowly shipping clerk. But my, how he loved me. He was mad for me. I heard later that he made his fortune abroad, in the colonies, of all places, and now he's wealthier than Midas. Imagine that. He was terribly angry when I refused him. Nearly strangled me. I was so frightened. But what choice had I? A duke or a shipping clerk."

Dalton had never heard her speak of this beau before. Something she had said jarred his mind. O'Roarke nearly strangled her? That didn't sound right.

"Tell me more," Dalton urged. "Did this O'Roarke hate my father for stealing you away?"

"Oh yes. Called him a devil and an evil British oppressor. Said he'd never make me happy, as he could. Said I'd live to regret my folly. And so would the duke. He was all red about the face. Truly he scared me. But why didn't I listen to him? Why didn't we run away together?"

The hairs on the backs of his arms stood on end. That gave O'Roarke a motive. He'd hated the duke for stealing his bride.

Hated him enough to murder his son?

Love made people do desperate things.

The murderer had left a note stuck under a rock on the barren stretch of shoreline.

You stole what was mine, so I stole something of yours.

Abigail lifted her head and tears began streaming down her cheeks. "Why, why did I marry your father?" The cat on her lap gave a frightened yowl and leapt away, startling the cat by Dalton's feet.

The two offended felines tore out of the room.

"He was so cruel," she moaned, clutching at her collar. "His fault. Poor Alec . . . poor, sweet boy. He had to pay the price."

Dalton sprang out of his chair and offered his handkerchief, discreetly pulling the bell for the nurse.

This was how it began. There was nothing more he could do. He'd tried. But anything he did at this point would only make it worse.

When his mother was safely in bed and feeling calmer, Dalton walked back to his apartments.

This was the best lead he'd had in years.

He'd go to Ireland to find this Patrick O'Roarke. Or America, if he had to. Question him. Break him, if necessary.

Perhaps Con would be seeing his brown-eyed Bronagh soon, after all. If O'Roarke still had ties to County Cork, Dalton needed to be there.

They'd leave tomorrow, slipping away in the early morning. He couldn't risk Trent seeing him with this slash across his jaw, or hearing about it from someone else.

Actually, a journey out of town was exactly what the doctor ordered.

And there was irony for you, he thought as he ascended the stairs to his chambers. Lady Dorothea would certainly be interested to know he was planning to visit Ireland.

Of course, she'd never know.

"You're late."

"I . . . am?" Thea blinked at the tall, broad-shouldered older man who'd opened the door of the duke's town house before she'd even finished knocking.

Emphatic nose, bristly gray beard with reddish streaks, no cravat—was he even a butler?

"Well, don't just stand there, love." The man gestured impatiently toward the shadowy entrance hall. "He's waiting."

Love? Just who did this disreputable-looking butler think was at his door? Thea hesitated on the threshold, a sliver of misgiving intruding into the indignant resolve that had driven her here.

She'd slipped downstairs when her mother retired for the evening and left by the side entrance on King Street, swathed in a hooded gray cloak over her pelisse.

Skirting St. James's Square instead of taking the direct route across, she'd traversed the back streets as stealthily as possible, her mission made easier by the fact that the duke still lived in his more modest bachelor apartments instead of in the nearby grand residence of Osborne Court itself.

One thought had pulsed through her mind, sweeping away hesitation and propelling her to his door.

The duke had ruined all her plans. And he would just have to repair them.

She simply couldn't be a success. And she *wouldn't* live with her grandmother.

It extinguished all hope of the unobtrusive season she'd planned, the quiet escape back to Ireland, a quiet, blissfully husband-free life with her aunt.

"Well?" The man crossed his brawny arms and stared down at her, drawing his thick gray eyebrows together. "Are you going to stand there all night? You *are* Miss Inga Olofsson, are you not? From Madame Signe's? Here for the usual?"

"Erm . . ." Apparently she'd been mistaken for a Swedish courtesan.

Maybe now would be a good time to tell the unkempt butler the truth.

I'm Lady Dorothea Beaumont and I'm here to deliver the scathing reprimand your master so richly deserves.

That wouldn't get her past the door.

She'd be whomever the butler wanted her to be if it would gain her entrance to the lion's den. "That's right, I'm Inga Olofsson." She gave a confident nod, adding a *ja?* for good measure.

The butler grinned. "Follow me, *Olofsson*." He strode across the entrance hall and up a wide spiral staircase.

Dark and cavernous, the hall held little furniture. Thea paused for a moment. There were no paintings on the wall. None whatsoever.

She'd never seen walls so very bare and devoid of art.

She had to trot to catch up. The wavering light from his lantern was the only illumination keeping her from tumbling down the black-and-white marble stairs and breaking her neck. The duke certainly preferred his house dark.

The butler paused outside a massive carved wood door. "He's unclothed and ready."

Thea stared. Surely he hadn't said *unclothed*.

A low moan emanated from inside the room, the eerie sound reminding Thea of nothing so much as a caged wild animal. She shivered.

"Not frightened, are you?" The butler's whiskers bristled when he grinned. "He's quite harmless, really," he whispered conspiratorially. "Only devours two or three young ladies per day."

Ladies? Thea searched the butler's face. "I'm not frightened," she said, attempting to believe it was true.

The flood of righteous resentment that had swept her here began to flow again. *The duke ruined everything on purpose. He had no right to interfere with my plans.*

She straightened her shoulders. "Lead on, sir."

"In you go then, love." The butler opened the door. "Remove those boots and climb aboard."

Climb aboard?

Heavens. What on earth had she agreed to do?

"Er," Thea whispered desperately. "There's been a mistake. I'm not really—"

"I'll leave you now, *Olofsson*," the butler said loudly. He gave her a little push into the room.

The door closed with an ominous thud. Thea nearly dove for the knob and ran straight back across the square. This had been a spectacularly bad idea. Perhaps she should pen an excoriating letter instead. She'd be assured of choosing precisely the perfect invectives that way.

You're not scared, are you?

Thea took a deep breath.

Fear had dictated her actions too long.

She had a right to be here after what the duke had done. A right to speak her mind, demand that he make reparations. Ensure she could retire to Ireland as planned.

She stood at a crossroads.

The well-worn path of silence and obedience stretched back to her house, to the unbearable weight of her family's expectations, and beyond, to a loveless, miserable marriage.

The path of courage and adventure lay ahead.

In the duke's bedchamber.

She pivoted toward the majestic, towering bed that dominated the center of the room.

What she saw upon that bed nearly stole what remained of her bravery.

Miles and miles of duke. Face down.

Very much unclothed.

Well, there was a thin linen sheet covering his lower half, but it didn't do much to hide the lines of his taut, rounded backside and powerful thighs.

Thea's first sight of a nude male not carved from marble or fashioned from bronze quite took her breath away. All those ridges and valleys on the vast landscape of his back, shadowed and gleaming in the firelight.

So much powerful virility.

So much overbearing arrogance, she reminded herself.

And then the true enormity of her task became clear.

She was meant to climb.

On top.

Of a duke.

She should have brought a rope and pickaxe. This wasn't a crossroads—it was a mountain expedition.

Thea unlaced her boots. She'd probably be unceremoniously ejected the second the duke saw her face. Best to continue the charade as long as possible. Find just the right moment to spring her demands upon him.

She approached the bed on wobbly, yet determined, limbs.

"You're late, Olofsson," the duke growled, not bothering to raise his head. "It's the right shoulder again. Seized up so I can barely move it." He flexed the bulging muscles in his shoulder and moaned. "Work your magic."

Er, what magic was that?

If Olofsson ministered to his shoulder, and not *other* parts of his anatomy, then she was a . . . nurse?

Thea must mount him and . . . then what? What exactly did this Olofsson person do?

When she was closer she could see by the light from the thick candles in bronze stands on either side of the bed that his eyes were tightly closed.

There was a thin red line along his jawline that hadn't been there last night when they waltzed. Had he fought a duel? It was entirely possible. Some of the married ladies he dallied with must have jealous husbands.

"I haven't got all night, Olofsson," the duke said impatiently. "I promise not to bite. Climb up and walk around."

Right, then. She could do this.

Thea stepped onto a low wooden stool and hoisted herself onto the bed, then, cautiously, she crawled onto his back on her knees and slowly, very slowly, rose until she was standing.

The hard hillocks of his muscles made it difficult to find a flat resting place.

"Walk, Olofsson, walk!"

She clung to the velvet bed hangings for support as she trod across the enormous expanse of his back toward his shoulder.

"Ah," he moaned. "Yes, that's the location. Stay there a moment."

She bore down on his right shoulder. How could one man possess so much solid, knotted muscle?

"That's right. With your heels."

This must be hurting him dreadfully. His profile was carved from granite and stood out in firm relief against the white of the bedclothes. He never glanced at her, never looked up. His eyes were squeezed shut and his mouth compressed. His breath came in short gasps.

She pressed down on his shoulder blade with her stockinged heel.

He moaned and clenched his eyes tighter.

"That's it," he said. "Just like that."

She worked her foot back and forth, shifting her weight from toe to heel.

The grunting noises he made sounded almost as if he were enjoying the pain.

So this was what he paid women to do. Not exactly what she'd been expecting. Although who knew what he did with them after they finished battering his back.

"You feel lighter," the duke said. "Have you been reducing?"

"I apologize, Your Grace." Thea shifted all her weight to her right foot and dug her heel into the space below his right shoulder blade.

"Oof."

"Too much, Your Grace?"

"Not at all," he grunted. "Do your worst, Olofsson. Do your worst."

She bounced harder.

He gasped.

She was actually beginning to enjoy herself now.

Waltz with her. Make her popular. Fill her foyer with flowers from lecherous old lords.

She used all her strength to grind her heels into the ridges of his back.

"Christ," he grunted. "Easy now."

"Am I hurting you, Your Grace?" she asked sweetly, redoubling her efforts.

"Hold a moment," he said, low and dangerous. "I know that voice . . ."

With one swift movement he twisted, setting her off balance. He caught her by the waist and forced her knees to either side of him, pressing her down against him.

"What in all the fiery blazes of hell are *you* doing here? Con," he bellowed. "I'm going to bloody well murder you."

Chapter 5

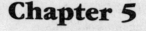

Thea heard the sound of distant laughter.

She squirmed in a useless attempt to break free, grabbing the velvet drapes for leverage, but the duke's large hands clamped around her waist and held her immobile above him.

"Your Grace," she gasped. "Didn't you receive my note? Why are you surprised to see me?"

His eyes narrowed ominously. "Because I told my feckless, good-for-nothing manservant to oust you speedily if you darkened my doorway."

Her limbs were spread to either side of him, her knees flat against the bed, her body pressed against his solid length.

This was far worse for her sanity than waltzing with him. "Ah . . . apparently he mistook me for this Olofsson person and ushered me inside."

He snorted. "There's no chance he mistook you for her. She has shoulders nearly as wide as mine." His gaze shifted from her face to her torso. "While you are delicate and rounded and soft." His gaze intensified, lingering over her chest. "Everywhere."

She had the sense that he was seeing her, truly seeing her for the very first time.

Then his eyes hardened. "Your mother had

better not be outside, waiting to burst in upon us. I know she likes to do that."

At the reference to her mother's role in attempting to force the Duke of Harland into marriage, Thea's jaw clenched with fury and she shoved against his chest with her palms. "I'm not trying to trap you, Your Grace. I wouldn't marry you if you were the last male left on God's green earth."

His lips twitched. "Is that so?"

"Yes, it is. Now please release me."

"I don't think so. Not yet." One of his hands left her waist and untied her cloak. He slid the garment off her shoulders and threw it to the floor.

There was a subtle shift in the air.

She felt his desire.

Well, literally, she felt it, hard and firm against her inner thigh, but it was also in the atmosphere between them.

Perhaps men lost their faculties of reason when they had ladies on top of their half-nude bodies.

"I repeat. Why are you here, Lady Dorothea?" the duke asked.

Obviously she wasn't going to extricate herself by force. She must use words. She took a deep, steadying breath.

"Because I was gravely mistaken. Your preference was sufficient to annihilate years of failure. And I'm so tired of everyone using me for their own purposes. You can't just run around willynilly transforming near-spinsters into successes at whim."

It seemed Thea had discovered the secret to conversing with gentlemen and it was fury. Outrage made her quite loquacious. "First you deny my sincere petition to catalogue your art collection with no explanation, and then you wreck all my plans on purpose. I know it was on purpose, don't bother denying it."

"Oh, I'm not denying anything," he said with a smug smile, settling her more firmly against him. "I knew if I chose you for the first waltz you would be inundated by suitors and wouldn't need to chase me. It was all part of my plan to rid myself of you forever."

"You . . . you," she sputtered. She beat her fists against his chest. "You manipulative, egotistical, flint-hearted *rakehell*."

He captured her fists in his hands. "What about pompous arse?" he suggested helpfully. "Or how about puffed-up bastard?"

Thea had never used such crude language. But there was a first time for everything. "Arrogant arse," she whispered.

He laughed. "Louder, please."

Teasing her, was he? "Arrogant *arse*," she proclaimed.

Without warning, he lifted her up and reversed their positions, rolling her onto her back and pinning her against the bed with the weight of his thighs.

"Oh," she cried. "You'll crush me."

"I'll teach you a lesson about why it's not wise to enter a duke's chamber, climb into his bed, and hurl insults at him."

The bulk of his body imprinted her into the

bed. He held both of her hands trapped above her head with one of his large hands.

Why, exactly, did that send thrills chasing along every vertebra of her spine?

She wasn't frightened; he was only teasing her, teaching her a lesson, but her body reacted in uncharacteristic ways.

Lifting and arching kinds of ways.

His lips drew closer. Such sensual lips. Firm on top with a hint of flare to the bottom.

"Lady Dorothea, you're staring at my lips." A teasing spark lit his eyes. "That generally means a woman wants kissing."

"I don't want kissing," she said defensively. Which was a complete and utter falsehood. She *did* want kissing. Quite desperately.

Heat rushed to her cheeks.

Why did it have to be this arrogant, supremely self-confident beast of a duke who made her long to be kissed for the first time?

Of course she didn't want him to kiss her. That wouldn't solve anything.

Unless someone *saw* their lips locking. And then she'd be ruined instead of merely tainted by a jilting. That could work. But there were no witnesses tonight. He released her wrists. Brushing a curl away from her face, he skimmed his knuckles lightly down her cheek and over her neck, the possessive touch thrilling across the surface of her skin, forcing her senses to wake up and acknowledge that she was pinioned beneath an enormous, dangerous beast of a duke.

The vast terrain of his chest stretched above her, candlelight playing over relentless lines and inflexibly muscled ridges.

A thin brown leather cord hung from his neck, supporting what looked to be a bit of red rock tied at the end . . . wait a moment . . . She ran her finger over familiar sharp, jagged contours. "This is a *maërl* fossil, isn't it? From the beaches at Balfry Bay."

He snatched his hand away from her cheek. "No, it's not."

Why would he deny the fact? "I believe it is. I've walked those beaches many times and gathered pieces of this same bloodred coralline algae."

"Why exactly did you come here tonight, Lady Dorothea?" he said testily. "I mean other than to stomp upon my back, insult me, and contradict my every word?"

To be thoroughly kissed by an expert in the subject.
No, no, that wasn't it at all.

"You're a rake. You obviously know how to fool people into believing all that charm is sincere. So find a way to make me unpopular again. Make this right."

"How would I achieve that?"

"Spread rumors about me, say I threw myself at you. Say I begged to be ruined."

"Hmm." He nuzzled her neck, which did interesting, fizzy things to her belly. His teeth teased her earlobe, making her heart race.

"Are you asking to be ruined?" he breathed in her ear. "Because I could possibly make an exception . . . to the no-innocent-ladies rule."

He traced tempting hieroglyphics along her collarbone with one finger. "Just this once, mind you."

"It would only be *theoretical* ruining," she hastened to explain.

"How is this theoretical, exactly? Here I am above you." His weight shifted, to emphasize his extremely hard and pressing point. "And here you are, soft and yielding, under me."

"Let me explain the concept, Your Grace," she said with a chipper, cheery tone, as if they were discussing this over a nice cup of tea in a respectable drawing room.

She had to pretend the situation was ordinary, at least. Had to pretend there were no tremors in her belly and no melting sensation in her belly.

"Theoretical ruin, or make-believe despoiling, as it's sometimes known, is quite simple really." She adopted a schoolmarm tone. "*You* spread rumors of my wanton behavior. *I* confirm the rumors, thereby exonerating you of any guilt in the matter. *I* am ruined. And *you* are free to continue climbing the rose trellises of London's thrill-seeking widows and wives."

A small snort emitted from the beast. "Why the hell don't you want to be a success? Isn't that every well-bred lady's goal? Shouldn't you be thanking me?"

His gaze heated her skin from the inside out like coals filling an iron bed-warmer. "I could think of several ways you might show your . . . gratitude, now that you're here."

Thea squeaked as his large, rough hands caressed down her flanks and settled her more firmly against his body.

Gracious! Perhaps this *was* a crossroads . . . leading straight to actual ruin.

"You don't understand, Your Grace," she said desperately. "I planned to endure one more season so my family would finally abandon hope and allow me to fade away to Ireland to live with my aunt in peace."

She closed her eyes, remembering her aunt Emma's dear, plump face and the way her clothing always smelled of rich clover honey and wood smoke.

"I was useful in Ireland. I had a purpose other than attracting unprincipled peers. I helped my aunt with her beekeeping. And with putting by her renowned marmalades. I was free from the dictates of society . . . I don't expect you to understand."

"You'd rather be stung by bees than marry. I understand completely."

Thea's eyes flew open. Forget the fact that she was in intimate contact with a man for the very first time and that the man in question was none other than London's most notorious rake. Forget that he was known for heartlessness and seduction.

He understood. She gave him a startled smile. "That's exactly it. I'll do anything to avoid my family's marriage machinations."

He propped himself up on one elbow, regarding her curiously. "You truly don't wish for a titled husband and a safe, cosseted life and dozens of servants to fulfill every whim? You have no need for French perfumes and clusters of diamonds?"

"Oh, I've never wanted diamonds, Your Grace." She sighed. "My mother has piles of cold, inert diamonds and they certainly don't improve her marriage . . . or give her happiness."

He propped his great, square jaw on his chin, on the side without that livid cut.

She wondered again how he'd got that cut. It was the exact red shade of the fossil dangling from the leather cord around his neck.

"A privileged young lady of good breeding who doesn't long for a perfect match." He shook his head. "No. It still makes no kind of sense. I'm sorry you didn't approve of the results, but I truly thought that in my own brutish way, I was doing you a kindness."

Thea pushed at his chest, attempting to roll him off. "Thanks to your *kindness,* my grandmother has announced that I must go and live under her strict supervision tomorrow morning, with the goal of betrothing me to the Duke of Foxford or the Earl of Marwood. Both of whom I would rather die than marry."

The duke went still. "Foxford?" He rolled off her in one lithe, swift motion and jumped off the bed.

Grabbing a poker, he stirred the logs on the fire. "You'll not be shackled to that lecherous old toad. I won't allow it."

The sight of him standing in front of the fireplace, licked by flickering flames and forbidding her to marry Foxford, was nearly more than a girl could stand.

He was only wearing his smallclothes. And they seemed to be too, well, *small* to contain certain parts of him.

Parts she wouldn't mind seeing in the flesh.

Thea sat up so fast her head spun. What was wrong with her? She'd never had thoughts like this before.

She straightened her bodice, smoothed her skirts, and swung her legs over the high edge of the bed, managing to hop down without falling flat on her face.

A small triumph.

She found her boots. "Precisely my goal in coming here. *Not* to marry Foxford. Now will you agree to theoretically ruin me so Foxford drops me like a hot coal?"

The duke jabbed savagely at a half-burned log and orange sparks flew into the air. "I'm not going to ruin you, theoretically or otherwise." He set down the poker and grabbed a green silk dressing gown from a chair back.

Thea barely suppressed a forlorn sigh of disappointment when he tied the dressing gown around his waist, covering all that smooth, muscled chest.

"If you won't theoretically ruin me, you'll just have to arrange safe passage for me back to Ireland. Tonight preferably. I won't go and live with my grandmother tomorrow." She placed her hands on her hips. "And I refuse to marry Fox-ford."

Lady Dorothea met his gaze with unwavering, steel-flecked blue eyes.

Dalton had the distinct impression he'd just been challenged to a duel.

The Duke of Osborne's bedchamber. Half past eleven. Choose your weapon.

Had he thought her delicate and fragile?

He'd been wrong. She may appear to be fashioned from silk and soft curves, but she had the same steel backbone as her mother.

"Lady Dorothea, you appear to be suffering from a delusion of potential success."

He stalked to the sideboard and poured himself a glass of brandy. "There's no chance I'll ruin you, theoretically or otherwise, or help you run away to Ireland. I couldn't have known you didn't wish for success. I thought I was doing you a great service."

"Oh yes, deigning to dance with me. The handsome duke granting a wallflower a charity dance to lift her from the mire of obscurity. And keep her from pestering you." She tossed her head. "Well, I don't want your charity. All I want is to live my life in peace, far from domineering grandmothers and lecherous old peers. And you're going to help me achieve that dream."

Satisfaction or death. Walk ten paces and level your pistol.

Dalton jammed a hand through his hair.

Lady Dorothea had managed to surprise him.

And that wasn't easy.

There was a part of him that enjoyed battling with her far more than going through the tiresome motions of courting the vapid Mrs. Renwick.

But he had far bigger problems on his mind than finding ways to help wallflowers become spinsters.

Not that Lady Dorothea would ever make a proper spinster.

Damn, she was a vision by firelight.

All those butter-and-marmalade curls spilling around her shoulders. It made him hungry.

Had he even eaten dinner?

He shouldn't have drunk so much, but it eased the ache of his shoulder.

She'd be a good way to ease your pain.

Hellfire. That was the brandy talking.

"You dull your pain with spirits, Your Grace," she observed. "Perhaps you should try confronting it head-on for a change."

"You don't know anything about me," he growled.

Was he truly standing in his smalls, arguing with an infuriating lady?

Dalton tugged the sash of his dressing gown tighter. "This conversation is over." He turned on his heel and walked three paces.

Tap. Tap.

Seriously?

He whirled around. "What now?"

"Three little words, Your Grace."

Three words. *Bed me now.* No, that wouldn't be it. *I'm dangerously addled.* That was more like it.

She rose onto her tiptoes and steadied herself with a small hand against his chest.

Silken curls tickled his chin and the scent of roses swirled into his mind.

Soft. Flowery.

Deranged.

Her wide, blue-gray eyes flashed with determination. "I demand satisfaction."

Certain suggestive parts of his anatomy south of the sash greeted this with unbridled enthusiasm. *She wants satisfying!*

He jabbed a finger at the door. "Out."

She raised her small chin and looked him in the eyes. "Not until you agree."

There was a knock and Con entered the room. When Dalton saw the urgency in his expression he quickly crossed the room. "What is it?" he asked in a low voice, so the lady wouldn't hear.

Con glanced behind him. "Trent," he whispered. "Been asking about you at the club. Said he'll pay you a visit. Maybe tonight."

"Damn it!" He couldn't risk Trent seeing the slash on his jaw, yet he had no taste for hiding like a rat in a hole.

Dalton made a split-second decision. Better to be on the road, away from the threat of exposure. "We leave now. Tonight. I can't risk discovery."

Con nodded. "The traveling coach is ready."

"Traveling coach? Where are you going?" a soft voice asked.

Dalton spun. Lady Dorothea had snuck up

behind him. She gave *meddlesome* a new definition. "That's none of your con—"

"Why, love, didn't His Grace inform you?" Con ignored Dalton's frantic silencing gestures. "We're off to the green shores of Ireland."

Dalton groaned. Why, oh why, hadn't he sacked Con before now?

Lady Dorothea's eyes lit. "You're going to Ireland? You didn't mention that. Why? Why would you go there? Are you visiting Balfry House?"

Too many questions. "Con, escort Lady Dorothea to the door."

"Who's after you?" she persisted. "A jealous husband?"

"Precisely right. A jealous husband. Dangerous fellow. Loose cannon. You have to leave. Now." Dalton attempted to herd her to the door.

"But why Ireland?"

"Because"—he searched his brandy-and Lady Dorothea–addled mind—"of a widow," he finished triumphantly. That ought to send her running back to Mama. "A lovely, lonely widow with flaming red hair and emerald eyes. She's pining for me. Happens all the time, you know. Poor thing."

She narrowed her eyes. "Pining for you from across an ocean?"

"Her rose trellis wants climbing."

There was a strangled noise from Con, who was watching their exchange with a gleeful expression, as if he were watching a holiday pantomime.

Lady Dorothea advanced until her eyes were

inches from his chin. "Take me with you. You owe me an escape route, if you won't repair the damage you caused."

"I don't owe you a damned thing." Dalton retrieved her cloak and threw it around her shoulders.

She drew herself up, all five petite, curvaceous feet of her, her eyes flickering with blue fire, like the heart of a gas flame. "You refuse to make me unpopular, and you won't take me with you. Very well then. It will be more complicated, but I'll find my own way back to Ireland tonight."

She couldn't be serious. "With what funds? In what conveyance?"

"I have some pin money here in my reticule." She drew the small velvet pouch from her cloak pocket. "I'll buy a ticket on the mail coach. I'm sure there's one leaving in a few hours."

The mail coach? She couldn't travel by coach. She was so achingly beautiful and innocent.

And far too trusting. She'd climbed on top of his naked torso, for God's sake. The lady obviously had no idea of the dangers inherent in scrambling into rakes' beds.

There were highwaymen, fortune hunters, jewel thieves, and cutthroats just waiting for naïve young heiresses with eyes as wide as an ocean crossing.

"You can't travel by mail coach. Not with all that"—he gestured helplessly toward her luxurious curls—"and those . . ." He waved at her full, pink lips, having lost the ability to speak in complete sentences.

Con snorted. "Chalk it down, Duke. A lady can't travel by coach. She'd be a target."

Right now Dalton felt as though he was at the center of an archery target. And she'd pierced him. Straight through the conscience he hadn't even known he possessed.

Every second they stood here arguing could mean Trent arriving at his doorstep, asking questions, making demands.

A warrior never ran from a fight, but by staying he would risk everything.

Seemed it came down to a contest between facing Trent or traveling with Lady Dorothea. At least she was of a more manageable size. And there'd be no danger of *her* uncovering his secret. She had no idea he was anything other than the careless, pleasure-seeking, wager-happy rake society believed him to be.

Con winked at Lady Dorothea. "We've plenty of room in the traveling chariot, isn't that right, Duke?"

Thea glanced askance at Con. She'd never encountered an insubordinate old reprobate thinly veiled as a servant.

"It's only twenty hours to Bristol," Lady Dorothea said, by way of attempting to convince Dalton to stuff her in his carriage.

Damn it. He was going to regret this. He opened his mouth to reluctantly agree, but the lady cut him off.

"If you don't provide an escape for me I'll . . . I'll . . ." She curled her small hands into fists that wouldn't leave a dent in the ripe insides of a cantaloupe. "I'll camp outside your front door and explain to anyone who arrives that you're taking the Great West Road to Bristol."

Mother of God.

Dalton thudded his fist onto the sideboard and brandy snifters jigged precariously. "You, Lady Dorothea, are a plague and a pestilence."

"Then you'll take me!" Her lips curved into a masterpiece of a counterfeit smile. "Thanks ever so, Your Grace."

Con smirked. "The duke would never refuse a damsel in distress." He dropped a courtly, flourishing bow that Dalton had no idea Con even knew how to perform. "Your carriage awaits, my lady," he said in a nasally British accent, a far cry from his usual lilting brogue.

"Why, thank you," Lady Dorothea replied, lifting the hem of her gown and cloak and sailing across the carpet looking every inch as imperious as her formidable mother.

"I'll just follow your servant down to the carriage, shall I?" she asked, turning back toward Dalton. "I'm sure you need to do something about that." She waved a hand in the direction of his face. "And . . . *those.*" She flicked a disdainful glance at his bare legs, visible beneath his dressing gown.

The two of them left, clearly conspirators in a war against his sanity.

Dalton was left sputtering, clutching a half-empty glass of brandy and cursing himself for an addlepated fool. He downed the rest of the brandy in one fiery, fortifying gulp.

What had just happened? Had he actually agreed to escort an innocent young lady to Ireland? All because of the execrable crime of *waltzing* with her?

It made no sense. None whatsoever.

He surveyed his chamber dolefully. Since Con was his only manservant (bad, *bad* idea, that) he'd have to collect the necessary items himself.

What he required: non-ducal clothing, since he'd be traveling anonymously. His knives. His pistol case.

What he did not need: a runaway wallflower in his carriage with theoretical ruining on her entirely too clever and nimble mind.

It seemed he hadn't solved the Lady Dorothea problem at all.

He'd only made it worse.

Chapter 6

Thea followed the duke's unconventional man-servant out to the stable yard, shivering in the cold, damp air.

Here she was, fleeing a forced marriage in the dead of night, all because of one seductive smile in a ballroom that she hadn't been strong enough to resist.

If only she hadn't danced with the duke she would still be a failure.

Her plans for an uneventful final season and an unnoticed exit from society would still be intact.

Now she had no time to plan her escape. She'd wanted to bring certain items back with her when she returned to Ireland.

A carriage-full of books for her young friend Molly, the daughter of one of the tenant farmers on a neighboring estate, a voracious reader who couldn't afford a library. They'd forged an unlikely alliance while Thea was in Ireland. Books kept Molly out of trouble. She was the type to get into scrapes if her quick mind wasn't kept occupied.

Ah well. Thea could always purchase books for

her in Dublin. Or there was the duke's library at Balfry House. A grand affair with towering ceilings and breathtaking expanses of leather-bound spines.

First the paintings . . . then the books, Thea thought with a smile.

She certainly had her work cut out for her on this journey.

But she'd wear him down.

She must.

She glanced back in the direction of her house where her mother slumbered in her lonely bed, dreaming of her daughter becoming a duchess at long last . . . and at any price.

Thea was an heiress with the promise of a very large portion when she married. She couldn't imagine any other outcome from this precipitous departure except . . . disinheritance. Perhaps she'd never even see her father's town house again.

"Not thinking of changing your mind, are you, my lady?" the duke's unusual manservant asked, noting the direction of her gaze.

"Never." Wrapping her cloak closer, she trudged after the man's huge, lumbering frame.

Running away would be seen as the ultimate betrayal.

Worse than years of disappointing society appearances.

Worse than speaking the truth that day in the church with the Duke of Harland.

But living under the suffocating control of her grandmother and marrying the gentleman she chose based on rank and social position, with no consideration for basic human decency, was simply not an option.

Somehow, Thea felt that her unconventional half sister Charlene would understand the choice Thea was making. Not for the first time, Thea wished she could talk to Charlene, seek her advice, but she was in Surrey with the duke and her newborn son.

They owned a cocoa manufactory, of all things. And Thea had heard the manufactory doubled as a sanctuary for destitute young girls. She'd also heard that lessons were taught to the girls in how to defend themselves against unwanted advances from men.

Thea might need lessons of that sort . . . if she were to live alone with her aunt forever in Ireland. Someday . . . well, perhaps she could go and visit Charlene. And if Thea ever did come by her inheritance someday, she'd be proud to invest in her charitable ventures.

"What's your name?" Thea asked the duke's servant as they approached a waiting carriage.

"Everyone calls me Con, my lady."

"I'm in your debt, Con. Thank you."

He may be gruff, unkempt, and unmannerly, but if it weren't for him, she'd have been thrown out on her ear. She'd be eternally grateful for his aid.

He ducked his head and the ends of his graying red beard disappeared into the upturned collar of his coat. "Don't be thanking me, now.

You needed an escape route. We happened to be going your way."

Glass-paned lamps mounted on either side of the front windows of the sleek, black carriage cast a brave yellow glow in the darkness.

Thea caught Con's eye. "His Grace made it quite clear I'm unwelcome."

Con reached for the brass door pull. "Pay no attention to his grumbling. Has a shell tough as a walnut, he does. What he wants is a good cracking. And a good—"

"Servant who isn't openly insubordinate." The duke's bass voice startled Thea as he appeared from behind the carriage, setting her heart beating faster. "That's what he wants."

A challenging look passed between the duke and Con, signaling that they clashed often and never knew who would emerge the victor.

Con had implied the duke might be soft and sweet inside.

He obviously had it all wrong.

In the lamplight, Osborne's face was formed from obdurate angles and foreboding shadows, as if the playful cleft in the middle of his chin had wandered there from someone else's visage and lost the way home.

His attire was as brooding as his expression.

Tall black boots, dark brown breeches, a black greatcoat, and a simple black beaver hat with a curved brim. Everything clearly of the finest quality, but rugged, unpolished, and a far cry from his fashionable ballroom attire.

The carriage didn't bear his crest, Thea noted.

Perhaps the sober clothing and unmarked carriage meant he wished to remain incognito to evade more possessive husbands.

Could be scores of jealous rivals to elude.

Everyone knew he burned through mistresses as if they were kindling and he aimed to start a bonfire large enough to incinerate London.

"Last opportunity to change your mind, Lady Dorothea." Osborne slapped a pair of black leather riding gloves against his open palm. "I'll have a groom escort you safely home to your doting mother and your safe featherbed."

Hardly doting, her mother. Not when Thea had turned out to be such a disappointment.

She wouldn't let the duke intimidate her with those mocking midnight eyes.

And he most certainly wasn't going to make any decisions on her behalf.

Thea lifted her shoulders higher. "I'm afraid you're saddled with me for the journey, Your Grace."

"And I was afraid you'd say that, Lady Dorothea." He crumpled his gloves in one fist. "Then let's be off. I've no time to waste."

Con offered his hand. "Up you go, my lady."

Thea mounted the carriage step, but where there should have been a floor to receive her there was only a . . .

"Bed," she said in bewilderment, staring at the striped blue-and-cream-silk cushions plumped cozily together atop a flat, angled wooden surface. "It's a bed."

She balanced atop the step, not quite certain

what she was meant to do. Surely it wouldn't be proper to mount into a traveling . . . *bed* . . . with a duke.

There's nothing proper about any of this, she reminded herself. *You're leaving proper far, far behind.*

"What's all this, then?" the duke asked in an exasperated tone.

His huge presence loomed behind her as he bent to survey the inside of the carriage.

"In you go, my lady." Con gave her hand a quick tug, setting her off balance, and she lurched unceremoniously into the carriage. "Aren't these traveling chariots ingenious?" He slapped the wall of the carriage. "Fold-down panels for nighttime journeys."

It was difficult to tell under those whiskers, but Thea was certain that was a sly smile on Con's face.

The duke surveyed Thea as she righted her bonnet and reordered her skirts after the precipitous entry.

Abruptly, he backed away. "Change it back to a seat," he barked at Con.

"Too late. No time. We must leave immediately."

"I'll ride out, then."

"Can't. Someone might recognize you."

The duke swore under his breath and flung himself into the carriage, landing beside Thea with a thump that shook the entire wood-and-steel structure.

Con winked at Thea and slammed the door shut. By the ominous furrowing of his brow, she could tell the duke was in no mood for further provocation.

He could only be described as thunderous. With a strong chance of lightning and torrential floods.

But nothing was going to drown the exhilarating surge of hope Thea experienced as the horses began to trot and the wheels to turn.

Back to Ballybrack Cottage.

Where the humming of the bees in her aunt's woven dome basket hives filled the air, and pots of orange-and-honey marmalade bubbled on the range, filling the air with spice.

She'd wasted enough time attempting to be perfect and then castigating herself when she fell short. In Ireland she'd have the liberty to determine who she was, not who her mother ordained her to be.

And Thea already knew she'd choose to be flawed and tart and imperfect, like the coarse orange marmalade with only a touch of honey to temper the bitter fruit peel.

Thea settled onto the cushions in as dignified a manner as possible, tucking a red plaid woolen blanket around her legs and untying her bonnet.

The duke sprawled on the cushions, his long legs stretching all the way into the hollow boot of the carriage.

The swaying of the carriage over the city streets nudged them closer together, and Thea had to hold on to the curtains in order to stay firmly on her side.

He could still decide to pitch her out on her ear.

Best to give him some breathing space, at least until they left London. Then she could renew her campaign to persuade him to unveil his art collection.

There had to be another painting by Artemisia somewhere in that attic, she just knew it.

A lost work of genius.

A painting so heart-wrenching and lush that historians would be forced to grant Artemisia a more prominent place in the canon of art history.

And if it turned out to be a self-portrait, Thea would finally be able to meet her favorite painter, in a fashion.

She had a day in the carriage to Bristol, and then another day on a ship bound for Ireland, to make the duke change his mind. At least she could convince him to see the *Sleeping Venus* for himself, before he absolutely forbade further discovery.

It should be sufficient time to crack his resolve.

It would have to be.

Thea glanced at the duke from the corner of her eyes. If the force of his presence was overwhelming from across a ballroom, it was devastating in this tiny space.

Thea shivered.

"Cold, Lady Dorothea?"

Thea met his hooded gaze in the gloom of the carriage. "A bit." She wrapped her blanket tighter. "I was just thinking about your manservant. He's quite . . . singular."

"I'd choose another adjective." Osborne glared out the window, obviously imagining several slow, torturous deaths for Con. "He does enjoy his little pranks."

"Has he been properly trained as a gentleman's gentleman?"

"There's nothing remotely gentlemanly about him. I would think you could have discerned that by now."

"Where on earth did you find him?"

"He's . . ." The duke shifted toward her, propping himself up on one elbow. "He's really none of your concern."

"I'm sure there's no hope of making you see why I'm doing this, why I need to leave London. Why I won't submit to my grandmother's governance and marry a man of my family's choosing."

"I thought you were doing this to plague me."

Not a hint of a smile. Where had all that famous charm gone? At least he could pretend to be gallant, to make her feel more at ease.

"It's not *my* fault I'm here." She couldn't help the accusatory tone. Surely he must guess how difficult this was for her.

"Not your fault?" He made a disbelieving sound. "Not your fault? Who climbed into my bed this evening and stomped on me? Who practically blackmailed their way into this carriage?"

Thea reminded herself to breathe, to smile graciously.

Ladies never lose their tempers, her mother admonished in her mind. *If you must give in to pique, do so in private. Then reemerge with a tranquil smile upon your face.*

"Ah, but who ruined all my plans, Your Grace?" she asked lightly. "Who filled my house with roses from lascivious old peers?"

"Surely there were a few flowers from less objectionable gentlemen. No doubt you could take your pick of many."

"My grandmother is set on Foxford or Marwood. Which is not a choice she will make on my behalf."

He regarded her for a moment, his hair glinting with copper in the passing glow from streetlamps. "This is a rash impulse. You're going to regret this when you're older."

Spoken as if he were her father's age, when he couldn't be much more than nine and twenty. "You think me incapable of making my own decisions."

"I think you haven't thought the consequences through."

A typical male, freely gifting his opinion without truly listening to anyone else.

Her father was the same. From time to time he made some blustery command to appease his ego, when everyone knew the running of the London household, and of his entire holdings, was overseen by her mother's iron control.

"Why should I not be free to choose my own destiny?" Thea asked. "If I want to become a spinster, I won't let a duke stop me."

A smile played over his lips. "You'll never be

a spinster, Lady Dorothea." His eyes flicked to her lips. "You're not made for the role." His gaze slid lower, as if he could see through the blanket. "Trust me."

Oh dear. There was the captivating smile that had landed her in this predicament in the first place.

"It's just that I don't fit with your view of the world. I don't occupy a neat niche for you to place me in and then forget all about me," she persisted.

"Niches." He smiled wolfishly. "I like niches."

His ungloved fingers slid over the fringe of the blanket, inches above her arm.

His smile wrapped her in heat, dispelling the chill more swiftly than the woolen blanket.

She couldn't decide whether the glowering or the smiling was worse for her mental equilibrium.

Just then, the carriage wheels rattled over a bump in the road, ripping the drapery from her grip and flinging her against a solid wall of duke.

One couldn't be faulted if a carriage jostled one against a duke, now could one?

His strong arms surrounded her, holding her against his chest.

"Gracious," she said.

"Are you all right?"

"I'm fine." But she wasn't. A sudden urge to nestle closer attacked her defenses. Slide her hands under his coat, under all that wool and linen, seek the smooth, muscled flesh she knew awaited her there.

Dorothea Beaumont. Stop that immediately. Refined

young ladies never allow their minds to wander down ribald paths.

Maybe she just needed to be held. To be reassured that these uncharted waters might be rough but she didn't have to negotiate them alone.

Absurd.

The duke may have agreed to escort her, but only grudgingly.

"We seem to be spending an awful lot of time in bed together, Your Grace. And on such a short acquaintance." She gave an uneasy laugh because she needed to break the tension, chase away the yearning to be held.

To be kissed.

"We'll be in Hounslow in less than two hours. I'll have the carriage converted back to a seat," he said gruffly.

Oh no, don't do that, she barely stopped herself from saying.

The carriage shook again and he held her closer.

He'd force the most virtuous lady's mind to wander the path of iniquity. Make her fingers itch to wander as well. Make her have . . . urges.

Stop that this instant. A lady never itches . . . and she most certainly never succumbs to urges.

But why was it that gentlemen were allowed, even expected, to act upon their urges and ladies must suppress theirs?

Goodness, Thea. What would the duke think if he could read your thoughts?

He'd think she wanted to lure him into a forced marriage.

And he wouldn't be more wrong.

She staunchly refused to be just another one of his silly, fluttering admirers, flinging themselves in his path in the vain hope of becoming his duchess.

She'd stepped in his path for a very clear purpose.

Escape. Freedom.

And the chance to study his art collection.

It had nothing to do with his sensual lips, or that alluring cleft in his chin . . . or the rock-solid arms that held her.

Nothing whatsoever.

Dalton settled Lady Dorothea more firmly against his chest as they traversed a rough stretch of cobblestones.

He couldn't let her rattle around the carriage collecting bruises and scrapes, now could he? They must be nearing Ludgate Hill. Soon the road would be better maintained.

Then he'd set her over on her side of the carriage.

Roll his greatcoat into a bolster and wedge between their bodies.

He touched her shoulder. "It's late. You may as well try to sleep. The journey will be easier once we reach the West Road."

Heavily fringed lashes fluttered onto pale cheeks.

Did she have to smell so delectable? A man couldn't sleep in a carriage scented with rose petals and warm woman.

Somehow just listening to the rhythm of her breathing was unbearably erotic.

Each inhale made her chest lift under the blanket. He was only a man. He couldn't help thinking about what lay beneath the plaid wool.

They wouldn't overflow his hands, her breasts. They'd shelter inside, perfectly filling the cup of his palms. And when he clasped her nipples between his thumbs and forefingers she would gasp with surprise and arch into him.

If he slid his hands down the curve of her hips he could easily drag her on top of him.

Hold her pinioned there while he pleasured her with his hands, his lips, his tongue, and his . . .

Dalton gave himself a swift mental kick.

Troublesome she may be, but she was an innocent.

Not one of his worldly widows.

Nor one of the wives he chose to bed whose husbands were notoriously unfaithful and cruel. Women who sought him for solace and revenge.

They received pleasure, and the reassurance that they were beautiful and meant to be treasured, while he listened to them talk of their husbands.

The powerful peers and corrupt men of business who ruled London's underworld.

He and the wives and widows used each other for mutual gain, and no one got hurt.

They understood he had no heart to give.

It would be far too easy to hurt Lady Dorothea.

"Your Grace, are you asleep?" she whispered drowsily.

"I was," he lied.

"You weren't. If you'd been asleep, you wouldn't have heard me ask you that question."

"I was attempting to sleep and I had nearly achieved success. I suggest you do the same."

She yawned, curling against him, one of her small fists settling near his earlobe.

A light touch along his neck.

One soft, tentative touch and he was hard and raw with need. He stopped breathing.

He always needed physical release after a night at the hells, when his blood still pulsed with danger and his mind pounded with the need for dominion.

Gently, he lifted her fingers, preparing to move her across the carriage. He had to create distance.

In direct contradiction to his movements, the carriage wheels jarred, shaking the planks beneath them and sinking Lady Dorothea more firmly into his arms.

"How did you receive this slash?" she murmured, glancing at his jaw. "Was it the possessive husband you're running from?"

So convenient, how the papers crowed about the duels he fought. The duels he manufactured from hints and well-placed rumors.

"Tavern accident. Shard of broken glass. Nothing as dramatic as a duel."

"Really," she said, clearly skeptical.

People drew their own conclusions about his bruises and cuts. Of course he wasn't marked often. He was too swift for that. He'd been careless with Trent. He'd let his guard down.

It would never happen again.

"Can I ask you one thing, Your Grace?"

"No, you cannot." But even as his lips remonstrated, his hands encouraged her boldness.

He realized with consternation that he'd been stroking her hair. Running those strands of honey through his fingers.

"Go to sleep, Lady Dorothea."

"I only want to know this. What is it about amorous dalliances that justifies every risk?"

Don't answer that, Dalton. Don't—"Some things are worth any cost, any price."

Your spun red-gold curls for example. Priceless.

The way you fit in my arms, tucking your head beneath my chin.

Jesus. What was wrong with him?

It was the darkness. And the bed.

And the warm, sleepy bundle of woman in his arms.

"But what *exactly* is it about conquest, about claiming a woman, making her yours, and then discarding her and moving to the next, that compels you so? Is it the power? The pleasure?"

Hellfire. "That's not a conversation we'll have. Ever."

"I'm genuinely curious. Pretend I'm a man. Pretend we're having a conversation over a pint in a pub."

There was no way he'd ever be able to pretend that. Not with her soft curves pressed against him.

"I'm your best friend," she continued, lowering her speech to an adorably husky baritone. "I say,

Osborne, time for a new mistress, then? Tired of that Renwick bird? Who's it going to be next?"

He choked back laughter. What did she know about mistresses, anyway?

And then he remembered. Her father, the Earl of Desmond, was a notorious profligate. His by-blows were scattered the length and breadth of England.

Dalton's friend James had married one.

Was she equating Dalton with her father?

The thought heated his blood with anger. He wasn't anything like Desmond.

But of course he could never explain that to her. He'd cultivated his dissipated reputation with diligence over the years.

The gossip about his amours kept gazes turned away from his other nocturnal activities.

He owed her some explanation, though.

"Men aren't complicated. We like smashing things, drinking to oblivion, and pleasuring women. It's that simple."

It wasn't that simple, of course. The need for revenge was stronger than the need for love. And he'd do well to remind himself of that truth right now, in this carriage, with Lady Dorothea tucked into his arms.

He never should have agreed to escort her to Ireland. She'd only been bluffing. She wouldn't have told Trent where to find him.

An image of Foxford's withered hands pawing at her roiled through his mind like last night's brandy still souring his stomach.

He fisted one hand against her waist. She'd never marry Foxford. Dalton would never let that happen.

His ruthless mission continued but she was under his protection now until she reached her aunt's house. He was strong enough to accomplish both tasks.

She tilted her head. "Are you saying that men are compelled by primitive needs . . . animal urges . . . and perish the consequences?"

"Something like that."

She nestled closer, burying her chin in his neck. "You don't feel those urges . . . right now?" she whispered softly.

Oh, he felt them. He felt them and drowned in them and longed to unleash the ferocity of them. "Please go to sleep," he said desperately.

"You don't desire . . . *me?*"

He'd explode soon.

They'd find bits of him all the way back to London.

"It doesn't matter if I desire you or not. Now go to sleep or I'll tie this cravat around your mouth."

"Humph." She rolled onto her side, away from him. "I'm only trying to comprehend the male mind."

"Women generally want more from men than we're willing to give," he said more gently.

"I know."

Such bleakness. He nearly shivered.

"My father taught me that lesson," she said. "He's never taken the slightest interest in me. He probably won't even notice I'm gone."

"But your mother, won't she be worried?"

"Furious, more like. She's wrapped all her hopes and dreams in me, instead of living her own life. I realized that some time ago."

"And so you're running away."

"I hope to make something of my life. Be useful in some more meaningful way."

Ah yes . . . here it came. She wanted something from him.

Something he could never give her.

"Why won't you allow me to unwrap those paintings in your attic? Where's the harm? There could be priceless lost treasures hiding there. Did your father purchase them at art auctions in Europe?"

"They weren't purchased. They were settlement for gambling debts. Sometimes he won entire estates, other times ancestral art collections."

"Aren't you at least curious about the value of the collection? I have a feeling they'd fetch a staggering sum if you decided to sell."

"No."

"But why? What possible harm could it do?" she persisted.

"I won't go back to Balfry." The words burst from some buried part of his soul. "My brother, Alec, drowned there when he was five. In the cold waters of the bay. He . . . fell off a cliff."

Society still thought it had been a tragic accident, if they ever thought about it all.

There was a moment of stunned silence. A tentative touch on his arm. "I'm so sorry," she whispered. "I truly had no idea."

Dalton knew that soft tone. That's what happened when a man made an intimate confession, and a woman began to think he could be saved.

He tensed, the muscles in his forearm cording into hard ropes. "Society has forgotten. My family never could. Especially my mother. She's never been back since the death."

Damn it all. Even worse. He couldn't speak about his mother. That would give her even more hope.

He needed to shut his mouth now. And keep it firmly closed.

He was a danger to her.

"Have you thought that visiting the house might chase away the ghosts, instead of drawing them nearer?" Lady Dorothea said softly.

"I've no wish to relive the past."

"That's very sad."

"I don't need your sympathy, Lady Dorothea. I only told you so you'd see why I have no interest in cataloguing the house's contents."

She wrapped the blanket more tightly around her shoulders and curled up on her side of the carriage. "I'll pester you no more, then."

Now he'd angered her. But what else could he do? He had nothing to give her except his protection on this brief journey.

Her breathing grew regular and easy.

She tempted him to uncharacteristic revelations with her trusting eyes and innocently teasing questions.

He couldn't be distracted.

He must be sharp and ready for what lay ahead. Confronting O'Roarke.

Remain focused. Driven.

Lady Dorothea sighed in her sleep, a small sound of release that wound him even tighter.

Obviously, there'd be no sleep for him until this bed became a seat again.

She was tempting but he was strong enough to resist.

Even if she begged him to kiss her. Even if she wound those curls of hers around his shaft and asked him to teach her how to pleasure him through the satin curtain of her hair.

What the devil's wrong with you? Pull yourself together, man.

Her beauty was bone deep and something precious. Not for him to sully.

Not for him to possess.

She was under his protection now.

He would never lose control.

Chapter 7

A touch on his face jolted Dalton awake. In an instant he had his assailant pinned, squirming and helpless beneath him.

"Your Grace." A muffled, indignant female voice. "Your Grace, it's *me*."

A pause. Several disoriented breaths. A lady in his bed. Daylight.

He never slept the night with a female . . . much less a lady.

Not his bed.

Cramped space.

Carriage.

He rolled off Lady Dorothea, the events of last night crashing through his skull like a left hook from a prizefighter.

By daylight, the situation was even more objectionable. What in holy hell had he been thinking? He never should have agreed to escort her anywhere other than straight back across the square to the countess.

He was more of a danger to her than controlling grandmothers.

Damn. Damn. Damn!

"Well," huffed Lady Dorothea, adjusting her bonnet. "You needn't *crush* a person."

"You touched me. My reaction was an instinct."

"I was trying to wake you. We've stopped to change horses." She wrinkled her nose. "I smell stable."

Judging by the light, he'd slumbered through at least three well-lit inn yards, a host of stable hands changing horses, new postilions arriving and old ones leaving. It was a disconcerting realization.

How long had she been awake?

He slanted a glance in her direction.

Blunder. Don't stare at her. Don't . . .

Riot of spun-sugar curls. Faint dark smudges under brilliant rainy-sky eyes. Tempting sliver of collarbone visible beneath gray-green patterned silk.

Dalton ripped his gaze away, retied his cravat in a simple knot, and ran a hand through his unruly hair.

Time to make his escape from tumbled and freshly bedded–looking beauties with bold, searching gazes.

"We'll not stay long." He searched for his hat in this rumpled excuse for a hired chariot. "We'll have stopped at a second-rate inn. Could be unsavory characters about."

And he chief among them.

He'd spent far too many hours last night imagining all the depraved things he wanted to do with her. She'd be safer with a highwayman.

She fastened hidden hooks under the embroidered satin of her pale green slim-fitting coat. "I'm *that* famished." She tied her long dove-gray bonnet ribbons into a pert bow beneath her sharp little chin. "Now then. We need a story, Your Grace. In the event anyone at the inn asks questions. Whose traveling chariot are we riding in?"

"Con rented it from a merchant named Jones, I believe." He located his hat. Even more deflated now. Had he slept on it? "What difference does it make?"

"It means that you're the quite ordinary and humble Mr. Jones. And I'm the estimable Mrs. Jones. Let's see . . ." She fingered her bonnet ribbon, staring out the window at the bustle of activity in the inn yard while he groped around the carriage for his greatcoat.

"Mr. Jones owns a chain of prosperous dry-goods shops. Flour . . . grains . . . oats, that sort of thing. Horses have to eat, you know. Bread must be baked. And we've got three children waiting in Bristol. Their names are . . . Melisande, Mirabelle, and . . . Michaelmas."

Dalton blinked. He hadn't had his morning coffee yet. It was far too early for children. "Michaelmas?"

"She was born on the holy day, poor thing."

"Michaelmas is a *girl?*" Dalton jerked on his greatcoat and plopped his crushed hat on his head. "We don't need a story." He opened the door and leapt down from the carriage. "Because you're not going to speak to anyone."

Grasping her about the waist, he lifted her to

the ground. Not strictly necessary, but expedient. Except that his hands didn't want to relinquish her slender waist. Where was that voluminous gray cloak she'd been wrapped in last night?

There, balled in a corner of the coach. Too wrinkled to wear.

Her eyes lit with a saucy glint. "Would you rather we had a boy, Mr. Jones?"

Dalton snatched his hands away and took a step backward. "I'd rather not have this conversation at all."

Thankfully, everyone else in the stable yard went about their business, saddling horses and hauling feed buckets, too industrious to notice the insurrection being mounted before their eyes.

This was supposed to be a quiet, uneventful journey.

She tilted her head back so she could see him more clearly from under her bonnet brim. "Then pray inform me who you have traveling with you on your carriage bed. *Olofsson* of the talented feet?"

He slammed the carriage door and marched her toward the inn. "You're decorous Lady Dorothea. I encountered you desperate and alone by the side of the road, the mail coach you so rashly hired having left you behind when you stopped too long at an inn to pester the innkeeper with questions."

Lady Dorothea smiled triumphantly. "You're making up stories, Your Grace. But I like mine better, don't you? Mr. Jones is such a very prosaic and *agreeable* sort of fellow. Why, he never scolds his darling wife. And he never, ever glowers. Or growls."

Dalton glowered. And then he growled. "I'm begging you to go inside quietly and sip your tea swiftly. *Lady Dorothea.*"

"Oh, do call me Thea, Mr. Jones. I should think with three children I might grant you that liberty."

Dangerous words, those.

Ladies named Dorothea would never speak to tradesmen in a second-rate inn and attract too much attention. But recalcitrant *Theas* might very well make a scene.

He shook his head. "Not Thea. Not Mrs. Jones," he muttered.

Her eyes narrowed in the watery morning light.

Dalton ignored the warning and hastened her toward the doorway of the inn.

A man in the sober black clothing and white collar of the clergy emerged and walked past them.

"Caro mio! Che bella giornata!" Lady Dorothea shouted, sweeping her hand toward the lowering sky.

The clergyman craned his neck to stare at them.

"What in God's name was that?" Dalton whispered when the clergyman was safely past.

"If I'm not the wife, I must be the mistress. And staid Mr. Jones prefers passionate opera singers," she announced.

There went her fingers again, rubbing the length of bonnet ribbon silk. "I do speak perfect Italian, you know. And my lyric soprano is quite good."

And he was the damned archbishop. "You're as English as Yorkshire pudding. No one will believe you're Italian." He marched her to the door. "Now go inside. Quietly. No more Italian. And no more stories. Do you understand?"

She frowned. "I used to sit in the town square in Florence and observe the conversations. It's all in the hand gestures, you know."

She raised her arm with a dramatic flourish. "I'm Dame Gabrielli, the famous coloratura from Florence." She cocked her hip and placed a fist on the resulting swell.

A stable hand turned, his gaze caught by her unguarded movements and captured by the buttercup curls spilling over her shoulders.

Dalton gritted his teeth. "If you long for adulation you should return to London, where your adoring public waits to heap roses at your feet."

The glow in her eyes extinguished. "I don't want adulation. I want freedom." She tossed her head. "I want to sing at the top of my lungs. I want to . . . I want to *live*."

Something tightened in Dalton's chest. It was only natural for her to fabricate other realities when she'd been living under her mother's stern control her entire existence.

But her burgeoning rebellion wasn't convenient for his plans. He nudged her toward the doorway. "We need to reach Bristol swiftly, attracting no notice. If we meet anyone we know you'll be ruined instantly. It's dangerous for you, surely you acknowledge that much."

"Do you truly think me witless? Of course I

know that. But the story can only help us. If the travelers at this second-rate inn, who are hardly likely to recognize us, believe they've encountered an opera singer and a prosperous merchant, they'll have no tales to tell of"—she lowered her voice to a whisper—"dukes and spinsters."

There was some sense to that. No . . . no, there wasn't. It was always best to simply keep one's mouth closed.

Let people make up their own stories.

"You're going inside and I'm going to the stables." He handed her some coins from his waistcoat pocket. "I'll pay for your tea. You'll sip it swiftly."

Her fingers closed around the coins. "Whatever you desire, *caro mio*," she said in that affected Italian accent with a sugary smile pasted on her lips. "Your wish is my command."

The obedient act didn't fool him.

There wasn't an obedient bone in that slim, curvaceous body of hers. And her next words proved it.

"I'll try not to serenade the good folk at the inn with more than one or two arias." Her hips swished in a suspiciously operatic fashion as she disappeared through the doorway of the inn.

Too many people around to hoist the lady over his shoulder, bind her wrists with his cravat, and bundle her back in a carriage to London with Con.

Dalton could ride the rest of the way to Bristol on horseback. Alone.

On second thought, better let Con do the tying, because thinking of something so intimate with the lady shot an arrow of pure lust to his groin.

His stomach growled. He could do with breakfast. But they needed to be on the road again swiftly, to minimize the risk of the news of his whereabouts reaching London.

Dalton didn't know why Trent had been searching for him. But he certainly didn't want him to hear about the cut across his face.

Gingerly, he probed the wound. It could do with a washing.

He strode to the stables and sluiced cold water from the pump over his face.

His mind cleared with the shock of the bracing water, the sound of horses pawing. Brisk smell of horse dung. Leather. Straw. Simple smells with no hint of spiced rose petals.

He followed the sound of Con's whistling to one of the stalls.

Con's grizzled face split into a grin when he saw him. "Well now, if it isn't Sleeping Beauty. Finally decided to awaken, eh? Where's your lady suitor?"

"You can wipe that smirk off your face. Nothing happened. And that was an infantile trick to play with the bed."

"Can't think what you mean." Con wasn't very good at appearing innocent. Too hairy.

"You know very well what I mean." Dalton gave him a disgusted look.

"You mean she didn't have her way with you?

I thought a persistent thing like her might teach you a thing or two you didn't learn at Cambridge."

"Oh, ha ha." Dalton grimaced as his skin cracked over the cut. "It's really not a laughing matter. The lady will be ruined if anyone recognizes us."

Con snapped a horse bridle between his hands, testing the strength. He never left anything to chance, preferring to personally oversee the details of their excursions. "As long as you don't ruin her, she'll survive."

"Leave off. You know I'd never debauch an innocent." Although it had been exquisite torture holding her warm curves against his chest.

You don't feel those urges . . . right now?

A less principled man would've taken those words as a clear invitation to seduction.

"Sure and I wasn't talking about debauching. I was thinking more of wooing. Composing treacly verses about her eyes, that sort of thing. Making her love you and then abandoning her." His blue eyes sharpened. "I won't have you doing that. I like the lady."

Dalton sighed. "I like her, too, damn her scorched butter curls. Even though she has the most irritating habit of not listening to a word I say . . . and then disarming me by making me laugh."

Con shook his head, his whiskers twitching with barely concealed mirth. "Can't have her making you laugh, now. That won't do."

Dalton was an expert at tracking criminals

through the crooked maze of London's back lanes. He could fell a man with one blow. Find a vulnerable neck with his blade in five seconds flat.

But he was beginning to suspect there were far more treacherous predicaments.

Being confined in small spaces with the most vexing and desirable woman he'd ever met, for one.

Wallflowers bursting into impassioned Italian in courtyards, for another.

She longed to be free from her mother's control. He'd met the countess and certainly wouldn't want her telling *him* what to do, but he couldn't allow the lady to increase the risks inherent in confusing the strict boundaries between his two worlds . . . the rake and the Hellhound.

It was too dangerous. For his plans. And for her safety.

"We've a killer to hunt," Dalton said sternly. "Or have you forgotten?"

"I haven't forgotten." Con ran his hand over the leather horse tack, testing the bridles and reins. "Though I'm none too happy about going back to Ireland. Never thought I'd see those shores again. Too many painful memories."

It was the same with Dalton. They were both returning to their troubled pasts.

"Do you have other family left in Cork?" he asked Con.

Con jerked his head. "Nah, not anymore."

Dalton had never seen Con shaken like this. It wasn't fair to ask him to do this, he realized. "You should return to London. I'll carry on alone."

Con grunted, giving a harness a last tug. "I've come this far. Besides, it's damned entertaining watching that slip of a lady wedge herself so thoroughly under your skin."

"Like a patch of poison ivy," Dalton said bleakly. "Scratching only makes it worse. She's probably in the breakfast room right now serenading everyone with a bleeding aria."

Con grinned. "Arias, is it?"

"Wants to make up stories about us. I'm Mr. Jones and she's a famous opera singer. Been repressed by that overbearing mother of hers her whole life and now she's breaking free."

"Like I said, damned entertaining. Wouldn't miss it for the world." Con gestured for a stable hand to come and take the horse tack. "I'll finish up here. Go fetch the opera singer and we'll be on our way."

Someone had to corral the lady back to the carriage.

And then he'd have to climb in after her because of the risk of a nobleman seeing him with this telltale crimson slash across his jaw in the daylight.

At least there'd be no more beds involved in their brief acquaintance. He'd convert the makeshift bed back to a seat immediately.

Though that was small protection.

Something about her brought out the beast in him.

When he entered the inn, he saw her immediately, across the smoky, low-beamed room, as if the other people were underwater, their features blurred, while she glowed in sharp relief.

Weak sunlight filtering through streaked glass caressed strands of honey and amber in her hair, and rested on her skin because it had the right to touch her, to warm her.

He wanted to touch her. Right now. Claim her as his.

And it looked like he wasn't the only one. A gangly fair-haired young man in a high, starched collar that left only the scarlet tips of his ears visible approached her table and stopped to address her in an unforgivably familiar manner. A hot wash of rage swept through Dalton's chest before he reminded himself that he couldn't possibly be jealous of a pup who'd barely started shaving.

He wasn't the jealous type. He never felt possessive about a woman. They were transitory diversions. No more his than the moon or the stars.

He never gave them any illusions about his intentions. And they never left dissatisfied.

So it wasn't jealousy he felt, it was mere protectiveness.

The same kind of protectiveness he would feel for any small, helpless creature that ventured across his path.

Except that she wasn't helpless. She'd bent him to her purposes easily enough.

Still, some dangers were too much for even a determined and thoroughly resourceful lady.

That pup may look harmless, but the first rule of traveling was never to talk to inquisitive strangers. Especially if they wanted to know what route you were taking, or when you planned to depart.

She'd been too sheltered. She had no protective shell.

She smiled at the pup in the high collar.

Dalton's hands tightened into fists and he crossed the room in three strides.

"Oh, there you are, Mr. Jones." She smiled at Dalton. "I was beginning to think you'd fallen into the horse trough. Coffee?"

She didn't wait for him to answer but poured him a cup from the silver pot on the table. "I know you take your coffee strong. Wouldn't do to weaken it with milk or anything as indulgent as sugar."

The boy in the starched collar took one look at Dalton's face, stammered his apologies, and made a hasty retreat back to his own table. As well he should.

Dalton took his place across from Lady Dorothea and accepted a cup of strong, black coffee. He could use a cup. Or five.

For the first time he noticed she must have borrowed a traveling writing desk, and appeared to be composing a note.

Dalton gulped his coffee down in two swallows. "Writing a letter to someone?"

"My mother." The nib of her pen scratched across the page.

Dalton's cup banged against the saucer. "No mention of me, I trust?"

"None whatsoever," she said breezily. "Not everything is about *you*, you know."

A stout man in a striped waistcoat glanced their way. Far too many people who might remember his face, the cut across his jaw.

Dalton ripped a roll in half and slathered it with butter. He'd give her two more minutes.

In the morning light, in the low-ceilinged room, Osborne was truly monolithic.

One glance from him and other men scurried away like terrified mice.

One glance *at* him and her mind simmered with forbidden desires.

She remembered the feel of his muscular arms embracing her, steadying her against his chest. The moment when he'd told her he thought she was beautiful.

Her hand shook and ink splotched across the paper.

Foolish girl. You mustn't let him seep into your thoughts and leave an indelible stain.

She'd woken hours before him and lain in the jostling carriage, watching him sleep. Watching morning light tease bronze from his hair and play across the rugged landscape of his face.

He reached for another roll. He ate in the same way he approached everything: swallowing it nearly whole, taking no time to savor, simply devouring as his due all that life laid before him.

She bent back over her letter. Only a few more lines.

The duke wiped his fingers on a napkin. "I was just contemplating removing my neck cloth, tying you up, and bundling you back to your mother. How about that instead of a letter?"

Thea's head snapped up. "You wouldn't do that."

"Oh, wouldn't I?" His fingers moved to his cravat, tugging the end just a bit, drawing her eye to the threat. "Don't tempt me," he said darkly. "I only want one more reason. One more minuscule reason."

"I'd only find another way to escape London."

"That what starched collar over there is? Another way to leave?" He turned that ferocious glare toward the man who had lent her his writing desk.

His glowering stare sent a naughty quiver through her. He was so clearly asserting his claim to be by her side.

"I'll have you know Mr. Cooper is a respectable clerk."

"Don't like the look of him. Too crimson about the ears. Like an underdone suckling pig."

"He blushes when he speaks to me. I think it's sweet. I required the means to write a letter. He loaned me this traveling desk. Very *obliging* of him."

Dark blue eyes narrowed. "Promise me you'll not accept favors from strangers. Under that earnest, starched collar could beat the charred heart of a hardened criminal. One with ulterior motives and nefarious designs."

Really, the gentleman had an overactive imagination. "I hardly think Mr. Cooper was contemplating anything too wicked."

"No, but he was contemplating your figure. Couldn't tear his gaze away from you."

"You're staring rather rudely yourself," she rejoined.

Of course his goal in all this rudeness was to goad her into an unbecoming fit of pique. He wanted her to act like a spoiled princess. Beg him to send her back to the comforts of London.

She would never give him that satisfaction.

Certain things had been expected of Thea.

To wed. To be a mother. To swim along with the inexorable tide of generations of women just like her moving toward the same destination.

Now here she was turning midstream and fighting her way against the current. It wouldn't be easy.

And there was a large, duke-sized obstruction currently blocking her path.

"Mr. Jones." She set down her quill. "Never say you're jealous of a poor clerk."

He backed away so quickly his chair nearly overturned. "Jealous of that pup? Preposterous. Finish your letter."

She hid a smile, finished the last sentence, signed her name, blotted the pen, and placed it carefully back in its case.

"I'll return that." The duke reassembled the case.

Thea rose, wiping away crumbs, and folded the letter.

When they reached the table of the poor, terrorized Mr. Cooper, she bent near him. "Thank you ever so much for lending me the writing kit, Mr. Cooper."

The man blushed, then trembled when Osborne glared at him, then blushed some more. Thea gave the clerk her brightest smile. "I pray you, pay no attention whatsoever to Mr. Jones. He ate a bad oyster last evening."

Thea patted the duke on the shoulder. "Poor man is suffering dreadfully. Turns him into an uncivil beast."

Oh, how she enjoyed the murderous look on Osborne's face.

Vexing dukes might just be her new favorite pastime.

Thea thrust her letter into his great paws. "Be a dear and post this for me, won't you, Mr. Jones? There's an obliging fellow."

Chapter 8

The Great Wall of Duke sprawled next to Thea, the crown of his black hat brushing against the blue-striped silk ceiling, his sheer physical bulk relegating her to a thin wedge of carriage seat.

Thea did her best to concentrate on the rolling hills and quaint stone farmhouses of the passing countryside but found it impossible.

He was too near. And there was that distracting possibility of their bodies meeting . . . conversing . . . while they remained silent.

He hadn't said more than two words to her since they left the White Hart Inn. Probably still sore about her sending him on a menial errand such as posting her letter.

Ordering him about in front of a clerk had gone against her entire upbringing. She'd almost gone back and apologized on the spot.

Dukes take precedence unless a member of the Royal Family is present. Etiquette rules etched into her mind since birth, much like the Ten Commandments.

But Thea had been apologizing for one thing or another her entire life, and being here in this carriage marked a declaration of independence of sorts. So maybe the rules didn't apply anymore.

In this brave new motherless world maybe dukes did *not* take precedence.

Maybe they were simply men. Maybe they didn't deserve her respect or adulation based solely on their birthright.

He'd lectured her on the impropriety of speaking with a respectable clerk, in a public dining room, for heaven's sake, when he'd dallied with half the widows and a goodly portion of the wives in London.

The enormity of the unfairness of that galled her.

She'd watched him during her first two seasons, as a hen watched a fox circling its sturdy enclosure, aware of the dangerous charm, but safe behind the barrier of her own drabness.

In the ballrooms of London he'd exuded charisma that seduced every female in his path. But he'd never even spared the wallflowers one glance. He was the king of intrigues, scandals, and careless arrogance.

A far cry from the brooding man beside her. What was he thinking about? Something vexing, judging by the way he furrowed his brow and tapped his foot.

Tap, tap, tap. Three times for displeasure.

Probably plotting how to get rid of her at the next posting inn. He'd said he wanted to tie her up and send her back to London.

Obviously he cared nothing for her good opinion. She was a temporary problem for him. Another day and a half and he could wash his hands of her.

She stole a glance at those hands where they rested on his thighs, ungloved and interestingly unpolished.

Who ever heard of a duke with roughened hands and a hint of dirt under his nails? And that jagged cut along his jaw gave him a dastardly look, exacerbated by the brown stubble of beard he was allowing to grow unchecked.

He was too . . . well, he was simply too *everything*. Too large, too distracting, and too accustomed to having his way in all matters.

He glanced up and caught her staring. "I didn't post your letter, you know," he remarked nonchalantly.

"I beg your pardon? Not post my letter? Why ever not? It was a very simple task. Even a duke could perform it."

He gave her a tight half smile. "You don't truly want to send that letter."

"How do you know what I want? Did you read my private correspondence?"

"Of course I read it," he scoffed. "You *wanted* me to read it."

"I most certainly did not." Thea didn't even attempt to modulate her tones to a ladylike volume. "And please stop presuming to know my mind better than I know it myself."

"If you didn't want me to read it you would have posted it yourself."

"I only gave you the letter because you were Mr. Jones. I've always imagined that's what a solicitous gentleman might do for his paramour, small acts of kindness, to show he cared."

His eyes narrowed. "May I remind you, madam, that I did not seek your company on this journey? The moment you set foot inside my carriage you became my responsibility."

"Your carriage was merely convenient." Thea kept her gaze steady, even though she wanted to shrink away from him. "I don't need your protection, or your censure, or you obstructing my mail. Now give me back my letter." She held out her hand.

He loomed closer, inches from her now.

Let him advance. She would never retreat. Never cede victory.

His needs didn't take precedence. He didn't know what was best for her.

"And besides," Thea continued, "it's not your carriage, it's Mr. Jones's carriage, so I'm not your responsibility."

"A mere technicality." The duke veered nearer, his arms bracketing her on the seat.

Thea reconsidered her no-retreat strategy.

Those dark blue eyes threatened to drown her resolve, cast her into a maelstrom of capitulation and longing.

How could one small-sized proven disaster of an almost spinster hope to hold her own with such an arrogant beast?

She must try. She could no longer be meek and obedient Lady Dorothea.

She could battle an overbearing duke and emerge the victor.

She looked him squarely in the eyes. "Give me back the letter. I'll post it myself."

"No." He prolonged the vowel, clearly issuing a challenge with that one short word.

"Give it here." She reached for the lapel of his coat, intending to find the inner pocket.

He caught her wrist. His touch made her mind steam over, like a mirror next to a copper bathing tub.

His eyes softened. "Do you honestly want to communicate such a lie? It will destroy your reputation."

Taken aback by the concern in his eyes, Thea paused. "If the letter isn't posted my mother will think I've been abducted. She'll launch a search party."

"And if it's posted, you'll break your mother's heart." A note of real worry snuck into his voice.

"I broke my mother's heart years ago, when I wasn't the success she'd groomed me to be." She searched for a way to make him understand. "She meant for me to dazzle, to awe, to inspire applause and adoration, like a fireworks display over Vauxhall. But instead I fizzled with a damp plop and never left the ground."

"But an actor in a traveling company? You honestly think your mother will believe a story like that?"

"Why shouldn't I have fallen in love and been compromised by a traveling player? They are paid to portray passion on the stage."

"Most of them have false teeth and wear wigs and more paint than a Covent Garden bawd. At least you could invent a middle-aged country squire."

"That would give my mother too much hope. This will allow her to grieve. And move on to finding perfect matches for my brothers."

His grip on her wrist loosened, and his thumb brushed over the pulse in her wrist. "You make it sound so dire, as if you're already an old maid. You needn't throw everything away. Your life is full of promise. I'm not sure you're aware of how astonishingly beautiful you are, Thea. And coupled with that brilliant mind of yours . . . it's a lethal combination."

When he turned on the charm it was as if a streetlamp flared to life inside his eyes, burning with sensual promise. He was the lethal one.

She licked her suddenly dry lips and his gaze lowered to her mouth.

"So beautiful." He captured her other wrist as well and soothed his finger over the sensitive skin of her inner wrist.

Low and silver-edged, that voice.

And those fingers on the insides of her wrists, stroking, soothing.

What were they even arguing about?

Maybe the letter *had* been penned hastily.

Do not *let him distract you with his practiced charm. Concentrate, Thea. This is too important.*

It was only that she kept having these compelling glimpses of something under his surface. Something that wasn't rakish or glib at all.

Something genuine and honest and concerned with more than his immediate pleasure.

"I do appreciate your concern for my welfare, Your Grace, but this is my life. And I'm free to live how I choose."

"Two ladies shouldn't live alone in the wilds of Ireland. You'll be easy prey for opportunists and rogues. And if you're disinherited you'll be penniless, as well as helpless and defenseless."

And then he said something infuriating like that and ruined everything.

Thea jerked her wrists away, irritation stiffening her shoulders. "It's hardly the wilds, and I'm not helpless. I'm highly educated and trained to manage a much larger household. And I'm perfectly capable of earning my own income should the need arise."

He crossed thick arms over his formidable chest. "Tell me you don't want luxury and comfort. I've never known a woman not to want that. I'll wager you like fine linen bedclothes and French-milled soap as much as the next lady. You smell as if you do."

"I'll learn to live without. I'll do whatever it takes. Anything is better than marrying a man of my mother's choosing. A loveless marriage. Bondage to a man who loathes me."

"What's she going to do, shackle you to the vicar?"

"You don't know my mother."

"Actually, I do. Remember I was there, at James . . . at the Duke of Harland's estate last year.

I know she's a formidable foe. Are you sure you're ready to incur her wrath? And what will you do for income?"

She had a plan in that regard. Of course that plan involved the paintings in his attic.

It wouldn't be in her interests to antagonize him too far.

"Flawless Italian won't pay creditors," he continued. "And you're far too lovely and delicate to rusticate in a cottage the rest of your life."

Delicate? She wasn't *delicate.* At least not anymore.

Don't lose your temper. You need to study his paintings. Don't lose your . . .

Thea lost her temper.

"You," she sputtered. "You pompous, autocratic, controlling . . ."

"You forgot *arrogant.*"

". . . arrogant arse!"

"What age is your aunt?"

"What's that got to do with anything?"

"Is the cottage entailed? How many servants does she keep? Is there a sturdy gate around the estate?"

Thea glowered at him. "I never should have trusted you with my mail."

"Exactly." His gaze darkened. "That's exactly the lesson I'm trying to teach you. Never trust a man, Thea. We're wolves, every last one of us. From the clerks to the dukes. We'll take your letters and we won't mail them. We'll tell you we love you, and we won't mean it. We'll eat you for breakfast and spit out your bones."

"And yet you think I should marry."

"A husband may be neglectful, but he'd be sworn to protect you."

Thea nearly laughed in his face. Sworn to protect? Her father had never protected anything in his life, save his own interests.

"I used to think marrying would be my best chance of escape from my mother's control. I even had foolish notions of finding someone to love. But after my first season I gave up those silly dreams. You don't need to teach me about not trusting men. That's not a lesson I need to learn."

"And yet you trusted that young clerk enough to accept a favor. And you handed over your letter to me like a credulous lamb."

She drew her shoulders up in an attempt to seem more substantial. "You don't need to warn me about big, bad wolves. I can take care of myself, thank you very much"

Something in his gaze shifted. "Can you, lamb?" His eyes darkened and grew serious. "I would worry about you, all alone next to that wide, bleak ocean."

A sudden thought occurred to her. That small branch of fossil he wore around his neck. It was from the beaches of Balfry Bay.

The place where he'd said his brother drowned.

In the wide, bleak ocean.

Thea's heart squeezed thinking that this strong, invincible man carried so much hurt inside him. So much pain he'd been avoiding for so long.

If she could convince him to visit Balfry

House there'd be more for him to find than
ancient masterpieces. He may very well find
surcease from the horrifying memories of his
brother's death.

If he could visit the scene again. Face his anguish head-on.

Confront his emotions.

Unable to suppress the urge, she touched his
cheek as well, the stubble across his jaw scratching the sensitive skin of her palm, their arms
crossing, elbows touching.

"I'm not afraid of the future, Your Grace," she
said softly. "This isn't only a whim. It's not the
moon growing full. It won't wane back to a sliver
again. I've thought this through very carefully.
I've chosen this path."

He turned his face and his lips touched her
palm for one moment. Not a kiss, only the briefest
of touches, but it set her heart racing.

"There's another way," he said. "Go back to
London. Tell your mother you refuse to marry
Foxford."

Thea shook her head. "If it's not Foxford it'll only
be someone else. My mother and grandmother
are desperate for me to fulfill their dreams. You
witnessed how my mother hired my half sister
Miss Beckett in an attempt to land Harland. If
that's not desperate, I've no idea what is."

Thea dropped her hand back into her lap, the
imprint of his hint of a beard still tingling along
her palm. "It's not enough to have run away. I
must have done something irrevocable."

They could do something irrevocable right now, Dalton thought.

In this carriage. On this seat.

Get rid of that bonnet. Too much stiff straw and silk ribbons in his path.

Work on the cleverly concealed hooks under the quilted embroidery on her pelisse.

Make short work of the gown. The petticoats. The stays.

His gaze slid down her slim figure. She'd have pert, tip-tilted breasts. Smallish, but round and perfect for his palm. They'd jounce in his hands, firm and smooth.

He'd leave the garters and stockings.

He liked to see a woman in garters and nothing else. The contrast of those silk ribbons on smooth thighs never failed to make him stiff as iron.

Speaking of which . . . he shifted, easing his erection into a more comfortable position along his thigh, hoping she didn't glance down.

Hoping she *would* glance down and see what she did to him.

She didn't think she was perfect? She was.

Perfectly made to test his resolutions.

He wanted to kiss her. Somehow his hand had become tangled in her butter-and-marmalade curls.

Wild bramble roses with thin petals. That's what she smelled like.

Her lips were a pale pink color, like the small French strawberries that used to grow wild in the fields near Balfry. Would they taste like strawberries, those lips?

He fought the need to claim her lips.

She'd be so sweet. So dangerously sweet.

He wanted all that sweetness for his own.

What would it be like to have a woman like her waiting for him when he came home from a night at the hells, bruised and aching?

Her innocence was strong enough to wash his pain away.

No. That was all wrong.

His pain was strong enough to destroy her innocence.

Her chest rose and fell rapidly. And those strawberry lips parted slightly. "Do you understand why I must mail the letter?"

Ah yes, the letter.

The one where she informed her mother that she could no longer live a lie, that she'd been compromised in Ireland by a traveling actor, of all the ridiculous lies.

When he'd read it, he'd experienced a sudden, visceral rage. Then he'd realized it was a complete falsehood.

But who was he to tell her not to ruin her life if that's what she chose to do?

As long as he didn't do the ruining. He cleared his throat and extricated his fingers from her hair.

Nothing irrevocable happening here. Nothing at all.

"I'll post your letter at the next inn," he said.

Eyes the color of raindrops hitting ocean waves searched his face. "You will?"

He nodded. "If that's what you truly desire."

A smile lit her eyes and curved across her lush lips. "Why, thank you."

He basked for a moment in the approving light of her smile.

"Now see, that wasn't so difficult, was it?" Her smile widened. "You don't always have to be so disagreeable."

Make another request. Anything. Ask me to ruin you in a completely non-theoretical way. Dalton drew a deep breath to chase away those thoughts.

Control. Stoicism. *Disagreeableness.* Because charm in this situation might get them both into trouble.

And none of this surreptitious touching. The burst of sensation that coursed through his entire body when his lips merely brushed her palm.

He edged closer to the opposite side of the carriage.

He had to find that center again. The still heart of vengeance. Razor-edged, single-minded purpose.

Trent had shaken him, made him doubt himself for the first time in years.

An enemy's blade.

A moment of weakness in a carriage.

They were one and the same.

They both left telltale scars.

After helping Con tend to the gear, Dalton entered the inn in Chippenham fully intending to keep his promise and post Thea's letter. But then he glimpsed her resting in an armchair by the fireplace in the great room. Shoulders hunched, hands folded, gaze trained on her red leather boots.

She looked lonely. Her oval face filled with uncertainty, brow wrinkled.

Informing her mother that she'd been ruined would change her life immediately. The societal stigma for fallen women of good breeding was severe. She'd be cut off from society. Unable to return to her family if she changed her mind.

What if she developed regrets? What if she wished to return to London?

A new thought struck him. What if her aunt didn't want her to be there in Ireland . . . or what if her aunt suddenly passed? Then what would happen to her?

Disinherited. Friendless.

Alone.

The thought made his throat constrict.

She should never be alone. She was made for laughter. For everything good and sweet.

For love.

Dalton backed out of the room without attracting her notice.

On his request, a jolly-looking innkeeper who obviously enjoyed his porter of an evening brought Dalton pen and an ink pot.

"Will there be anything else, sir?" the innkeeper asked.

"The lady in the great room, the one sitting by the fire. Bring her a cup of your finest drinking chocolate."

The innkeeper's eyes twinkled. "Admire the lady, do you, sir? Shall I tell her it's from you?"

"No." Dalton shook his head. "Tell her it's from the cook."

The innkeeper nodded sagely. "Of course, Sir."

Swiftly, Dalton composed a letter of his own.

He refused to be the means of delivering Thea to a lifetime of doubt and could-have-beens.

He knew enough about regrets to know they ate away at you, hollowed you out, like termites attacking the inside of a fallen log.

One veiled threat from Dalton to the countess that if Thea were forced to marry Foxford, or another peer of his ilk, Dalton would make life difficult for the countess in society, as only a duke could, ought to do the trick.

And a few lines informing the countess that Thea . . . *When had he started thinking of her as Thea? In the carriage just now?*

Informing the countess that her precious daughter, Lady Dorothea, was unharmed and would be delivered safely to Ireland.

Though he couldn't guarantee her safety past that point, since he'd be hunting O'Roarke.

He finished scrawling the brief note and handed it, along with Thea's letter, to the innkeeper to post.

Strictly speaking, he followed Thea's wishes.

He posted her letter.

He just happened to post one of his own as well. Which missive Lady Desmond chose to believe was entirely up to that humorless lady.

Chapter 9

Halfway to Bath now. Legs cramped from sitting on the carriage seat. Mind bent with guilt.

Had he done the right thing by posting the letter? No point in wondering that now. What's done was done.

Thea hid behind one of the broadsheets she'd collected, which was probably just as well. Whenever they spoke to one another sparks flew. They'd start the carriage on fire if they weren't careful.

The broadsheet crackled as it lowered, and blue-gray eyes emerged over the edge. "There's an advertisement here for Duchess Cocoa, manufactured by your friend the Duke of Harland. I had some at the inn in Chippenham. I had no idea it was so very delicious."

"James is dedicated to creating the finest drinking chocolate on earth. Now he's managed to lower import duty taxes so even second-rate inns can afford to serve cocoa."

If he kissed her right now, she'd probably still taste like the spices in Harland's famous chocolate blend. Why did he keep having these thoughts?

Small, confined space.

Lovely, lovely Thea shimmering in fading afternoon light. He'd never seen her in the afternoon before.

To distract himself from thoughts like that, he asked her the first question that came to mind. "Have you had any contact with the Duchess of Harland since she . . ."

"Since she stole my intended?" Thea smiled. "I was banished to Ireland the day after I was supposed to have married the duke."

"That must have been difficult for you."

"Oh, I don't know. I didn't really want to marry Harland. No one seems to believe that, but it's the truth. I'd never even met the man."

"He's a good man." *Far better than me, Thea.*

"I'd like to see my half sister again some day."

Dalton nodded. He'd done the right thing. She didn't truly want to sever all connections with society. She didn't want to be lonely.

Thea readjusted the broadsheet.

Creaking of carriage wheels. Sound of horse hooves on gravel.

He sifted through what he knew of O'Roarke one more time, to keep himself from staring at trim ankles encased in supple red leather.

By his mother's account, O'Roarke had been a clerk in a shipping company and was now a wealthy merchant based out of New York. They should be able to find news of him and his shipping concern at Bristol Harbor.

Why had Dalton's father never considered O'Roarke a suspect? Perhaps he'd never even

known of his existence. His thoughts had immediately turned to all the men he'd ruined in the
gambling hells.

A lowly clerk hadn't made the list of suspects.

His father's theory had always been that one
of his enemies had followed him to Ireland from
London and struck the very day they arrived.

But it could have been O'Roarke, lying in wait
for years. Biding his time. Maybe he'd seen the
old duke as a symbol of oppression. Stealing
O'Roarke's love away. Robbing the Irish of their
ancestral estates.

"Ah . . ." Thea interrupted his thoughts. "Here's
something that should be of interest to the rake
about town. The Hellhound struck again. Outside
of the Crimson in Piccadilly. Says here he robbed
Lord Trent of his winnings and left him bleeding
in the street."

Dalton had been the one left bleeding.

*Don't move a muscle. Don't betray even the slightest
bit of interest.*

Or that might be too noticeable. He should
make some inane comment. "The streets are more
perilous than ever these days," he said with all the
nonchalance he could muster.

Steer the conversation along new lines. "My
mother hasn't left Osborne Court for nearly a
decade, can you credit that? She's too afraid to
venture into the streets of London."

Thea's mouth made a round, astonished shape.
"She hasn't set foot outside your house in ten
years? I knew they called her the . . ." She stopped
speaking.

"The Dowager Recluse. I know what she's called."

"I never did see her leave the house but I thought, well, I thought that perhaps she went out at odd hours, by the back entrance."

Dalton congratulated himself on a successful distraction. "My father tried to commit her to an asylum but I wouldn't let her be moved. They say she has anxiety of the most acute kind. She shrinks from the idea of leaving the house."

"How infinitely sad." Thea set aside the broadsheet. "Isn't there anything to be done?"

"I used to try to coax her out of doors. I'd bundle her up in a cloak and carry her to the front door. She'd scream so loudly I had to return her to her rooms. Her mind is still resolute and strong, but she's subject to bouts of despondency and fear."

"She's never been back to her home in Ireland?"

"Her sisters write to give her all the news, but she never visits them. And they've stopped visiting her. It's too painful for everyone involved."

"I'm sorry."

He turned his face away from the sympathy in her eyes. "She's not always unhappy. She likes to feed delicacies to her cats. And she takes exercise in the courtyard."

"But never to leave one's home? It's as if she's imprisoned."

"It's by her own choice."

The carriage filled with silence.

Dalton traced letters across the cold, hard surface of the window. Stopped when he realized whose name he was writing. Alec.

Thea cleared her throat delicately and he glanced at her.

"They say the Hellhound is an Irishman," she said cheerfully, probably thinking she was doing him a favor by changing the subject. "'He spoke with a strong Irish brogue,' it says in the paper."

Dalton caught his foot tapping and stilled it.

Don't betray too much interest. Not with clever Thea across from you.

Thea quirked her head to one side. "You frequent the gambling clubs, do you not? Have you ever encountered the Hellhound?"

"I only frequent the finer clubs. And the Hellhound is only a fiction invented to sell broadsheets."

She shook her head vehemently, sending golden curls twirling onto her shoulders. "I know he's real. I've met him."

Dalton gulped. What in hell was she talking about?

"Well, not personally," she clarified. "My eldest brother, Andrew, met him."

Dalton searched his mind for a Mr. Andrew Beaumont . . . ah yes. *That* Beaumont. *Bladdered* Beaumont, as he was known at the club.

"Your brother is, pardon my frankness, a drunkard. I met him on several occasions years ago and he was never parted from his cups for long. Most likely had his pockets cleaned as he stumbled home and had to embroider a more impressive tale to save his reputation."

An emphatic shake of that pointed chin. "That's not it at all."

Damn. Why hadn't he tied her up and sent her home when he had the chance?

"The Hellhound saved Andrew from gambling away his entire portion. I think the broadsheets have it all wrong. I think the Hellhound is more guardian angel than thieving rogue."

Dalton masked a surprised grunt with a cough. "If he's real he's a criminal. A marauding Irish scoundrel. They'll catch him one day and he'll hang, sure enough."

Was that too much? He didn't want to betray vehement sentiment of any kind. Something might give him away. A tremor. A nervous flinch. Arouse her suspicion.

"You're wrong." She shifted closer to him, clasping her hands, intent on convincing him of his error. "He's noble. Andrew nearly gambled away his entire portion, plus a property in Bedfordshire. I came home from a ball early and he was sitting in the parlor with no candles lit, his head in his hands. 'I nearly lost it all,' he said, his eyes burning. 'He saved me, Dorothea. He saved me.'"

Dalton remembered that night well. He'd been gambling at the same club, in his rake's guise, and he'd watched Beaumont lose half his fortune in the time it took to shake the dice box and spill doom upon the green baize.

Still young, but already going to seed, developing a paunch, with the red-rimmed eyes and juniper breath of a devoted drunk, Beaumont had grown increasingly reckless. When he'd left the club, shouting that he'd damn well try his luck at Old Crocky's next, Dalton had followed him outside.

Shed his evening clothes. Become the Hellhound.

He knew the darkness and the drink would mask his identity, and Beaumont had posed no threat.

Soft. Helpless.

Dalton hadn't even had to try. One growled word of warning and the fellow had started blubbering.

"He was ashen-faced, shaken," Thea said, her voice low and urgent. "He nearly spilled the glass of brandy he held, his fingers were trembling so. He isn't loquacious, my brother, but that night . . . I think he needed to tell someone, and I happened to be there."

She stared out the window. "He lost three thousand pounds in ten minutes. It was too horrible to be believed."

The man had been close to losing a lot more than three thousand pounds.

"Oh, look. We're nearly to the Bath turnpike." Dalton pointed to the signpost but she didn't even look.

Her mind was fixed firmly on his secrets.

"Andrew told me that one moment he was outside, catching his breath, and the next there was an elbow around his throat and he was up against a brick wall, a giant monster pushing his cheek against the brick. The Hellhound warned Andrew that next time he wouldn't be there to save him."

"How's that noble, exactly? Sounds brutish to me. Pushing your brother against a wall. Making threats."

"His methods may be unorthodox," she said primly, "but they are effective. Andrew never gambled again. And he stopped drinking as well. After he saved Andrew, I began to take an interest in the Hellhound's activities. I've been following his exploits in the papers for some time now."

Not good. Not good at all. "It looks as though the rain might be letting up," Dalton said desperately.

"There are patterns. He never attacks women or children, always men. And usually wealthy, corrupt men. And sometimes he saves poor souls like Andrew." She smoothed her skirts.

She gazed dreamily out the window. "Sometimes I wonder if Andrew imagined it all, because he needed to believe in something larger than himself. But no." She shook her head. "I believe the Hellhound's real. And I think he's heroic. Like Robin Hood."

"Imaginary," Dalton grated out. "He's definitely imaginary."

"He's noble."

"I hate to tell you, but you're wrong. There's no champion who can cure society's ills and defend the powerless. He's only a myth."

"You're the one who's wrong." She waved the broadsheet at him. "The Duke and Duchess of Harland champion the powerless, rescuing destitute young girls and providing training and occupation. That's noble. Why haven't *you* ever considered doing something like that with your fortune?"

She'd provided the change in topics this time, thankfully.

"As a matter of fact, I have quite an enormous sum invested in their charitable institution. Harland's my best friend. I believe in what he and Charlene are doing."

"Your Grace." She turned shining eyes on him. "I had no idea. How wonderful."

"It's nothing, really. I have friends who are better than I'll ever be. They make it easy for me to find a good use for my fortune."

"Well, if the Duke of Osborne, heartless rake, can invest in helping save powerless girls from the streets, then I definitely believe the Hellhound saved my brother."

What? Dalton nearly burst into a coughing fit. The lady had a narrowly focused mind and now she'd used both his titles in the same sentence.

Must distract her. Must create a diversion.

And so he did the only thing he could think of to stop the clever, inquisitive beauty from enumerating any more theories or making more comparisons.

He gathered her into his arms . . . and kissed her.

Well. *This is unexpected,* Thea had just enough time to think before the surprise of his firm, sensual lips meeting hers.

My very first kiss.

Which she'd always imagined would be an unmitigated disaster. She'd erupt into giggles.

Or knock her teeth against his chin.

Or . . . in an extreme nightmare she'd imagined during her first two seasons . . . vomit upon the gentleman's polished Hessians immediately following said kiss.

Yet Thea did none of the above. She simply . . . relaxed. Unwound. And allowed herself to thoroughly enjoy the foreign experience.

His lips were gentle, yet demanding, moving over her as a brush slid across a canvas.

She felt his kiss spread all the way down to her leather-encased toes, like a drop of Prussian-blue watercolor paint touched to a wash of water to create a hazy, cloud-strewn blue sky.

His lips demanded something very specific . . . and even more unexpected. They wanted her lips to open. They brushed and nudged until she complied and then, *oh,* was that his tongue sliding inside her mouth, unlocking a hidden portion of her mind that had been waiting for the answer to this question . . .

Why all the fuss? Why all the love sonnets?

Ah. *This.*

Powerful arm hooked around her waist. His other hand fumbling with bonnet ribbons and then flinging her bonnet aside, his lips never leaving hers.

Enormous hand surrounded the nape of her neck, tilting her head into the kiss and issuing more demands.

Tilt a little further back. Wrap your hands around my neck. Use your tongue as well. Talk to me without words.

Ever widening circles of bliss rippling through her body.

This floating feeling. This leap into the unknown.

His hands shaping her waist.

The roughness of his unshaven face scratching her cheeks and her chin.

Kissing the duke felt like viewing a life-changing painting in a gallery. The perception of a curtain opening on another world. Reality shifting, expanding.

She knocked his hat off and dipped her fingers into his thick, wavy hair, pulling him closer.

A lady certainly never knocked a gentleman's hat off his head. Or imagined ripping his coat off to expose the powerful chest she'd seen last evening.

My heavens. She was becoming a wanton.

And she loved every second of it.

Most of the time a kiss was just a kiss for Dalton. Lips meeting, seeking invitation, claiming acquaintance. A prelude to the act of lovemaking. A conversation that didn't require words.

Sometimes, very rarely, it became something more, a glimpse of heaven, of redemption.

And then there was *this*.

Dalton was lost from the moment his lips touched hers.

Lost to danger, lost to thought.

Her clever tongue matched him stroke for stroke as she opened wider, allowing him more access.

The noises she made. Soft little surprised moans. The way she pulled him toward her with her fingers threaded through his hair.

Where was the repression, the prudishness, the passivity? Weren't vestal virgins supposed to be timorous and unsure?

Thea took to kissing with an enthusiasm that had him harder than the carriage wheel spokes. All that repression must have primed her for this moment. And she was letting go.

Flying free and swift into passion.

He'd kissed her to stop her from talking. To distract her. Maybe even to frighten her a little. Take her out of her safe world of theoretical danger and into reality.

Stop that quick mind from uncovering his secrets.

And then he hadn't been thinking at all because she'd licked those plump, pink lips, so close to his, and he'd needed to taste, drink, claim.

He trailed the tip of his finger along the pulse in her neck, the hollow where his thumb fit perfectly in the depression.

She moaned and shut her eyes. He nibbled at her lip and she opened for him and then he slid inside again, tasting that sweet mixture of innocence and abandon.

Maybe this was his first kiss, not hers.

The strange thought came, unbidden, and wouldn't dislodge.

If there'd been enough room he would have pulled her onto his lap, but he couldn't, and the restriction acted as an aphrodisiac.

He cupped her cheek with his hand and stroked his thumb down across her lower lip while he kissed her.

Sensation without emotion.

The release of physical gratification without the need for intimacy.

Those were the principles that governed his dalliances.

He never truly gave himself to a woman. There was always a part of him watching from someplace outside his body. Observing. Remaining separate and untouchable.

But all that talk of the Hellhound . . . and Dalton had become him. The primal warrior. Balanced on the knife's edge of lust.

Full of raw, visceral need. The need for victory. For dominion.

His body had created some twisted idea that claiming her was his new purpose in life.

The window fogged over.

He nudged her lips apart with his thumb and deepened the kiss. Her soft breasts pressed against his chest.

She rubbed her velvety cheek against him like the brush of a cat's tail as it swished past him.

Hell, he wasn't strong enough to resist that invitation.

He kissed her neck, her flushed peach-colored cheeks, the delicate skin behind her ear.

His belly tensed and his cock strained against his breeches' flap.

Her small hands settled on his cheeks.

He thought she was stopping him, but instead, she leaned her head up and kissed the corners of his mouth. Then she kissed the indentation in his chin. "I've been wanting to do that since we waltzed," she breathed.

He closed his eyes.

She could teach some widows he knew a few lessons.

The carriage shuddered—or did he shudder? No, it was the carriage.

They slowed to a halt with a squeaking of wheels and a shouted *whoa, there* from the postilion.

Dalton drew away swiftly, calming his erratic breathing with an effort, and retrieved her bonnet from the floor.

The door opened and Con's face appeared, his nose red from the cold.

He took one quick look at Thea's rumpled hair and swollen lips and raised his thick eyebrows.

Dalton cleared his throat. "Ah, why have we stopped?" And when had it grown so dark? How long had they been kissing?

"Why don't you come see for yourself?" Con grunted. "It's the damn queerest sight I've seen in some time, begging your pardon, my lady." He lifted his cap to Thea.

"Quite all right, Con." Thea tied her bonnet ribbons, restoring at least a thin layer of propriety.

"I—I could use some fresh air," she said.

Con held out a hand to stop her from moving. "Best stay in the carriage, my lady."

"Why, what's the matter?"

"Your money or your life," came a thin voice from the side of the carriage.

Really? A highwayman? Dalton thought.

Didn't the fellow know those days were long past? It was becoming increasingly rare to encounter highwaymen with all the guarded turnpikes along the road.

Con's weathered face split into a grin. "We're being robbed at pistol point."

"And that's amusing because . . . ?"

"You should see the highwayman. Or should I say, highway *lad*. Can't be more than fifteen. Voice hasn't even changed yet. Sounds like a damned choirboy."

He'd rather face a dozen highwaymen than more of Thea's questions.

And her kisses were even more perilous.

Dalton turned to Thea. "Nothing to worry about, my lady. This will be over swiftly."

Chapter 10

God damn it, Dalton mentally kicked himself. *You're a beast. A rutting beast.*

Too occupied kissing the lady entrusted to his care and protection to notice they were being robbed by a highwayman.

A sorry excuse for a highwayman, but he held a pistol nonetheless and appeared to believe he might convince them to part with their money.

The hapless fellow couldn't be more than sixteen, with a round face covered in freckles, and fierce brown eyes. No doubt the son of an impoverished farmhand, driven to the act by hunger. A tall lad, but skin and bones. Hardly any shoulders to speak of.

"Hand over your coins," the lad said. "Don't want your bank notes."

Con had been right, the highwayman sounded like a girl. Poor fellow.

"Easy now," Dalton cautioned Con under his breath. "We don't want to frighten him. Pistols and jumpy, scared lads are never a good combination."

"Now then, my fine lad," Con said jovially. "No need to wave that thing about."

It was a rusty old pistol. Might not even be loaded.

But they had to assume it was.

Dalton and Con exchanged a quick glance.

Dalton would distract the lad, while Con moved to disarm him.

The hired postilion wisely stayed silent atop the carriage seat, attracting no attention.

Dalton fumbled for the coins in his waistcoat pocket. "Here you are, lad. More than enough for you." He held out a shiny guinea and the boy's eyes followed his fingers hungrily, while Con edged closer.

"Don't call me lad." The highwayman raised the pistol higher, aiming straight for Dalton's chest. "I'm the Dread Dark Baron, Knight of the Roads."

Dalton would have laughed if that pistol hadn't been staring him down.

"Why don't you lower that," he said soothingly. "We're armed to the grinders and twice your size. Take these coins and run back home to your mother."

Con was nearly there now, moving silently, preparing to strike. One quick jab with his wrist and he'd knock away the pistol.

In three . . . two . . .

"Why, you ought to be ashamed of yourself," an indignant female voice pronounced.

Thea. *Of course.* She'd exited the carriage and appeared to be marching toward the highwayman, her fists stuck onto her hips and her face forbidding.

Con wavered, unsure whether to strike.

"We're handling this, my lady," Dalton said, tensing in preparation to wrestle Thea out of harm's way when Con attacked.

Now what was the unpredictable female doing? Instead of following orders, she walked right up to the highwayman.

"Don't you know you're doing it all wrong?" Thea asked indignantly.

The highwayman gave her a guilty glance. "I . . . I am? I'm sorry."

Had he just apologized to her?

"You're supposed to wait until the cover of true nightfall," Thea said. "And you're most definitely supposed to wear a kerchief tied around your nose and mouth so that people can't see your features."

Was she *lecturing* the highwayman?

He should have Thea ride postilion with a pistol. She obviously didn't need *his* protection. "My lady," he warned sternly. "Con and I are in control of this situation."

Which generated about as much response as he'd assumed it would.

She marched to the highwayman and stuck out her open palm. "Give me that pistol."

The highwayman hung his head. "I'm sorry, my lady. I was that desperate."

"Give it here."

To Dalton's astonishment the lad placed his pistol in Thea's palm. She held the handle gingerly between her thumb and forefinger.

The highwayman's unlined face softened into

a near smile. "I'm sorry, Lady Dorothea. I didn't know what else to do. And I never thought I'd see someone I knew. You're the first carriage I tried, honest."

Dalton and Con exchanged puzzled glances. Had the highwayman just called her Lady Dorothea?

Dalton turned to Thea. "Do you, perchance, *know* this highwayman?"

She leaned forward and snatched off the highwayman's cap and two long black braids tumbled out. "Highway *hoyden*, more like. This is Molly. We met in Ireland. How on earth she ended up as a highwayman outside of Bath, I am sure she will enlighten us. Now come along, Molly. Into the carriage. Before anyone else sees you."

Molly glared at Con. "That one was sneaking up on me."

"You were waving a pistol about and attempting to rob him. Of course he was sneaking up on you."

"Not loaded."

"Well, he didn't know that."

"Molly," exclaimed Thea. "You climb in the carriage this instant. *Dread Dark Baron*. What utter nonsense."

Thea turned to Dalton. "She'll ride inside with me." She said it challengingly, as if he might contradict her.

"Suits me." He'd never trust himself alone in a carriage with her again. Not after the earth-shattering kiss they'd just shared.

Con approached Molly and leaned over so their faces were level. "Well then, Master Molly, is it? Or Miss Molly?"

Molly's brown eyes narrowed to slits. "You're Irish?"

"As the Blarney Stone. And what brings you to the Bath Road this fine evening?"

Molly crossed her thin arms, and her knobby elbows stuck out from a threadbare coat. "I had my money stolen. The unholy basta—" She glanced at Thea. "The bad man that stole my money ran off to Bristol."

"We'll take you to Bristol, no fare necessary. Now in you go." Con helped Thea and the girl formerly known as the Dread Dark Baron into the carriage.

Dalton mounted one of the horses.

They were only a few minutes from the Bath turnpike now, and it was nearly dark. Not much risk of discovery.

When they were under way again, Dalton caught Con's eye. "And then there were four," he said, shaking his head.

"I have to give the lady credit," Con replied, shouting across the horses. "Never a dull moment. Highly entertaining."

Dalton gripped the reins. *Entertaining* was one word for it.

He could think of others.

That kiss had shaken him, shifted his center of balance.

Branded him as plainly as the cut across his jaw.

He was losing the battle for control.

Beast, he thought disgustedly. *Couldn't control yourself, could you. Had to succumb to temptation.*

But she'd been talking about the Hellhound. He'd only kissed her to stop her theorizing.

Guilt seared his mind.

He'd just sent a letter to her *mother*, for Christ's sake. Vowed to deliver her safe and unharmed.

By God, if he did one thing in this life, he'd damn well keep his word.

There'd be no more intimate conversations.

And absolutely no more kissing.

Molly refused the handkerchief Thea offered her. "I never cry," she scoffed, wrinkling her freckle-spattered nose. "Used to drive Da mad that I didn't cry when he took the strap to me."

"What were you thinking, Molly? You could have been killed. Those are dangerous men out there."

There was something thoroughly unconventional about the rapport between the duke and his servant. She'd been watching their silent interaction. They would have had Molly disarmed within seconds.

"The red-and-silver-haired Irish bloke's all right, but I don't like the look of that big handsome one with the brooding eyes. Don't trust handsome fellows. You shouldn't be traveling with him, my lady. He's apt to steal your heart . . . and steal your money, too."

"Is that what happened to you, Molly? Why on earth are you here?"

"Something like," Molly muttered.

"Something like what?"

"I can't tell you." She crossed her arms stubbornly. "Don't try to make me."

The middle child in a family of eleven children who'd recently lost their father, Molly had been forced to take work at a silk factory in Cork.

"Why don't you tell me," Thea urged. "It may feel good to speak the words. May make your troubles seem lighter. Maybe it's not as bad as you think. Or perhaps I can help."

Thea and her aunt had often visited Molly's family cottage, bringing jars of honey, fresh-baked bread, toys, and handmade quilts to the harried mother with gray-streaked black hair, a care-lined face, and eleven mouths to feed. They were tenants of one of her aunt's neighbors, a callous gentleman who left the care of his estate to managers who bled the tenants for high rents and didn't see to basic repairs.

The duke's estate had no remaining tenants. Only a small staff of ancient retainers who were growing as old and knotty as the olive groves on his grounds. With all that land, he could provide good housing and arable land for a host of tenants. But he kept the house shut and dark as Pharaoh's tomb.

Thea shivered, remembering what he'd told her of his brother. Only five years old. But still, no reason to let such a magnificent property go to seed.

"It's bad." Molly blinked her brown eyes. "*I'm* bad." She stuffed her long braids back up under the floppy blue cap. "And I don't want to be a girl anymore. Girls have the short end of the stick, and that's certain sure. Think I'll wear trousers from now on. And keep my hair hidden." She jutted out her lip. "Don't try to stop me."

Thea smiled. "I wouldn't try to stop you. The Dread Dark Baron can do whatever she wants."

"That bit was good, don't you think? Had 'em quivering in their fancy boots."

"Oh, they were terrified."

Molly gave a wobbly smile. "I didn't know what else to do. I had no other options."

Thea nodded. "Just as I thought."

"'Twas one of the books you lent me, a history of Richard Turpin, the highwayman."

Molly had followed Thea home one evening, trailing two steps behind, watchful and wary. When Thea arrived back at the cottage, she'd headed straight for the bookshelves because she'd seen how Molly's eyes lit when she saw them.

From that moment on, Molly had spent all her spare time reading every book in the house. Thea had been drawn to the young girl who walked with a swagger and swore like a sailor and wanted to read every book in the world.

Molly arrived at the cottage in the evenings with her fingers stained bluish-purple from indigo silk dye, and her mind hungry for escape. She and Thea had read, side by side in front of the fireplace, during the long winter evenings.

"Oh, so now I'm responsible for your delinquency?" Thea asked.

"Course not," Molly said. "'Twas all Jack Raney's fault." She clapped a hand over her mouth, her lively eyes darting to Thea's face.

"Jack Raney? You may as well tell me now, Molly."

Molly sighed, her thin shoulders heaving. "I . . . can't."

"How about if I tell you a secret first?"

Molly leaned forward. "Go on."

"You mustn't tell anyone, but the handsome man with the dark blue eyes is none other than the Duke of Osborne. He's traveling in disguise as a merchant named Mr. Jones, because he's on the run from the jealous husband of one of the wives he dallied with."

"Osborne? You mean the Osborne of Balfry House?"

Thea nodded. "And I aim to convince him to open the house again."

"Well." Molly let out a surprised gush of breath. "I never thought *he'd* visit Ireland again." Molly glanced at her suspiciously. "But why are you traveling with him? You're not . . . are you and he . . . ?"

"Nothing like that," Thea hastened to assure her. "He's merely my escort back to Aunt Emma."

"Is that so?" Molly whistled disbelievingly. "I saw the way he looked at you."

"I told you my secret, now it's your turn."

Molly rolled her eyes. "Fair's fair. But first tell me why you left London. You've only been there a month or so."

"I missed Ireland too much. And I missed you, too. I was planning to bring you a carriage-full of books, but I left in a bit of a hurry."

"You missed me?" Molly smiled shyly. "You were going to bring me books?" Her face fell. "I can never go home again."

"Why?"

"He seemed my best option at the time, Jack did. The lying, cheating bastard. Excuse me, my lady. But it's true." She balled her hands into fists. "When I catch him he's going to wish he'd never been born, that's what."

"What happened?"

"One of the factory managers grabbed me and got a knee in his bollocks for his trouble." Molly propped her elbow on her knee. "I lost my position. Couldn't tell Mam. Had to run and I had no money. So I went with Jack to Bristol. He's a sailor and he said he'd find me work as a chamber maid at an inn in Bath."

"The scoundrel."

"You don't know everything yet," Molly said bitterly. "Jack said we needed money, to buy me a maid's uniform, said there were costs to be paid first. And so I . . . I stole the funds from me own mam. All the money buried under the yew hedge."

"Oh, Molly. You didn't."

"I told you I was bad. But I was going to replace it." She shook her head. "Jack took me to Bath and ran off with the money. He's back in Bristol making his runs between Bristol and Cork. Having his fun at the Anchor Tavern. Left me with nothing but an old pistol and a pair of his trousers."

Thea understood now. There were few options for a fallen girl, alone in a strange city.

"When we reach Bristol I'm going to find him," Molly said vehemently. "I'm going to find him and I'm going to get that money back."

She kicked the rusted pistol lying on the carriage floor. "First I'll have to learn how to load this pistol."

"No more pistols."

"Well, he's not going to part with the money if I say please and thank you. I'll have to scare it out of him."

"That's a terrible idea. I'll talk to the duke. Maybe he'll be able to help."

Molly regarded her warily. "He didn't make you any promises, did he?"

"None whatsoever. Quite the opposite. He's gone out of his way to show me how very much he dislikes me."

Of course there had been that kiss. Quite promising, that kiss. Thea wanted to know more.

In London, a kiss such as that would have meant she'd been compromised.

But they weren't in London anymore.

When she thought of the kiss, it was as though she'd wrapped it up in brown paper, tied it with a bow, and given it to herself as a gift.

She'd undo the ribbon later, in privacy, when she had time to relive the memory in all its perplexing glory.

"Let's not worry about the future now," Thea said. "First things first. A hot meal for you. You're awfully hungry-looking."

She took both of Molly's cold hands and chafed them between her hands. "When was the last time you ate a full meal?"

"Two days, I think." Molly's eyelids drifted down across cheeks scattered with pale brown freckles.

How could a man have wanted to steal her virtue? And her money?

How lucky it had been their carriage Molly had chosen. Her life hadn't been easy, and her bluster and tough talk were the shell she'd developed to survive.

Molly leaned her head against the carriage wall. "I do feel tired, my lady."

"Rest now. We'll be in Bath soon enough."

Molly curled up against the wall and Thea wrapped her cloak over her.

Why did the duke have such a hard shell? Must be his brother's death. And his mother's illness. Thea knew his father had been notoriously cruel and ruthless, and he'd owned several exclusive gambling clubs.

Maybe the duke's life wasn't as carefree and self-serving as she'd assumed.

The carriage rolled to a stop outside an inn in Bath.

Thea had been so engrossed in her thoughts she hadn't even noticed the streets becoming crowded with other carriages.

Thea didn't want to wake Molly just yet. She looked so exhausted and pale, poor thing.

The coachman helped Thea alight, and she shivered in the nighttime cold.

The duke dismounted and whispered something to his tired horse, smoothing its flank. He didn't glance her way.

The upstairs room of the inn was full of cheerful light, and the faint sound of fiddling and stomping feet drifted down.

"Is there a festivity?" Thea asked a stable boy.

"A dance, ma'am."

The boy stared behind her, at the carriage. "Your carriage has yellow wheels. With red trim. What's the gentleman's name, ma'am, if I may be so bold?"

Thea glanced at the duke. Best to maintain their fiction. "His name is Mr. Jones."

The stable boy nearly jumped out of his skin. "Mr. Jones, you say? Thank you, ma'am. I must be going now." He hurried away toward the inn without another word.

Odd. Wasn't he supposed to stay and help Con with the horses?

Con arrived, his breath visible as he spoke. "Where's the dread highway hoyden?"

"She's sleeping, poor thing. We'll need to find her a hot meal."

Con nodded. "We should all have some sustenance . . ."

He was interrupted by the door of the inn bursting open to reveal two heavyset men with red, angry faces.

"Jones," one of them roared, shaking his fists. "Which one of you lot is Jones?"

Chapter 11

What now? Couldn't they just have a nice quiet journey to Bristol? Why did there have to be all of these forbidden kisses in carriages? And country lasses dressed as highwaymen?

And now these two buffoons.

Beady eyes glaring, ham fists raised, mouths twisted into sneers, shouting for Jones.

"Now then, gents," Dalton said in a deliberately jocular tone. There's been a mistake. You see, I'm not Jones."

Con moved to stand beside him.

"Eager to rent us the carriage, was he, your Mr. Jones?" he whispered to Con.

Con gave a small shrug. "Suppose we know why now."

The man with bushy black side whiskers and a scrunched-up face like a bulldog, who was obviously the leader, stepped forward, halting a mere foot away from Dalton. "You've a black traveling chariot with yellow-painted wheels and red trim." He spat into the sawdust. "And that bit o' muslin"—he jerked his head in Thea's direction— "identified you as Jones, didn't she?"

"Aye, that she did," said his equally sullen companion, who wore a ragged red neck cloth.

Dalton groaned inwardly. *Of course.*

"I told a lie," Thea piped in. "His name isn't Jones."

Bulldog turned. "What's 'is name, then, love?"

"It's . . . it's . . ." Thea began, obviously searching her mind for a new story.

Oh, now that was truly helpful.

"You're Jones," the man roared, rounding on Dalton. "And you're going to pay what you owe to Mr. Gatling."

"Sorry to disappoint you, my fine fellows. I'm not Jones. I rented this carriage from him, though. Now, if you'll excuse us, we need to find a hot meal."

Why were there no other people in the stable yard? Seemed to be some sort of festivity occurring in the inn. There were candles blazing from an upstairs window, and the sound of music.

Bulldog followed his gaze. "Everyone's dancing and drinking punch. No one's likely to hear your cries."

Dalton laughed.

"What you think he's got to laugh about?" the man in a wrinkled red neck cloth asked.

"I'm happy because it's such a nice night," Dalton said. "Crisp and cool. With the smell of new leaves on the air. Spring will be here soon and even miscreants such as you will feel a lift in your steps and a song in your blighted hearts."

"Who are you calling blighted?" Bulldog lurched closer.

"I *never* have a lift in my step," Red Neck Cloth asserted.

Not a bright duo, but brawny. Enough muscle between the two of them to subdue an elephant.

"How much does Mr. Jones owe you?" Dalton asked.

"He owes Mr. Gatling one hundred pounds, what he stole from him cheating at cards a week ago."

"I see. Disreputable character, this Jones?"

"Mean as they . . . say now." Bulldog squinted. "*You're* Jones. Stop with the trickery and hand over the money."

"There's been a mistake, gentlemen," Thea began, but before she could finish that thought, Molly emerged from the carriage, blinking and rubbing her eyes.

"What's happening out here?" Molly asked.

"None of your concern, lad," growled the man in the red neck cloth. "Unless you've got our hundred quid."

"I don't feel well." Molly swayed on her feet. Thea laid a hand on her arm.

Molly's face was ghostly white in the yard lamps and her brow had a sheen of sweat.

Thea slid an arm around her shoulders. "What's the matter?"

"I think . . . I think I'm going to . . . faint."

Con leapt to her side and propped her up. He felt her brow. "She's got a fever," he stated.

"*She?*" Bulldog asked. "A *she* wearing trousers?"

"We need a physician," Thea said.

Dalton longed to go to her side, but he had to deal with these blunder-heads. "Con, take the women inside. I'll continue conversing with these fine fellows."

Con hoisted Molly into his arms.

"That girl's wearing trousers," Bulldog observed.

"What strange things are you up to, Jones?" Red Neck Cloth asked.

Dalton made certain Thea was inside the inn, away from harm, before he turned back to the men. He couldn't let her see this. She was already so suspicious, he didn't want her to see him flatten these fellows in under twenty seconds.

He'd have to prolong it a bit, just in case she witnessed from a window.

Allow them to land a few blows, so it wouldn't seem too easy.

"Now then, gents." He shrugged out of his coat. Rolled up his shirtsleeves. "This won't take long."

There were answering guffaws.

"Not take long 'e says. There's two of us and one of him."

"I like those odds," Dalton said.

The laughter died. "Right cocky for a man who's about to be beaten to a bloody pulp."

"Who'll be first, then?" Dalton asked. "Come on, don't be shy. Bare knuckles. Queensbury's rules."

He knew the one with the red neck cloth had a knife—he could tell by the way his fingers twitched over his pocket. But Bulldog had the look of a professional prizefighter and wouldn't be able to resist a bare-knuckles challenge.

The men squared, set to, and Dalton moved closer.

He'd let them take the first blow, to give them confidence.

The evening breeze carried the sound of hands clapping and fiddles sawing.

Dalton had no choice but to put up his fists.

And dance.

"Hit me," he taunted. "Hit me, you bloody imbeciles."

Dalton took the full force of the first blow on his jaw. His head whipped to the side and he staggered a few steps.

Bulldog went for the gut this time, his meaty fist connecting with Dalton's muscled stomach.

It stung, but he'd been conditioned for this.

The *thud crack* of bone against bone.

Spittle and blood flying.

Dalton spat a thick ribbon of crimson onto the sawdust. He blinked in the sudden salt sting of sweat.

He'd taken a blow that would have felled any other man.

But this was why he trained every day.

Punished his body and his mind.

So that he could recover from blows like this.

Each blow that connected with his flesh made him want to shout with wild laughter.

This was real. Real pain. The kind that made him forget everything else.

He could do this all night.

Absorb this pain.

Wait for just the right moment to strike back. Wear them down, lull them into thinking they'd beaten him.

This was his talent, fighting.

Well, this and pleasuring women.

Pain and pleasure.

He'd wait a respectable amount of time and then finish them. He had to seem suitably battered. Enough to calm Thea's suspicions.

He was reeling from a blow and didn't even notice her enter the yard.

He did notice when Bulldog's fist stopped halfway to his abdomen.

Dalton turned to see what had stopped Bulldog from striking.

It was Thea. Standing in the middle of the stable yard, hair completely unbound and streaming down her back, no bonnet, no pelisse, no gloves. Just rosy, delectable woman in gray-and-green patterned silk.

Hips swaying and eyes flashing.

One graceful arm lifted as if giving the scene her benediction. "I am *La Gabrielli*," she proclaimed. "Audiences weep uncontrollably when I sing Rossini and soar to a high F."

She kissed her fingertips, making loud smacking noises. "'*Che voce divina!*' they shout."

"Guh," Bulldog made a confused noise and straightened away from Dalton. He elbowed Red Neck Cloth. "What d'you think she said?"

Red Neck Cloth's mouth flapped open. "Dunno. But she's pretty."

"Silenzio!" Thea commanded in her overblown Italian. "It is your lucky night, gentlemen. La Gabrielli, she will sing for you now."

She flung her arms wide, shook her long, shimmering curls, and sucked in a deep breath that swelled her breasts above her bodice. Then she began to sing.

Must be Rossini, because she'd mentioned him earlier. Dalton didn't know his opera from his elbow, but Thea sounded good.

More than good.

She had a high, agile voice that trilled with warmth and richness.

His erstwhile assailants stood with jaws gaping, rendered mute and harmless by her beauty and the effortless grace of that voice.

All that golden hair glinting in the moonlight, her arms outstretched, and that surprisingly soulful, buttery soprano caressing their ears.

Her eyes sparked blue and silver, and in that dress with her curls tumbling around her shoulders no one would have even recognized her as the same woman garbed in white and tightly wound pearls that he'd danced with only a few evenings past.

He had a feeling he was seeing the true Thea for the very first time tonight. All of her movements were bigger, more careless, less restricted.

She was on stage and she reveled in the power she held.

He couldn't stop staring at her. Why would he ever want to stop?

She was the loveliest sight he'd ever beheld and he knew that this vision would be emblazoned on his mind forever.

Time slowed. Men stared.

She thought she was rescuing him. Why that pinched his chest he didn't know. It was . . . adorable. And brave.

And it was working, too.

Actually, he wasn't very pleased about how well it was working.

He didn't like those brutes undressing her with their eyes, dumbfounded by her moonlit passion, practically panting with lust as they watched her sway and warble. Head back, breasts heaving.

Make that *three* brutes.

The aria built to a dramatic, passionate crest and then tipped down into silence.

Thea swept toward them.

Bulldog blinked. "Guh . . . you're pretty."

"Why, thank you." Thea gifted him with a smile so dazzling, the man actually staggered back two steps.

"Now that I have your attention, gentlemen, I have one question, and one question only," she said in that ridiculous Italian accent of hers.

"What's that Mrs. Gab . . . er . . ."

"Gabrielli." She favored Bulldog with a censorious frown. "That's Dame Gabrielli to you, sir." She rounded on the other man. "The question is this . . . isn't there anyone inside this inn who may have seen this Mr. Jones and could perhaps confirm that my husband, Mr. Gabrielli here, is not the man you seek revenge upon?"

Her *husband*? Christ.

Thea drew close enough to touch.

"And just what do you think you're doing?" Dalton asked under his breath.

"Rescuing you, of course." She smiled brightly. "If you hadn't noticed, you're being pulverized. I've seen debutantes duel more effectively than that."

Bulldog scratched his chin. "Well now, I suppose Betsy would know Jones. Seeing as how she, er, *entertained* him."

Why hadn't Dalton thought of that solution?

"Men," Thea said disgustedly. "Always rushing in with their fists first. Never taking time to think things through. I shall go and fetch this Betsy. Do not move even one finger." She glared at each of them in turn, including Dalton, then glided imperiously back into the inn.

Dalton raised his eyebrows.

Red Neck Cloth gave him a sheepish shrug.

Thea reappeared shortly with a round, apple-cheeked young woman with thick light brown hair. "Is that gentleman Mr. Jones?" she asked Betsy, pointing at Dalton.

Betsy looked him up and down and whistled appreciatively. "Lordy. If that were Jones, I would have stowed away in his carriage and followed him to London."

"But this is Jones's carriage," protested Bulldog.

"I told you," Dalton wheezed, clutching at his rib cage. "I rented the carriage from him."

Red Neck Cloth cleared his throat. "Uh . . . no harm done, eh, Mr. Gabrielli?" He held out a huge paw in a conciliatory gesture.

"Come inside, *caro esposo*," Thea trilled. "Did they hurt you, those bad men? Should we call for the night watch?"

Bulldog shook his shaggy head. "No need for that, now. Just a misunderstanding."

"You numbskull, Brown," chided Betsy. "And you, Morgan, attacking the wrong man. Mr. Gatling will hear of this."

The men hung their head like schoolboys who'd had their hands rapped by a ruler.

Thea smiled at Dalton. *See?* That smile clearly said *my way was better.*

"Come along, *caro esposo*." She hooked her elbow through his. "These nice gentlemen are going to purchase our repast."

"Say, you're a brick, you are, Gabrielli. Got a stomach like a steel hull." Bulldog placed his arms around Dalton's shoulder, suddenly his best friend. "Let me make it up to you. What's your pleasure? Brandy? Wine?"

Dalton grunted. "Whiskey."

Bulldog grinned. "The finest Ireland has to offer. I'll have it sent to your room."

"We'll need your best chamber," Thea commanded. "Hot water, fresh linens, ointment for his cuts and bruises." She glared at the men and they hung their heads.

"Will there be anything else, Mrs. Gabrielli?" Betsy asked.

"You," Dalton whispered, low and intense so only Thea could hear. "He'll need you."

Too many direct hits to the skull.

Only explanation for those words.

"That will be all, thank you, Betsy." Thea blushed.

"I'll bring the physician who's attending Molly to you," Thea said as they climbed the stairs after Betsy.

"No," Dalton growled. "No physicians."

"But . . . you're cut. And bleeding."

"It's nothing." He winced. "There were two of them is all."

"It's a good thing I came along when I did. What do you call that boxing technique? Flop and drop?"

"Ha." Dalton winced as pain shot through his ribs. "Stop making me laugh. It hurts too much."

"I'm serious. When you return to London you should take lessons at Gentleman Jackson's. You should learn how to defend yourself."

Oh, the endless irony of *that*.

He could have flattened those bumbling brutes within ten seconds with both hands tied behind his back.

Of course he could never tell her that. She would ask far too many questions.

Ten minutes later Dalton was settled in a low red velvet chair by a crackling fire in the most spacious chamber the inn had to offer. They were eager to stop him from complaining.

The accommodating Betsy brought a basin of hot water, some fresh linens, and ointment. "I'll send your meal soon. If you need me to help wash your wounds, Mr. Gabrielli, or if you need anything at all"—she gave him a flirtatious wink—"just ask for Betsy."

Thea frowned. "That will be all," she said firmly, showing Betsy to the door.

Dalton smiled. She didn't like Betsy winking at him. He had no idea why that pleased him, but it did.

Thea turned back to him. "Those men gave you quite a pounding."

Ah . . . the things he did to stop clever wallflowers from learning his secrets.

"Only a few scratches and bruises. No more than usual." He winced as pain spread through his abdomen. "May have a cracked rib or two. Nothing to worry about. Go and see to Molly now. I'll be fine."

"Are you quite sure?"

She bit her lower lip, leaving a small patch of darker pink that drew his gaze and made him remember their interrupted kiss in the carriage. He'd like to finish that kiss.

End it properly.

True concern filled her eyes. "If you're truly injured I'll have to send for the physician. I won't take no for an answer, Your Grace."

"Nothing a few swallows of whiskey won't cure. Hand me that bottle, will you, lamb?"

When potent grain and honey heated his belly and Thea and her tempting lips left the room, Dalton stretched his legs in front of the fire and closed his eyes.

The spirits dulled the pain of his bruised ribs.

But the whiskey did nothing for the ache of wanting Thea so badly.

Chapter 12

The merry sound of dancing fiddles sounded faintly in Molly's chamber.

Con stood watch next to her bed, greeting Thea with a raised hand when she entered.

"How's she getting on?" Thea whispered, smoothing a strand of Molly's hair back from her forehead. She slept peacefully, though her face was still white and her lips pinched.

"Doctor gave her a sleeping draft," Con whispered. "Said she'll be fine. Only half-starved and exhausted."

"Did she eat anything before she fell asleep?"

Con nodded. "Drank some hearty beef tea and devoured six rolls." He glanced at Molly with a strangely tender expression. "You know her, don't you?"

"She comes from a large family of tenant farmers near the town of Balfry. Eleven mouths to feed. I'm not sure how Mrs. Barton manages."

Con's blue eyes widened slightly in his wrinkled and bewhiskered face. "Mrs. Barton, you say?"

"A widow."

"Wouldn't happen to know her Christian name, would you?"

Thea thought back. She'd only ever referred to Molly's mother as Mrs. Barton. She shook her head. "I'm afraid not."

"Never mind, then." Con's eyes crinkled as he looked at Molly. "Reminds me of someone I once knew. Has the same fierce brown eyes." His gaze returned to Thea. "Well then, and how did His Grace fare with those two blighters? They didn't know what hit them, eh?"

Thea tilted a glance at Con. "On the contrary, His Grace received battered ribs, a cut over one eye, and quite a few other bruises I've no doubt."

Con's bushy eyebrows climbed. "Really now? In that event, perhaps you'd best go and tend to him. I'll stay here and watch Molly. She'll be fine, don't you worry."

Had she ever thought Con rough and unmannerly? Quite the opposite was true. She touched his sleeve. "Thank you."

He cleared his throat. "Go on with you now, my lady. You've an injured beast to soothe."

Thea's stomach did nervous flips as she traversed the hallway.

The prudent course of action would be to request separate chambers. For propriety's sake.

She stopped walking.

Only a short time before she'd been singing an aria under the moonlight for an audience of ruffians.

Not much propriety in that.

Right then. One more step down the path of adventure.

And then another.

And then she knocked upon the duke's door.

"Enter," came the deep, gruff command.

He'd loosened his bloodstained cravat, and his coat was unbuttoned, but it seemed he hadn't made any progress on washing the blood from his face.

Too busy drinking whiskey, apparently. The level of the amber liquid inside the bottle had lowered significantly.

"How are you feeling, Your Grace?"

"I've been worse."

"Let's have a look at those injuries, shall we?" She spoke briskly, as she imagined a trained nurse might speak to a patient.

Purely medical interest. Completely aboveboard and irreproachable.

He grunted.

"Right, then." She unbuttoned the cuffs of her long sleeves and rolled them over her wrists. "You'll have to move to the bed. I can't wash your wounds when you're all scrunched up like that."

He lifted his eyes and the floor tilted under her feet.

Such a deep, deep blue. And filled with pain. She reached her hand toward him and then snapped it back to her side.

"I can't lift you, Your Grace. You'll have to rouse yourself. Our meal will be here soon."

"You want me on the bed, do you?" he asked, his eyes glinting.

Heat flushed her cheeks. "For purely medical purposes, you understand."

"Oh, aye, I understand." He lurched to his feet, gasping slightly, but refusing her offer of support.

He removed his coat.

Thea's turn to gasp. "There's blood on your shirt."

"Is there?" He glanced down. "So there is. One of them had a knife."

"Gracious. You could have been killed."

"Not likely." He grinned wolfishly. "I've got a tough hide."

He lowered himself onto the bed. "Do your worst, Thea. Do your worst." He swallowed more whiskey.

Thea undid the buttons at the top of his white linen shirt.

He pulled a laborious breath through the sides of his teeth as she gently worked the shirt up his arms and over his head.

Thea caught her breath at the sight of his powerful chest and hard, ridged abdomen.

She washed blood from the cut over his eye with a cloth dipped in hot water and he winced and caught her by the wrist.

"I'm sorry, Your Grace."

"Call me Dalton." He gazed at her steadily, searching her face. "And don't apologize, Thea. A woman who rescues dukes by singing moonlit arias should never apologize . . . for anything."

Her heart skipped a beat. "Dalton? But aren't you Osborne now?"

"My former courtesy title stuck with me even though I'm the duke now, since I was Dalton for so long."

Dalton . . . Did that make them . . . *intimates*?

She scrubbed blood from the shallow cut on his chest.

How different men's bodies were. Her fingers brushed over the golden-brown hair dusting his chest and one flat, round nipple.

He had other scars. The ghosts of other wounds.

"You're a damned sight more attractive than my usual nurse, you know that?" His lips quirked. "It's Con who usually tends me after a few rounds of pugilism."

Thea scrubbed a spot of blood off his cheek. "I've never understood the allure of pugilism. Men beating each other with their fists for sport. Isn't there enough violence in the world? Do you need to ritualize it?"

"I told you, Thea, men aren't complicated. We like smashing things. It's in our blood. After my brother drowned I felt vulnerable. As soon as I was old enough, I learned boxing and fencing to make myself stronger."

"You maybe should have studied the boxing a bit harder."

He smirked. "Oh, I was just warming up. Another five minutes and I would have delivered the knockouts."

"Mm-hm."

"You don't believe me?"

"It's just that . . . well, you weren't hitting them."

"Ah, but that was my strategy. Wear 'em down, tire 'em out, and then *boom*." His fist thudded on top of the bed. He groaned, the jarring motion obviously hurting his ribs.

"Stop flailing about," Thea remonstrated.

She spread ointment over the cut on his chest, her fingers sliding across smooth flesh and solid muscle. "Sit up, please. I'm going to wrap some linen around this scratch."

He propped himself up on his elbow. He was so very wide. It took her a long time to wrap the cloth around his torso. She had to lean so close to do it.

It made her want to wrap more than cloth around his powerful frame.

Thea drew her hand away. "I'll send for a fresh shirt," she said, turning away and scooting off the bed so he wouldn't see the longing in her eyes.

He caught her wrist and pulled her back to face him. "Don't." His eyes glowed boldly in the candlelight. "I always sleep nude."

And there were those waves of heat again, spreading from her belly up into her cheeks.

Something wild and bold caught hold of Thea. If he slept nude, she should remove his breeches as well.

Her fingers hovered, itching to move down to his breeches' flap.

Good gracious. She needed to walk around the stable yard in the cold air. Splash some icy water on her face.

"I'll just go and inquire after our meal," she

said to hide her confusion. To cover the fact that her entire body had gone liquid with longing and she'd been seconds away from ripping off his breeches.

Which was not even remotely a ladylike thought.

Outside the room, she leaned against the wall, catching her breath.

Betsy appeared at the top of the stairs, bearing a silver tray laden with dishes. "And how's Mr. Gabrielli? No serious injuries, I trust."

"Half-clothed at the moment, I'm afraid. Please have fresh linen delivered."

"Of course, Mrs. Gabrielli."

"I'll take that tray now, thank you, Betsy."

Thea grasped the edge of the tray.

Betsy held on. "Oh, now, it's too heavy for you. I'll just bring it in, shall I?"

In other words, she wanted a glimpse of unclothed Dalton.

"It's not too heavy." Thea pulled harder and Betsy reluctantly relinquished the tray.

"I'll just open the door for you then, shall I?" Betsy opened the door, craning her neck toward the bed, but she couldn't see around the bed curtains.

Whatever was on that tray smelled like heaven. Thea realized how ravenous she was. And not just for dukes.

Thea set the tray on the table and showed the curious Betsy to the door.

Dalton hoisted himself out of bed and sat in the chair across from her, wearing only buckskin breeches and the linen strip she'd wrapped around his chest.

"She's sending up a shirt for you." Heat flooded Thea's cheeks. She couldn't help blushing. She'd never sat across from a half-naked man during a meal before. How did that disreputable stubble along his jaw and the bluish bruise on his cheek somehow make him more devastatingly handsome and his eyes even more blue?

Thea distracted herself by concentrating on the simple beef-and-carrot stew and good, thick crusty bread and butter. She didn't care about manners tonight. She even mopped up some stew with her bread.

Dalton ate heartily as well and for a time silence reigned as they satisfied their appetites.

"Have you noticed how hunger can make simple fare more delectable than the finest society feast?" Thea asked, wiping her hands across a napkin. "What are you drinking? It smells rather"—she leaned over and sniffed the bottle—"mossy."

"That's a good word for it." He held up the bottle. "This is fine triple-distilled malted barley Irish whiskey."

"Is it very strong?"

"I wouldn't say it's Thea-strength."

Thea frowned. "What does that mean?"

"Only that young ladies usually prefer sipping a light sherry. No shame in that. I enjoy a fine sherry myself occasionally."

She straightened in her chair. "I'll have some whiskey, please."

May as well. The novel experience might help

her ignore the firm planes of his chest. And how large his hands looked surrounding the tiny glass as he poured her a finger's width of whiskey.

She took a tiny sip, proud that she didn't even sputter. Then another. It settled in her belly, warming her and loosening the knot between her shoulder blades.

"Beef stew and whiskey. My how the lady is coming down in the world," he teased.

"I suppose I am." Thea glanced around her at the plain furnishings. "Definitely the inn art has lowered a notch."

"Inn art?"

"You know, the same five reproductions of classic paintings on the walls of every inn across England. There must be hundreds of apprentice painters madly copying those same five paintings, day after day."

He shook his head. "Can't say I've noticed."

She waved her whiskey glass at the wall. "A Gainsborough, of course. It never fails. Inns always choose the most innocuous landscapes. Fluffy clouds. A church spire in the distance. Puffs of grazing sheep on a hillside. It's comforting, wouldn't you say?"

He narrowed his eyes at the landscape and Thea took the opportunity to pour more whiskey and drink it down.

"I don't like it," Dalton pronounced. "Not enough goddesses."

Thea laughed. "You didn't like the Titian on the ballroom wall, either. Are you truly not a connoisseur of art?"

"Haven't thought about it much."

"Have you thought any more about your art collection at Balfry?"

"I may be coming around to the idea." His eyes glowed in the candlelight.

There was knock at the door and Thea rose to collect Dalton's fresh shirt and cravat—wouldn't do for him to answer the door half-naked. Might give Betsy heart palpitations.

Though it truly *was* a shame to cover him up, she thought as he slipped the shirt over his head.

Obviously, that was the whiskey talking.

He tied his cravat only loosely.

"I find I like whiskey," Thea said. "Truly a marvelous invention."

Whiskey gave her the courage to do things like *this* . . . She piled her hair on top of her head, arching her back until her bosom thrust forward.

He watched hungrily and she reveled in the power she held over him.

She dropped her hair and shook her head, loving the weight of her hair against her back, its soft brushing against her neck.

There was more than one way to convince a duke to unveil his art collection.

The wayward thought settled through her mind like the whiskey warming her belly.

Dalton clenched his fork, attempting to ignore her and failing miserably.

She shook out her hair, and the firelight teased it into flame.

Despite his best efforts to relegate her to that part of his mind reserved for Problems, Perils, and Plagues, he found her too desirable, and too intriguing.

Her conversation sparked with wit, and a natural, easy sensuality infused her every movement.

He admired her courage as well. Defying her fire-breathing dragon of a mother and leaving her safe, cosseted life behind was a very brave thing.

"Oh, look," she said, lifting the lid off the last silver dish. "Trifle!" She dipped her finger into the dessert in a decidedly unladylike fashion and then . . . oh, God, then she licked her finger.

And Dalton was lost. Maybe they could sleep together on the same bed. Have just a taste of fun. Not too much.

"Mmm," she said, closing her eyes. "Sponge cake." She licked her finger again. "Apricot jam. Sweet cream flavored with sweet wine." She licked the last morsel away. "A hint of lemon, and frothy egg whites. Luscious."

She was luscious. Her eyes closed, her cheeks flushed from the whiskey and the heat of the fire. Those apricot and lemon curls spreading across the red velvet back of the chair.

She scooped a spoonful of trifle directly from the dish. "I'm going to devour this."

The *trifle*, he amended for the benefit of his ever-ready and ever-hopeful prick.

"Oh, that is . . . there are no words." She took another bite and this time her eyeballs fluttered beneath her eyelids.

Did the woman have to act like the trifle was

bringing her to ecstasy? "I gather you like it," he said harshly.

"It's perfect." She frowned. "You don't want any? You really should try it." She took another bite and her tongue darted out to catch a stray bit of fluffy egg whites.

His cock danced hopefully.

"Here." She scooped up a gooey bite of trifle and held it out to him. "Please try some."

He shut his lips tightly. "I don't like trifle."

"Have you ever tried trifle?"

"No."

"Just one bite."

And that's how all the trouble in the world began. He had to open his mouth, if only because of the fact that she held the bite toward his lips and he wanted to taste something she offered . . . even if it was only her spoon.

She took another sip of whiskey and giggled softly.

"What's so humorous?" he asked.

"Remember when I walked on your back? 'Harder, Olofsson,' you said. 'Do your worst.'"

"I remember," Dalton said. "How could I forget?"

"And then, you should have seen the look on your face when you realized it was me and not Olofsson. You wanted to strangle me."

His frown only made her giggle harder.

"I think you've had enough." He reached for her glass but she pulled it away and swallowed the rest in one gulp.

"If you only could have seen your expression."

"I see myself every morning in the glass and that's quite enough," he growled.

She laughed harder. "Admit it was funny."

"It may have been." He was trying to hide a smile but it broke through anyway. "I'm man enough to admit it."

"What you did today." She sighed. "Agreeing to convey Molly to Bristol. Staying here tonight so she can recover." She twirled a long buttery curl around her fingers. "You're very sweet."

No, he wasn't. What he was thinking about doing to her right now wasn't sweet at all. It was primal and nearly uncontrollable.

"And Molly does need our help," she said, sobering.

"How did she come to be standing in those bushes on the side of the road with that rusty old pistol?"

"I can't tell you all the details but there are . . . extenuating circumstances. She was driven to attempt robbery by a series of unfortunate happenings. She needs our help to go back to her family in Cork."

"Molly may ride with us." Dalton leaned back in his chair. The whiskey was starting to work its magic now, spreading a warm, sleepy languor through his limbs. "As long as the pistol stays with me."

"Oh, you." Thea grinned mischievously. "You grumble but you don't really mean it. It's true what Con said."

"What?" he asked suspiciously. "What did Con say?"

"Only that you were soft and sweet inside, and only wanted a good cracking."

"That meddling son of a . . . I'll kill him with my bare hands," he fumed.

"But it's true." She stared at him with that smug tilt to her nose. "All this gruffness and heartlessness. It's only an act. I've been watching you on this journey, you know."

She took another bite of trifle. "Something rings false. Or should I say it rings true . . . as if you do have a heart, and you want to do the right thing."

Now she needed to stop talking.

Dalton shifted in his chair.

Maybe he should sleep in the stables. That would be the only safe course of action. She'd been under her mother's thumb too long and was beginning to test her powers . . . of seduction *and* deduction.

He relinquished his spoon and threw his napkin down. "I'd best be—"

"I'm also beginning to think you have a secret reason for going to Ireland," she announced, waving her spoon in the air.

He forced himself to stay still, not to move a muscle, or twitch even a corner of his mouth. If he ran away right now it would be too suspicious.

She couldn't possibly be going to say that he was a duke by day and a crusading justice fighter by night.

"Oh, I have secrets," he said, sitting back down,

smiling carelessly. "You caught me." He lifted his hands in a gesture of surrender. "I have a secret reason for going to Ireland."

"You do?" Her eyes widened and she leaned closer.

"I'm not going to Ireland to visit a widow."

"What's the reason then?" She slid to the edge of her seat, breathless with anticipation.

Why was he going to Ireland? Think, Dalton. Make it plausible. And distracting enough to deflect her interest. "I'm going to find a . . . wife."

She nearly dropped her spoon. "A *wife?*"

"That's right." Dalton sat back in his chair and crossed his ankle over his knee. "It's a tradition for the Dukes of Osborne to take an Irish bride. I'm the age my father was when he married."

She snapped her jaw shut. "Uh."

"What was that?"

"I . . . I thought you were never going to marry."

He shrugged. "My mother wants me to marry. I think perhaps if there were a child, a grandbaby, she'd find the will to leave the house. She's Irish, and so she'll approve of an Irish bride."

She looked hurt and indignant. Damn. He wanted to wrap his arms around her, whisper into her hair that it wasn't true.

He wasn't looking for a bride. He could never marry.

"Everyone in London says you'll never marry," she said lightly. "That you're a heartless, callous rakehell who'll never settle down and do his duty."

"And they're right . . . to an extent. I'm marrying more for my mother's sake than my own." He didn't like lying to her.

"So you're saying you're not a rake?"

"I'm London's premier rake," he said. "You know that."

"Do I? You're charming, it's true, but I've noticed your smile never truly reaches your eyes, even when you're kissing a girl."

"Have you been studying me like one of your paintings, Thea?"

"Perhaps. You do seem to have hidden layers."

"Are you saying I'm a masterpiece?" he quipped. He couldn't betray how much she rattled his calm.

She tilted her head and her gaze slid across from his chin to his . . . was the lady staring at his *crotch*?

"I'm saying you don't betray much with your words, but your body has involuntary signals. For example, the foot tapping."

Dalton stilled his foot.

Damn her quick mind.

"Your left foot taps when you're displeased," she continued. "Usually three times, like it tapped just now."

He froze. "You're very observant."

"And do you want to know something else?" She leaned closer, sliding her elbows into the space between his fingers. "I'll wager you're not even an honest-to-goodness rake. You're only pretending to be one, to keep the marriage-minded mamas at bay."

Dalton snatched his hands off the table. "That's a wager you'd speedily lose. Ask anyone in London. Ask the publisher of the *Times*. My exploits alone paid for his son's commission."

She shook her head and threw him a challenging look. "Not convinced."

How neatly she'd put him on the defensive. She was most likely the most formidable enemy he'd ever faced. He had to be careful with her. He couldn't betray any emotion.

Luckily, he was practiced in the art of subterfuge.

He leaned back in his chair. "All you need do is read the entries in the betting book at White's. The ones detailing my conquests. They tell the tale quite irrevocably."

She dipped her spoon directly into the trifle bowl, dispensing with civility completely. "I don't think so," she said calmly. "They only tell half the story. And I mean to discover the whole truth."

Dalton kept a cool, seductive smile on his lips. "Nothing to find," he said nonchalantly. "Hate to disappoint you, lamb, but I'm a rake through and through." He opened his arms wide. "There's no heart of gold here. No heart at all, actually."

Blue eyes narrowed. "Care to place a wager on that?"

"No, I don't." No wagers. Nothing to prove. He should leave now.

"Exhibit A." She pointed her spoon at his feet. "Your boots."

Now what? "What about my boots?"

"You haven't had them polished since we left London. Everyone knows rakes always have shiny, polished Hessians in which to admire their own reflections." She flourished the spoon through the air. "Therefore, you're not a rake."

Dalton snorted. "I'll have them polished tomorrow."

"Exhibit B." Thea scooped more trifle and licked it off her spoon. "You don't smell at all like a rake. I've been pressed against you and you simply don't smell like one." She tapped her forefinger against the table. "Spicy musk. Sandalwood. Pine forest. The aforementioned polished leather. Those are all acceptable scents for a rake. But if you must know the truth, you smell rather like the stables."

"That's because I've been tending our horses," Dalton sputtered.

"No." She smiled smugly. "That's because you're not a rake."

"For the love of—this is ridiculous." Dalton half rose from his chair. "I'm going to the stables now to be among my own kind."

"Wait!" She flourished her spoon through the air. "Exhibit C is Molly. You allowed a girl who aimed a pistol at you to join your traveling party. That means you're not heartless."

"I'm not going to leave a young girl dressed in trousers and recklessly waving a pistol on the highway. She could have been killed. Or she could have ended up hanging from a noose."

"Precisely. You care about those weaker and

less fortunate then you. And you definitely love your mother. And you care about Con. Which leads me to the final exhibit," she proclaimed.

"I think you've had too much whisk—"

"Exhibit D: you're in a bedchamber with slightly inebriated me and you haven't even tried to kiss me. You haven't even stared with dark intent upon my lips."

She set down her spoon with a bang. "So you're most definitely not a rake worth his salt."

She stood up from the table and bowed to the right and then to the left. "Esteemed gentlemen of the jury, the prosecution rests."

Dalton groaned. She'd be the death of him. The gauntlet had been thrown. The challenge issued.

She was playing with fire now. He'd like nothing better than to prove his rakehood.

On the hearth rug.

Then the bed.

Push those skirts up and that bodice down. Make her sigh and scream. Spark hotter than the fire.

There was only so much provocation a half-drunken duke could stand.

He stared at her lips with dark intent.

Reaching down, he grabbed the legs of her chair and dragged her toward him.

"Come here," he growled. "And I'll prove I'm a rake."

Chapter 13

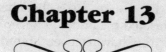

"Gracious," Thea exclaimed. A highly inadequate exclamation. Dalton grabbed her chair and yanked her around the table.

Perhaps she'd pushed him too far. Men must have breaking points.

But then she was beginning to think women might as well.

Pressure built inside her. Something reckless coiling at the base of her spine, waiting to unwind. She wanted his hands on her. Those large, roughened hands.

Thea had never had such urges.

She could satisfy those urges tonight.

The wicked thought buzzed like a bee flying too close to her ear, a secret, dangerous thrill. She had the rest of her life to be alone and untouched. Tonight she wanted to leave refined and proper far, far behind.

Another swift tug on her chair and her tightly closed knees were forced in between his powerful thighs.

Of course she knew he was a rake. He'd bedded half the widows and wives in London. Sophisticated, beautiful women. So of course he wouldn't find her all that tempting.

There were rumors he'd once seduced three ladies in a single evening and that he was the reason Miss Antonia Bradford now lived in a convent in France.

There were those who said he transformed into a wolf when the moon was full and prowled the streets of London in search of prey.

Well, that last bit she'd invented, but the myths surrounding him were enough to intrigue any lady with a newfound yen for adventure.

His hands settled to either side of her, surrounding her but not touching her. She stared at his neck, watching the pulse that beat so close she could have leaned forward and kissed the place.

"A rake might lift the hem of your gown now." His gaze followed his words, falling to her hem and then traveling upward.

But his hands never left the chair.

"Or he might command *you* to lift it." The seductive words rolled against her mind like waves breaking against distant cliffs.

"I would never do that." *Or would I?* came the reckless thought.

"You would." He smiled lazily. "Trust me, you would."

So confident and sure of himself.

The trouble was, when he spoke of lifting her hem, Thea imagined it happening, and it was only two short steps from imagination to longing, and another two steps to doing.

All that unwinding along her spine might travel to her hands and make her slide her gown up, inch by inch, over red leather boots and higher, over white stockings.

"I've been wondering what's under that demure gown." He tilted his head and a lock of hair fell across his brow. "Thin muslin, I'll wager. Something I could see the peaks of your breasts through."

Such crude language should offend, but her body responded to his words as if he'd touched her, the tips of her breasts stiffening and straining against the fabric of her shift.

He lifted his hands. She held her breath.

But he didn't reach for her. He reached for himself instead.

Slid off his coat. Loosened his cravat and untied the knot.

"Any rake worth his salt knows that a woman enjoys the sight of a well-formed male." He leaned back in his chair, thighs wide, hands spread. "Makes her wet and ready for him."

Ready for what? Thea's mind raced ahead, imagining all the possibilities, while her eyes drank in the sight of him.

Black leather boots creased with hard use. Buckskin trousers stretched across taut thighs. Cravat dangling loose around a thick, corded neck.

Severe jaw softened by that round indentation in the middle of his chin.

Bronzed hair, thick and wavy and impatient to fall in his eyes.

A stillness about him. A self-possession that drew the eye.

He commanded every room he entered. Ballroom or bedroom.

He controlled her responses right now. And just as she had when they waltzed, she longed to surrender.

He arched his eyebrows. "Had a thorough look?"

Thea gulped. "I . . . I've seen better."

"Have you now." He undid the buttons at the top of his shirt and slid it over his head, leaving only his untied cravat.

"Certainly. I've seen statues of . . . warriors." She'd been about to say gods and demigods, but that might make him even more conceited. The man truly had a high opinion of his charms.

Though it was an apt comparison.

He was cast from bronze, towering over the mere mortals who wandered near his feet.

The sound of his laughter rumbled like carriage wheels over gravel. "A rake knows when a woman's thinking about this." He cupped himself through his breeches in a terribly obscene gesture. "Care for a glimpse?"

Thea gasped. He was trying to shock her into ending the game. Admitting he was a rake and she was out of her depth.

"It might be diverting." She tilted her chin higher. "But I've seen such sights before."

His jaw flapped open. "Excuse me?"

Finally shocked him, Thea thought. *Two could play this game.*

"One cannot be a student of art without viewing the male form," she said primly. "In Caravaggio's painting of Zeus, for example, his . . . manly bits . . . float directly in the viewer's face."

"Float in your face?"

"Well, not literally. I only mean the perspective of the painting is such that it's the first thing the viewer notices."

"I'm sure it's the first thing young ladies notice."

"It's not all that impressive, really. It's floating, you see. *Zeus* is floating. On a cloud."

"Sounds rather . . . *flaccid.* I can assure you there'd be no floating here."

"I've seen other examples," she said flippantly. "On the wall of a temple in Rome. An etching of the god Priapus. His attributes were . . . most impressive. Far more impressive than yours, I'm sure."

"Have a care, Thea. Some gentlemen might take that as an invitation to stage a comparison."

"And some ladies might take that challenge."

Young ladies don't take challenges. Or stare at a man's breeches. Or . . .

Break all the rules! Every single one, something in Thea urged.

Could she? Did she dare?

Tentatively, her heart beating rapidly, Thea reached out her fingers . . . and broke a very big rule indeed.

He jumped back as if her touch had scalded him. "Oh no." He shook his head. "Not yet, little lamb. Moving too quickly is against the rake's code of conduct."

He slid his cravat from around his neck, snapping the linen tie between his fists, and muscles bunched and rippled in his arms.

"Hold out your wrists," he commanded.

What was he going to do? Thea widened her eyes as he lifted her wrists and wrapped the cravat around them, tying it in a loose knot.

"Ladies who break the rules must suffer the consequences." He gave one last tug and drew away, leaving her trussed and breathless.

He reached for his whiskey glass and swallowed the rest of the liquid.

He hadn't even touched *her* yet. Except on her wrists as he tied them.

He'd gripped the chair legs, stroked his own chest as he removed his coat, and now he was caressing his glass like it was one of his dratted widows.

Maddening.

And she couldn't even touch him now because her wrists were tied with his cravat. Why did that make her body heat and her thighs clench?

"Raise your arms over your head," he commanded.

Her arms drifted higher until her knotted wrists hung in the air over her head.

"That's nice," he murmured approvingly. "Very nice." He skimmed his fingertips over the tops of her breasts where they pushed against her bodice. She arched shamelessly into his touch.

His fingers traced a path up her neck and along the inside of her upstretched arm.

He pulled down her sleeve, exposing the inside of her arm.

The uncoiling wasn't only in her spine now. He'd said a woman became wet and now she knew what he'd meant.

Warmth and heat pooled between her thighs. She shifted in her chair, clenching her thighs together in an effort to assuage the need building there.

His thumbs traced the skin of her inner elbow. She was captured, unable to break free, but not because of the cravat tied around her wrists.

Because she wanted more.

He kissed the inside of her elbow and she nearly moaned aloud.

So vulnerable, the inside of an elbow. Such an unexpected place to be kissed.

He repeated the action on the other side, his tongue flicking over the pulse in her inner elbow. The soft touch of his lips reverberated through her entire body and set her pulse hammering and her belly humming.

"When I touch you here"—he brushed his thumbs across the inside of her elbows—"you want me to touch you here." His fingers skimmed lightly over the fabric covering the juncture of her thighs.

That brief contact burned through the layers of cotton, more suggestive and devastating than an actual caress.

Her arms ached from holding them over her head.

"Your arms are trembling. You want to lower them," he said. "You want to wrap them around my neck. Your lips part slightly. You take one breath, a quick one, and you fill your lungs and then exhale."

The man was a practiced seducer, no doubt about it.

She shook her hair back, away from her neck, keeping her arms raised overhead.

What would it take to make him lose control and break his own rules?

"If I do this"—she thrust her breasts forward and bent her head back, exposing her throat— "you want to touch me."

His breathing quickened.

"You want to twine your fingers into my hair." The words flowed from some primal spring in her mind. "More than anything."

He moaned softly and cupped her cheek with his palm.

Promising.

She turned her head and brushed her lips across the inside of his palm. Her tongue darted out to taste him. Salt. Skin.

The unfamiliar taste of a man.

Strong arms strained as he tilted her chair until she tumbled into his arms and he caught her. Lifted her. Settled her legs to either side of him, dangling over the sides of the wooden chair.

He wrapped her arms over his head, still tied, and took her mouth with his lips, kissing her thirstily. She tasted a hint of metallic blood and smelled the clean scent of the birch soap she'd used to wash his wounds.

Sensation uncoiled along her spine, sliding and nudging desire to life. She was a glass jar full of captured fireflies, whirring with sensation and light, wanting to break free and fly.

His fingers nestled into her hair, massaging her scalp and guiding her into his kiss.

Savored, surrounded, treasured, his hands framed her face as he pulled back and kissed the edges of her mouth. The soft grazing of his teeth on her lip made her squirm with pleasure.

This was the legendary Duke of Osborne. Not glimpsed across a crowded ballroom.

Here.

Kissing her hot and deep. Pleasure slithering along her spine.

A melting sensation, like butter meeting the surface of a heated saucepan.

A cry of pleasure torn from her throat and swallowed by his mouth.

Heat settled in the center of her thighs, pooling into wetness.

She moaned into his lips, straining toward him, craving more contact.

She knew he was trying to teach her a lesson about the depraved nature of men, but Thea refused to take heed.

She never wanted the kiss to end.

She wanted to thread her hands through his hair, bring his lips to her breasts, but she couldn't move her hands.

Move your mouth lower, Dalton. Please.

His breath tickled her flesh. She lifted her chest slightly, the tips of her breasts hard and unfamiliar feeling, tingling, begging for his attention, contracted to hard points. "Please . . ."

Finally he cupped her breasts through her shift, lifting them to his lips.

His skillful tongue claimed the tip of one breast through the thin cotton. Sensation shot through her whole body and she arched uncontrollably.

"Oh, that is . . . there are no words," she moaned.

"**T**hea," Dalton groaned, laying his head against her soft, supple breasts. "What am I going to do with you?"

He could think of fifty utterly debauched things. None of which he could do with a virgin entrusted to his protection. He didn't need whiskey to ease his bruised ribs. When he touched her, his body forgot all about the existence of pain.

He could blame it on the drink, or the lingering effects of those blows in the courtyard, or he could acknowledge the truth. He wanted to touch her satin skin . . . hear her trilling laugh . . . taste the apricot and whiskey on her tongue.

He wanted her with a longing so visceral it was a sixth sense.

Lifting her bound wrists from around his neck, he settled her back into her own chair and dropped to his knees in front of her.

Maybe he could have just a little taste.

"What are you doing?" she gasped as he pushed her skirts and petticoats slowly up her white stocking-clad legs.

Shapely legs with slender ankles.

He knelt to unlace her red leather half boots. Slowly. Drawing out her anticipation. She watched him with half-lidded eyes, the fringe of her lashes casting shadows on her cheeks.

She wore simple cotton drawers with a slit down the middle.

Easy access. He liked that.

No time to untie her drawers. He needed to taste her. Now.

She wiggled, attempting to escape, but he held her immobile.

She made a startled sound as his fingers slipped inside her drawers. Wet for him, slippery with wanting.

He gently spread that honeyed wetness over the outer lips of her sex, parting her, preparing her.

"Dalton, what are you . . . oh . . . my." She squirmed but he stilled her with an arm around her waist. Her body quivered when he touched the tip of his tongue to her, running it softly around the hood of her sex.

Only a hint. A promise.

She stilled. Waiting. She wanted more. He licked her again, sliding the hood up and down, not touching the heart of her directly yet.

He savored the smoky, sweet flavor, dipping his tongue inside to taste more, and then dragging his tongue back and forth over her core.

Her hips moved now in small, undulating circles, unconsciously disclosing the rhythm she preferred.

Letting go of her hips, he balled her shift up in one fist so he could see her moving above him. She was so perfect and beautiful.

He was fully hard now, as rigid as he'd ever been. He couldn't help thinking about lifting her off that chair in one swift movement and sliding her down onto his shaft. She was so wet and slippery it would go easily, even though she was an innocent.

She tasted so good.

His cock twitched and begged for release while he pleasured her.

Pushing his fingers inside her, where his cock wanted to go, he worshipped her with his fingers and his tongue at the same time.

"Dalton?" There was a question, a quivering need. Inner muscles tensed around his fingers. She was very near now.

He couldn't answer, because his mouth was full of sweet, satisfying woman.

He thrust his fingers deeper and sucked gently, flicking her sex with his tongue at the same time.

She moaned, pressing against his lips, her entire body tensing and shaking.

"I . . . oh . . ."

Nearly there, Thea.

He sucked and flicked harder now, quickening the pace.

Her body tensed and jerked beneath his lips

and then her head fell backward. She slumped back in the chair and he rode the lingering tremors of her orgasm with his tongue and lips, prolonging her pleasure.

His Thea, his sensual goddess. Moaning with abandon, thighs spread.

He untied her wrists and flipped her gown back over her legs.

"Let that be a warning to you," he growled. "About why it's not wise to wager with a rake. You'll always lose."

"I'm woman enough to admit when I'm wrong," she said shakily, rubbing her fingers across her wrists.

"What was that?" Dalton sat in the chair opposite her and crossed his arms over his chest, striving to quiet his breathing. "I didn't quite hear you . . ."

He loved the pink tinge he'd brought to her cheeks and the way her lower lip was plump and swollen from his kisses.

That one small taste hadn't been nearly enough. He wanted more.

He sipped more whiskey, the earthy flavor flooding his mouth and mingling with the lingering sweet taste of Thea.

"You're definitely a rake worth your salt," she replied.

"And?"

"The condition of your boots doesn't signify."

"Then my job here is finished." That was his cue to leave. So why didn't his legs lift him out of the damn chair?

"Truly?" Smoky blue eyes gazed at him. "Did you . . . *finish?*"

Whiskey burned the wrong way down his throat and he coughed helplessly.

"Anything the matter?" she inquired innocently.

"That's not a conversation we'll have on this journey," he choked out.

She tilted forward and satin flesh mounded over the patterned silk of her gown. "But what happens next?"

Chapter 14

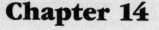

"**N**othing happens next." Dalton edged his chair away from her. "I go sleep in the stables."

"In the stables? With cracked ribs?"

"Or I'll sleep on the chair here, by the fire."

Her gaze flicked to the bed next to the window. "Or we could . . . share the bed."

"No more beds." Damn it, why was he always growling when he spoke to her?

As he'd observed earlier, she brought out the beast in him.

"I'm curious." She furrowed her brow. "How long does the . . . rest of it last? From the bits and pieces I've gleaned, it sounds like it would be a quick affair."

"There'd be nothing quick about it, I can assure you."

"Of course, since you've made the pursuit of pleasure your life's sole purpose I'm sure you've developed a certain . . . aptitude. Or perhaps women merely flatter you? Pretend to enjoy themselves?"

"Women never pretend their pleasure in my arms."

"How can you be so sure?" she asked with an arch smile.

Ah, he understood what was happening here. This was Thea constructing a barrier of humor and carelessness, pretending this interlude meant nothing more than physical pleasure to her.

"Believe me, Thea, if we made love, you wouldn't be pretending anything. And it would last all night. But that's completely beside the point because it will never happen. This will never happen again."

"And why not? What if I want it to happen?"

He reached over and cupped her chin in his palm. "Because with men, pleasure blows through us like a squall across an ocean. There one moment and gone the next. But it's different for women."

She moved her chin away from his hand. "Maybe I'm not like other women. Maybe I can take my pleasure and barricade my heart, just as men do."

"Life hasn't taught you yet to divorce this"—he touched her forehead—"from this." He brushed his fingers lightly across her chest, over her heart. "I sincerely hope it never does. And I'm too honorable to be the one to do it."

Her eyes narrowed. "Oh, you're so very honorable. Flaunting yourself in ballrooms, taunting the proper young ladies with your physical perfection. Behold my impressive musculature," she growled, imitating his deep tones and puffing out her chest, apparently pretending to be him.

She leapt up and thrust out her chin. "How do you like this devastating cleft in my chin?" She squared her shoulders. "Don't my strong, wide shoulders make you tingle?"

He reached for her skirts but she ducked away, a teasing light shining in her eyes. "Oh no, young ladies, you can look, but you can't touch."

He couldn't help chuckling. She disarmed him so completely. "Is that truly what the wallflowers were thinking?"

"Oh yes," she breathed. "And that's not all we thought about."

Sweet Lord. Her gaze dropped and his cock leapt to attention, straining to break free.

Rising from the chair, he lifted her into his arms and carried her to the bed, beyond caring about right and wrong. Only thinking of this . . . the soft curve of her lower lip. The even softer swell of her breasts beneath his chest.

She nestled into his touch with a sigh that he felt as a caress along the entire length of his stiff cock. Then she did something wholly unexpected. She pushed against his chest until he flopped onto his back on the bed.

She reared over him, tracing the hair that trailed down his stomach and disappeared into his breeches with her finger. "Do you want to know what else the wallflowers were thinking?"

Don't answer that. *Don't answer that.*

An incriminating moan escaped his lips.

She stared at his groin. "We wondered about *this.*" Her fingers drifted to his breeches' flap.

"Wondered if you padded your breeches, or if it was all real."

Sweet heaven above, he'd corrupted her mind. Unleashed a wanton. And it was glorious.

"Thea. You're going to kill me."

Her finger traced the line of hair that bisected his abdomen. "I want to know where this path leads."

He should stop her, but it felt so damned good.

And she'd accused him of being a tease. Couldn't have that, now could he?

The tables had been completely and utterly turned. He was at her mercy. A lusting fool praying she might follow words with actions.

"Thea," he groaned feverishly. With a quick flick of his wrist he undid a button and his cock sprang free. He gripped the root, offering himself to her. "Is this what you want to see?"

She nodded, her eyes going wide as she stared at his cock.

"Would you like to see me as well?" she asked, her voice soft and seductive.

He nodded, incapable of coherent speech.

She reached around and undid the buttons of her gown and slipped it over her head, leaving only white cotton stays over a simple white chemise.

Because he was desperate for the sight of her firm, high breasts, he tugged the edge of her chemise down and her breasts spilled over the edge of her stays.

"Jesus, Thea. You're too beautiful."

She glanced down at her own breasts. "You think so?"

He nodded, incoherent with need, tracing a finger along the delicate swell of her breasts over smooth skin and tight, rose-colored nipples.

She rose over him, propping herself on her wrists. Her hair swung in feathery circles over his chest. "I want to give you pleasure as well," she whispered.

Her hand brushed his chest and moved downward, over the tightness of his abdomen. Down . . . tentative, petal-soft brushing of fingers on the rim of his cock.

"Show me . . . show me how to pleasure you." Her fingers sheathed his cock.

He groaned. She gripped him tighter. And the fever took him.

He closed his hand over hers and guided it up and over the head of his cock and then back down the shaft.

Of course she easily learned the way of it. His hand fell away and she continued, sliding up over the crest, lubricated now by his sweat and the drops of his seed that signaled he wouldn't last long.

All that pleasure chasing away the pain.

It was the most erotic sight he'd ever seen. Thea's lips pursed and those big, blue-gray eyes focused in concentration as she slid her fingers along his shaft.

He moaned, showing her that she pleased him.

Mind screaming with need now. Hands fisted into the bedclothes on either side of his hips to stop from parting the folds of her sex with his fingers and plunging his cock to the hilt.

Wrap her legs around his back and lift her hips and rock in the cradle of her body.

She'd be his equal in passion. And inventiveness. She'd ride him . . . match his movements and improvise ones of her own.

Body tensing, muscles gripping, mind blanking.

He was too ready and she was too lovely with her breasts thrust over her stays and her golden curls streaming around her shoulders as she concentrated on what she was doing.

He reached for her neck and kissed her then, brushing his tongue against her tongue, deepening the kiss while she worked his cock with her smooth, soft fingers.

She tasted like honey. Like the sweetest substance in the world and he could get stuck in her and drown, drunk with pleasure.

Bruised ribs forgotten, he molded her softness against him, thrusting into her hand, lost to everything now but the driving need coursing through his veins.

"Faster," he gasped. And she pumped him faster. Harder.

He buried his face in her rose-scented hair, dripping with sweat, convulsing with need.

His climax hit him like a fist to the gut, splintering his control and bringing blood rushing through his body and pleasure screaming through every nerve.

Flopping back onto the bed, he drew Thea against his chest. Her curls mixing with his sweat. His seed on her hand, pooling across his abdomen.

Pleasure thudded through him, fainter now, like the fading drumbeat of a retreating army. He didn't want it to end.

He stroked her hair. "That was so good, Thea. Thank you."

"You're welcome." She raised her head, smiling shyly. "Was that . . . right?"

"More than right."

When he regained enough equilibrium he grabbed his old, torn linen shirt and wiped them clean.

In the candlelight her eyes had a lighter circle of gray, like a band of silver clasped around her pupil. How had he not noticed that before?

He banded his arms around her and settled her against his chest, drinking in the scent of warm, recently pleasured woman.

He wasn't going to examine why it felt so right. Or why he didn't even care about breaking his rules. Why shouldn't he sleep with Thea in his arms?

He could drift in this pleasure a few hours longer.

It was unexpected, this happiness.

Shouldn't her mother's imperious, recriminating tones be intruding into her head about now? Remonstrating. Scolding.

Instead there was only the sighing of Dalton's breath and the steady beat of his heart against her ear, and a pleasant hum of lingering, languid sensation in her limbs.

"I find I rather like bed sport," she said. "I think I have an affinity for it."

"Mmm." He nuzzled her ear with firm, questing lips. "I won't dispute that."

Goodness, she loved hearing his breath hitch. "What do you call it, anyway? The moment of . . . *completion*."

"My climax . . ." he murmured drowsily. "Crisis . . . coming . . . my pleasure." He stroked her hair. "*Our* pleasure."

She drifted, held tight in the warm circle of his arms. If she'd known he was this agreeable after having a crisis, then she should have given him one that first night. It would have made things easier.

Thea smiled against his chest.

The release . . . the *coming*. And then the discovery.

She'd never considered all the possibilities of this body of hers. How she could be so much more than something inert, silent, draped in satin and stuck with feathers to entice a mate.

There was so much more to her body.

Pleasure singing through blood and contracting muscles.

And there was more to this journey as well. A destination. Leading to more discovery.

"Dalton?"

A grunt. He was still awake.

"The painting I seek in your attic is a self-portrait by Artemisia, the Renaissance painter I told you about. Her letters mention a painting she was working on entitled *Self-portrait as the Allegory of Painting,* but it's been lost."

His fingers drifted lightly across her shoulder. "What would you do with the painting?"

"Write about it . . . perhaps an article for the British Institution. History has relegated her to a brief footnote. The seventeenth century wasn't ready for a fiery, opinionated woman who utilized her art to pass judgment on a society that restricted her freedoms."

"So you want to rewrite history."

"I'd like to think perhaps the world might be ready for the self-portrait now. Ready to acknowledge her bold, uncompromising talent."

"Perhaps. Though I wouldn't hold out much hope of that."

"Women's artwork was . . . still is . . . supposed to be feminine, and safe, and placid. Artemisia broke that mold. There's nothing pretty or safe about her mythological paintings. Blood spurts from the neck of her Holofernes, while a muscular, anguished Judith saws through bone and gristle."

He shifted above her. "Really? I'd like to see that."

"The painting's in a gallery in Florence. I think it's the reason I'm here instead of dutifully embroidering a sampler at my grandmother's house in London, waiting to be sold to Foxford. That painting proclaims that our fingers are no less skillful, our minds no less sharp and our sensibilities, the way we view the world, no less unique."

"There are others, you know," Dalton said
drowsily.

She searched his face in the darkness. "What
do you mean, there are others?"

"Other attics . . . rooms . . . entire estates filled
with artworks and antiquities my father won at
gambling. Stole, really."

"Truly?" Thea's heart pounded. "Where?"

Dalton's chest rose and fell beneath her like the
swell of a wave beneath a ship.

"When I was fifteen, home from Eton on holi-
days, my father brought me to a large town house
in Mayfair. The way he was acting, so furtive and
secretive, I thought perhaps he wanted to intro-
duce me to one of his mistresses. I was wrong."

His voice drifted into silence and Thea held her
breath, needing the story to continue, afraid he
might fall asleep first.

"The house was literally filled floor to ceiling
with treasure, like some mythological dragon's
lair. Marble statues . . . coffers of coins . . . piles of
priceless, ancient paintings . . ."

Thea's breath caught. "That must have been
quite a sight. What did he do with it all?"

"Nothing." A bitter note crept into Dalton's
deep voice. "Hoarded it. He had an eye for beauty,
the old duke, but he only wanted to claim, to possess, to become the wealthiest man in England."
His voice trailed off and his breathing deepened.

Thea brushed his rough, angular jaw, wanting
to soften this memory for him somehow. "It's all
still there?"

"Covered in dust," he murmured sleepily. "And

cobwebs . . . the attic at Balfry is only a taste. I've no idea what should be done with his hoard."

Her skin heated from his arms around her, and now her mind buzzed with possibilities. She'd gladly help him decide what to do with ancient masterpieces.

"Some noblemen donate ancestral artworks to the Institution," she whispered, keeping her voice even, not wanting to frighten him away with the excitement and fervor sparking in her mind. "The Institution exhibits the works for the public occasionally, and for students of art to copy and study."

"I like that idea." His arm twitched against her shoulder and his breathing grew rhythmic.

"Dalton?" she whispered.

No reply.

It was so unfamiliar to hear someone else breathing close to her. She'd never had anyone else in her bedchamber. No sisters. No friends who spent the night and crawled into bed to whisper secrets.

She'd always been alone.

What would she and Dalton say to each other tomorrow? How would she look at him without imagining the wicked, secret things they'd done?

Thea's entire body flashed hot, and then cold, thinking of it.

She'd truly broken loose from familial moorings now.

There was danger in that thought. Uncertainty.

But also excitement.

And a tantalizing taste of freedom.

Chapter 15

Damn, damn, damn.

Dalton woke with Thea's head nestled into his neck and her small fist tucked under his jaw. He counted one unforgivable sin for every breath she took against his chest.

Accepting a morsel of creamy trifle from her spoon.

Pouring her a tumbler of honeyed Irish whiskey.

Accepting her dare to prove he was a rake. Wrapping his cravat around her wrists.

Jesus. Had he really done that?

Lapping her creamy sweetness until she cried her release. Clasping his hand around her hand and teaching her to give him release.

And the worst crime of all?

Wrapping his arms around her and telling her that the paintings in the attic at Balfry were only a taste.

Stupid, heartless, triple-damned bastard.

He never slept the entire night with a woman in his arms, vulnerable and pleasure sated.

Last night he'd given in to a self-indulgent need

for connection he hadn't surrendered to since Cambridge when he'd fancied himself a poet and drank cheap wine in taverns and written verses even more unpalatable than the wine.

What happens next? she'd asked.

He'd been dying to show her exactly what happened next.

Ease inside. Find the rhythm, the angle, she needed. Sink deep. Deeper.

Pleasure bursting, ripe and fleeting as a summer's day.

That's right. Follow those thoughts to the logical conclusion. You wouldn't be able to offer for her and the guilt would tear you apart.

She was a danger to him because she made him feel. She dulled his edge.

And he was a grave danger to her because anyone close to him would become a target. Alec had been drowned to crush the old duke, punish him for his sins.

If Dalton's secret came to light, the powerful men who hated him for stealing their profits and scaring away their customers would attempt to control him in the same way.

They might try using Thea as a bargaining chip. A weapon to bring him to his knees.

He'd never forgive himself if anything happened to her because of her association with him.

He wanted to be the one to fulfill her every dream. But he wasn't that man.

She moved in his arms, sighing softly and nestling closer, warm curves heating his skin. He recognized her yearning for love, for acceptance. Recognized it, and couldn't do a damn thing about it.

Because he could never be what she needed and he'd have to say goodbye soon.

And he'd have to dream about this moment for the rest of his lonely life.

How she looked all curled up, dark fringe of eyelashes across her cheeks, one smooth shoulder exposed.

Need to leave. Now.

Gingerly, he lifted her off his chest and set her back upon the bed.

He lifted the bedclothes, preparing to leave.

Blunder.

She'd removed her stays and her lovely breasts were clearly visible beneath the thin cambric of her chemise. The garment had ridden up her legs and was twisted between her thighs. He could see her shapely legs, the dark patch between her thighs.

The sight sent a shock of longing down his arms, along his fingertips, and deeper, into his chest, somewhere in the region of where his heart should be.

He leapt off the bed, not caring anymore if she heard him, and grabbed his clothing and boots.

Hand on the door. Push it open. Don't look back.

In the hallway, Dalton slammed his back against the wall, aching to go back into that room.

Peel off her shift to reveal high curving breasts, slender waist and flaring hips.

She'd lift her hair off her shoulders and turn to catch his eye, silver-ringed eyes framed by gold waves.

Shy invitation in that glance. Not yet. Can't touch her yet.

Maybe she needed a wash. She might be sticky still from last night's abandon.

Dip a cloth in warm water. Smooth a cake of rose-scented soap and smooth it over the scrolling lines of her neck, her back, her shoulders.

Use the soap instead of his fingers.

Make her wait . . . make her breathing falter . . . bring the soap around now. Over her nipples, under the swell of her breasts. Down to her belly button, fingers gripping the soap harder now.

Slide the soap lower . . . between her thighs. Where he wanted to be. Where he wanted to slide.

Heavy with need now. So close to losing control.

Take her over the edge until she cried his name and then . . . lift her into his arms and take her to bed.

He banged his head back against the wall. What the hell was he doing standing outside of her room, panting like a lusting fool?

"Mr. Gabrielli?"

He straightened. "Good morning, Betsy," he said gruffly, praying the woman didn't glance below his waistcoat. "Mrs. Gabrielli requires a pot of drinking chocolate for her breakfast."

He strode quickly down the stairs and headed for the stables.

He'd ride the remaining two hours to Bristol outside the carriage.

Separated from Thea by layers of wood and steel.

And impossibility.

"This is the place, my lady." Con handed first Thea, and then Molly, down from the carriage in front of the cheerful green-painted door in the orange brick façade of the Trumpeter Inn on St. Maryport Street in Bristol.

"You'll rest here until the ship sails tonight." Con noticed Thea craning her neck toward the horses. "The duke will be at the docks by now, seeing about the ship."

"Oh." Thea tried to hide her disappointment.

She'd thought maybe they'd have luncheon together. Dalton hadn't spoken to her since he'd slipped away while she was still sleeping. He'd ridden out, beside the carriage, and they hadn't stopped between Bath and Bristol.

Molly had slept most of the journey, still feeling tired. Leaving Thea more than two hours to remember every intimate, shattering detail of last night.

Thea had changed. Become aware of light and sound and taste in a new way.

The chocolate she'd sipped that morning had been impossibly rich. And when a breeze ruffled her bonnet ribbons across her cheek, the soft, silken contact triggered memories of his fingers brushing her cheek.

She shivered slightly.

"Could it be the duke's avoiding you for some reason?" There was a knowing twinkle in Con's blue eyes.

Thea's face heated. "Don't be ridiculous."

They knew, of course. Con and Molly knew she'd shared a room with Dalton.

What must they think of her? Her cheeks were going to burst into flames any second now.

Molly's freckles danced higher as she raised her eyebrows. "The lady doth protest too much, don't you think so, Con?"

Lending Molly the complete works of Mr. Shakespeare maybe hadn't been such a clever idea.

Con chuckled and regarded Thea with an amused smile. "She's turning quite an interesting hue. What would you call that color, Molly, my love?"

Molly pretended to deliberate. "Gooseberry?" She tilted her head. "Scarlet?"

"You know, Molly," Con said, "I've been hoping for a lady to come along and put that man in his place, good and proper like. And Lady Dorothea's the one to achieve it, and make no mistake. Nearly there, I'd say."

Thea opened her mouth to protest and then shut it again. Anything she said now would only be incriminating. "Humph." She tugged her bonnet lower to hide her face. "Are you two quite finished?"

A young porter with shiny brass buttons marching down his red jacket and even shinier red spots around his nose ushered them inside the inn.

Thea and Molly waited while Con made arrangements with a dour-faced innkeeper who had a drooping black moustache.

"Everything's settled," Con said jovially, rejoining them. "We'll be back soon, Mrs. Gabrielli." He winked at Thea. "And young Master Gabrielli." Another wink for Molly. He set his black cap back atop his ginger and gray head and strode away.

Molly glanced at the porter triumphantly, obviously reveling in the fact that no one at the inn seemed to take any notice of the fact that she was a girl garbed in male clothing.

She *was* tall and slender in the chest, but it wasn't that. Thea regarded her curiously. It was something about the way she held herself. She'd taken to standing with her legs parted and her shoulders thrust back just like the duke.

They followed the spotty-cheeked porter to their temporary chambers.

"So what happened last night after I fainted?" Molly whispered. "Did you and . . . *you know who* . . . share a room?"

"Don't look at me like that," Thea whispered back. "Nothing happened."

Well . . . not *nothing*. But Molly didn't need to know that.

"Never took the duke for a coward," Molly said with a sly smile.

Nor me for a wanton, Thea thought.

They reached Molly's chamber first. "I think I'll take another nap," she said.

"Still feeling weak?" Thea asked. There was

more color in Molly's cheeks now, which was a good sign.

"I'm fine. Just tired, that's all."

Thea made sure Molly was settled and then ordered hot water for a bath in her own chamber.

When the copper tub was filled, Thea sank gratefully into the steam, eager to wash away the travel grime. When she slid deeper beneath the water he was there, cradling her in his arms, saturating her body with liquid heat. When she shifted, the water sloshed across her body like Dalton's hands caressing her.

Last night had been revelatory. And so wondrously decadent.

She closed her eyes and leaned her head back. Slid fingers down her arms and across her breasts and then lower, over her belly.

She wanted to learn more about her body. He'd kissed her . . . *here*. Her fingers found the place, sliding over sensitive flesh.

Her limbs twitched beneath the water. One hand on her breast and the other under the water, inside the slippery opening of her body.

The pleasure that still pulsed.

She didn't have to live by her mother's rules any longer. She could be imprudent. Scandalous.

She could take a lover.

The shocking idea had never occurred to the proper, refined daughter of the Countess of Desmond. But the idea was definitely occurring to runaway Thea. Especially after the taste of pleasure she'd received last night.

Her plan had been to exit society quietly, unobtrusively. But now that she'd sent the letter to her mother claiming she'd been compromised, there was no hope of that.

There would be whispers about her precipitous departure from society.

One of the servants could read her letter and spread the rumor.

Artemisia had taken lovers and been branded promiscuous, her private life overshadowing her art.

Even Aunt Emma had a scandalous past. Thea didn't know all the details, but it was rumored she'd had an affair with a married earl whose wife was an invalid. Which explained why her aunt was never invited to London.

Her finger moved faster now, splashing across the hard button of flesh where all the sensation concentrated. She wanted to discover more on the ship to Ireland tonight, while waves rocked beneath them.

Talking. Laughing. And then . . . not talking.

She wanted to know what happened next.

She'd never considered the possibility of this much pleasure.

The waves undulating between her thighs, spreading into the center of her body. Tensing. Flicking faster with her fingers. Harder.

Belly tightening. The wave cresting, spilling pleasure through her body.

She moaned softly, her head falling over the rim of the tub.

This could become habit forming.

It was too short. It didn't last long enough and it created a need for more.

Like eating sugary trifle. Or drinking hot chocolate. Explosive spice and sweetness in her mouth. The distant cousin to these hot, melting waves of pleasure still crashing through her body.

A lady never eats more than one biscuit. A lady denies herself pleasure.

But Thea was most definitely no longer a lady.

There was a knock at the door. Her heart beat faster.

"Who is it?" she called.

"Jenkins, ma'am," a female voice answered.

The maid. Not Dalton.

"Enter," Thea replied.

"Is this your only gown, ma'am?" the sturdy maid with rosy cheeks asked, shaking out the patterned blue-and-gray silk.

"I'm afraid so."

"Well, never you mind, I'll brush it good as new. And these handsome boots." She lifted the red leather boots. "Once I've got the mud off they'll glow again, red as rubies."

Thea thanked the maid and she left.

Thea felt newly polished. She'd discovered quite a few things about herself already on this journey.

Hidden reserves of strength she hadn't known she possessed.

She'd severed ties with her mother. Faced a pistol. Defused a duel.

Driven an arrogant duke to distraction.

Her perspective had shifted, as if an artist had decided the pose she was in at the beginning of the journey wasn't right and had painted over her, a new, bolder outline, the ghost of her former self only barely discernible beneath layers of fresh paint.

Chapter 16

Dalton pushed open the door of the Anchor Tavern, and the stale smell of spilled gin and refuse rotting in the back alley assaulted his senses.

He chose a corner table where his back would be against the wall and the entranceway in his line of vision, and ordered a pint of double stout porter from a buxom barmaid with flaming copper hair and a flirtatious smile, to while away the time until Con joined him here.

He'd hired a merchant brigantine with the poetic name of the *Truth and Daylight*, whose dockers had been offloading wooden barrels bearing the Cork Butter Exchange stamp, negotiating terms with the ship's master to turn around immediately and sail back to Cork on the next tide.

He'd also purchased Thea and Molly first-class passage on Bristol's most luxurious steam packet. Con could meet them at the docks in Cork Harbor and provide them an escort to their families.

Dalton was a greater danger to Thea than anyone she'd meet in a respectable dining room on a steam packet.

What was Thea doing right now? Most likely having a bath. Submerged in steam with one shapely, elegant leg poking out of the tub, her hair wet and coiling around her shoulders.

Or she could be curled up in a soft bed taking a nap.

And now he needed to quench his thirst. Where was his beer?

Dalton looked up in time to see an unusually large man hoist a full keg effortlessly to the bar.

The barmaid tapped his pint and brought it to his table. "Name's Pearl," she announced with an appreciative glance at his arms. "Care for some company?"

Dalton shook his head. "Not today. Thanks all the same."

The barmaid leant over his table so his gaze was drawn to the curving expanse of her bosom. "Sure now?"

"Sure," Dalton said firmly.

He gulped the dark brown porter, thick and hearty as a slice of bread, as he thought back on the news he'd learned after he finished with the ship.

O'Roarke's ship, the *Rambler*, sailed back to New York from Cork Harbor in two days.

The large man from the bar approached Dalton's table. There was something familiar about his crooked nose, thick neck, and deeply inset blue eyes. "Do I know you?" Dalton asked.

"By reputation, I've no doubt." The man straightened his cravat. "Albertson, though most know me as the Bristol Basher." His fists were enormous and covered with purplish bruises. "You're in my establishment."

Dalton had seen the Basher fight once, many years ago. "And a fine place it is." He'd wanted to sit here and drink his pint in peace while he waited for Con, not talk to the proprietor. Dalton gave him a forbidding look.

Undeterred, Albertson leaned his elbows on the table. "What brings you to Bristol, Mr. . . . ?"

"Jones." Dalton said shortly. "Here on business."

"What kind of business?"

"Not yours."

"Oh, well now." Albertson backed away, huge hands raised. "Just a friendly question. Enjoy your pint."

Dalton watched Albertson closely as he lumbered away. Nothing unusual for a prizefighter to own a tavern. The dank courts and blind alleys of the rookeries surrounding the docks were full of quay rangers and prizefighters and other desperate characters.

But Dalton hadn't liked his questions.

He shook his head to clear his thoughts. It was probably nothing. He was rattled. He wasn't himself.

Con arrived and Dalton waved Pearl over for another pint.

"They're settled at the inn," Con said, taking a seat. "Lady Dorothea blushed five shades of crimson when I mentioned you. Something I should know about last night?"

"I don't want to talk about it." Dalton swallowed the rest of his porter in one gulp and gestured for another.

Con leaned back in his seat and hooked one boot over his knee. "I like that lady. She's got spirit and heart. And I won't see her hurt by you. If something happened—"

"She's still a maid."

Con stared challengingly for a few more beats and then relaxed. "And there's still time," he smirked. "She'll conquer you yet."

Ignoring that, Dalton accepted another pint. "We sail tonight. Found a brigantine unloading from Cork. The shipmaster said his crew would balk at turning straight back around but I offered him twenty percent over his usual profit to sail on the evening tide."

"Twenty percent over his normal voyage profit could be a tidy sum. Not worth that," Con groused. "Even with four extra passengers."

"Two."

Con's eyebrows spiked. "Two?"

"I booked separate passage for the ladies on a steam packet leaving tomorrow morning. They've no place on a merchant brig."

Con gave him a sharp look and set down his mug. "What are you so afraid of, then?"

"Nothing," Dalton scoffed.

Thea, he amended silently. He'd faced men who wanted to kill him but he was far more terrified of a slip of a thing with eyes the color of rainy skies and a smile like the first faint promise of a rainbow after it rained.

Con folded his arms across his chest. "You're not getting any younger, you know."

"Your point?"

"You should marry. Sire a brat."

"You know that's impossible."

"Man goes to his grave lonely. Man might have regrets."

"I'm not lonely. I've plenty of female companionship."

"Quit acting the maggot. That's not what I mean."

"You know I can never marry. Besides, you're one to talk. I don't hear you planning to visit Bronagh."

Con stared into his pint glass. "I've been thinking about that. I've a mind to maybe go and see her."

Dalton stopped with his pint glass half-raised.

"Least I can do is give her a chance to yell at me," Con said. "Might do her some good."

Was that a note of *hope* in his voice? "Might do you some good as well."

"I don't like Molly and the lady traveling alone."

"They won't be alone. I asked the ship's master to ensure they were under his personal protection, and the steam packet will be teeming with respectable matrons. You can meet them at the docks with a hired carriage and convey them to their destinations."

"About Molly's destination." Con swirled the dark brown liquid in his glass. "She's Bronagh's daughter."

"What?" Dalton thumped his glass against the

table and porter sloshed over his knuckles. "How do you know that?"

"I stayed with her last night, after she fainted, and we talked of her family." Con's eyes filled with a wondering light. "She's Seamus and Bronagh's daughter. My niece."

"Truly?"

Con nodded.

"That settles it, then. You're going to see Bronagh whether you want to or not. Here's to Uncle Con." Dalton raised his glass in a toast.

Con snorted. "Now don't be thinking I'm suddenly going soft and turning into a family man. Bronagh hates me for leaving. She'll probably chase me away with a rusty pistol. Like mother like daughter."

"Or she could welcome you with twenty years' worth of stored kisses."

"Ha."

Something about that slightly wavering *ha* spoke volumes. It said that maybe Con was hoping for kisses. That maybe he really would consider retiring and becoming an honest farmer. Settling down. Finding love.

Dalton glanced sideways at his old friend and conspirator, trying to imagine babes dandling on his knees. Little ones tugging at that long, gray-threaded beard and riding upon his boots.

And . . . *no.* Couldn't picture it.

The Con he knew avoided most human interaction, preferring solitude and shadows.

They sat in their customary silence for a few

minutes, drinking their porter. Dalton thinking how strange it was to picture Con plowing a field or milking a cow.

"Any news of O'Roarke?" Con asked.

Dalton leaned closer, keeping his voice low. "His ship's the *Rambler*, out of New York. Set to sail two days from now from Cork."

Con gripped his glass. "We've time to catch him."

"I think he's the one, Con. I can feel it." He'd been searching for so long. Consumed by the need for revenge.

Con grunted. "We'll see. But right now you have to go tell the lady why she won't be traveling with us." He smirked. "Give her a chance to yell at you."

Dalton rapped on Thea's chamber door.

He was here to inform her of his decision and nothing would cause him to waver. He was here to say goodbye.

At her command he entered, preparing himself for that first glimpse of lively blue-gray eyes and curved strawberry lips.

"Dalton." She stayed seated, but one of her hands rose and stretched toward him.

She smiled and he actually had to turn his face away, pretend a sudden interest in the carpeting. "Hello, Lady Dorothea."

"Lady?" she teased softly. "My, how formal we are today."

Her hair was still damp from a bath, and whatever she'd used to wash it smelled different. Sharper. Like roses that only bloomed at night.

He had to stop himself from leaning over and inhaling the scent.

There would be no easy way to do this.

He was a danger to her. Best to end this swiftly.

He cleared his throat and lifted his head. "I'm leaving."

"But you only just arrived," she laughed. "Sit down. Have some tea."

"No time. I'm off to Cork tonight."

Her brow creased. "Yes. I know that."

He still wanted her. Of course he did. That would never go away. Not today. Not until the day he died. But he could never have her.

"Con and I are continuing on alone and you and Molly will take a steam packet tomorrow morning."

She stretched out her hand again and he fought the urge to back away. If she touched him, he'd be lost.

"You promised to escort me to Ireland, if I remember correctly." Her eyes sparked. "That was the bargain. And you're a man of your word. Just read the betting book at White's, remember?"

Dalton clenched his jaw. "Remember what I told you? Never trust a man, Thea. We say we'll do one thing and then do another. I purchased you first-class passage on the finest steam packet to Cork. You'll have a luxurious dining saloon. A chamber music band for entertainment."

"You know I don't care about any of that."

"It will be more comfortable."

She narrowed her eyes. "Why are you doing this? Is it because of last night?"

Of course it was because of last night. "What happened between us last evening was—"

"Not something you need to apologize for." She tossed her unbound hair and the seductive scent filled the air. "I'm perfectly fine. More than fine."

He'd been prepared for tears, recriminations, at the very least bleary eyes and a whiskey headache. Not bright eyes and a seductive smile.

"You're far too good for this treatment, Thea. Too good for one night. Too good for me."

"You're afraid," she accused. "You think I'll use what happened between us last night to make demands."

That wasn't it at all. He was afraid of himself, of this ocean of longing that had opened in his chest, crashing down the walls he'd built, sweeping away anything but the tidal pull of Thea's arms.

"You think I don't know my own mind, but I do." Her hands gripped the chair arms. "I've always been on the edges of things. Schoolrooms. Ballrooms. I was never in the center, unless Mama pushed me there, and then I was apt to trip and fall. I find I want to be right in the heart of things. I want to know what life's all about. Can you trust me, Dalton?"

He couldn't trust *himself.*

"Thea, you're forcing me to speak very plainly."

He reached over and caught her chin in his hand, turning her to face him. "I can never marry you."

She pulled her chin away from his grip. "I'm well aware you're off to seek your Irish bride, with statuesque curves, flaming hair, and emerald eyes."

Damn. He'd completely forgotten about the fictitious wife search. He cleared his throat. "I never told you what she looked like."

"Oh." She waved her hand through the air. "You have a type. Tall. Fashionable. Showy. Abundant of bosom. Meager of mind."

Except that he had a new type now.

Petite, persistent, contrary . . . and smoldering with awakening sensuality.

"You picture me as some lonely, defenseless spinster in Ireland," she chided, "when that's simply not going to be the way of it at all." She gave a carefree laugh. "I'll be a *scandalous* spinster. I'll take a lover in Ireland. Maybe more than one."

Challenged flared in her eyes. "Handsome fellows in Ireland. Rather like your friend the Duke of Harland. Dark hair and green eyes. Well muscled." She glanced at his arms. "But not ostentatiously so."

Was she insulting his physique?

This conversation was going all wrong.

It didn't feel right telling her even one more lie. But he'd been lying so long that it was second nature. "I should leave now. I've a call to make on a"—the word stuck in his throat—"a widow I know in Bristol. Before my ship sails."

Thea's eyes darkened to stormy gray, just as he'd expected. "A widow?"

Blotches of color appeared on her cheeks, and the dangerous streaks of lightning in her eyes intensified. "You don't need any more widows."

"My widows understand me completely."

"All they understand is the size of your fortune."

"Are you moralizing, Thea? I thought you were adventurous and unconventional."

She tossed her head. "I am."

"The first rule of adventure is variety. When one path becomes restrictive you choose another. I understand the allure of thinking one path might be the answer." Dalton stared past her, his gaze finding the window, the brick building across the street. "But I'm nobody's answer."

"Why are you doing this?" she whispered.

Because it was better to make her hate him. Easier for her that way, in the long run.

"I thought you might need more proof that I'm a heartless rake. In the event that it hadn't been thoroughly established last night."

"What do you believe in, Dalton? Do you care about anything? Or is life just a game to you?"

"I believe the sun will set tonight and rise again tomorrow." He set his hat back on his head. "I believe that men chase sensation to stave off the knowledge that every breath brings us closer to death. That the devil lives in empty pockets and greed seduces men to sin. I believe that love is an illusion people invent to cheat the fear of death."

"I mean nothing to you," she said dully, all the laughter gone from her voice.

He couldn't answer that truthfully, so he remained silent.

The truth was she meant everything to him. And that's why he had to leave.

She deserved so much more from life.

Quiet nights reading together by a roaring fire. Uncorking a new French wine. The clink and covenant of glass against glass.

New paint for the nursery.

Everything tender and warm.

Everything he could never give her.

"Very well, seek your empty pleasures. Drown in a sea of accommodating widows." She pushed a still-damp lock of hair away from her eyes.

There. His job was done. She hated him, and that was for the best.

He turned to leave but the door swung open and Con strode into the room. "Where's Miss Molly? Can't find her anywhere."

"Having a rest," Thea said. "She slept the whole way in the carriage. Still a little ill, I believe."

Con shook his head. "She's not in her chamber and the bed's untouched. When was the last time you saw her?"

"An hour ago."

He paced across the floral carpet. "You don't think she would do anything . . . foolish, do you? She wouldn't pretend to be a highwayman again?"

"I have her pistol," Dalton said. "I don't think she'll get far without it."

"But this Raney character, the one who stole her money," Con pressed, "she told me last night that he's a sailor. You don't think she'd go searching for him?"

Thea's shoulders tensed. "I thought she was too exhausted to leave the inn but now that you ask, it does sounds exactly like the rash sort of thing Molly might do." She twisted her silk skirts in her hand. "I should have kept her with me. Kept an eye on her."

"It's not your fault," Dalton reassured her. "We'll find Molly. If Raney's a sailor he's bound to be near the docks."

"She did mention a tavern he frequents. Let's see . . . what was the name? Something nautical . . ." Thea's worried gaze moved to the grate, searching for the answer in the wavering flames. Her head snapped up. "The Anchor! That's the place."

Dalton and Con exchanged a glance. That was the tavern they'd just come from. And it was no place for a young girl.

Con clutched the brim of his hat. "We have to find her. There's no time to lose!" He spun on his heel and stalked out the door.

Chapter 17

"**F**aster, man. We haven't got all day," Con bellowed, poking his head out the window of the carriage.

Dalton knew Con well enough to know he'd take it very hard if anything happened to his niece on his watch.

They were caught in the tangle of carriages and farm carts attempting to funnel onto the smaller side streets that led to the St. Jude's rookeries.

Somehow Thea had managed to insinuate herself into the rescue mission, clamoring in after Con, so that the three of them were wedged onto the single seat of Jones's carriage. She'd said she wasn't about to sit by herself in the inn while Molly could be in peril.

This would be a swift affair. Dalton and Con would storm the Anchor, retrieve Molly, and they'd all be back on the way to the inn within ten minutes.

"This is taking too long." Con fidgeted on the seat, tapping his boots and clenching his fists atop his knees.

"We'll be there soon," Thea soothed.

Dalton didn't relish the idea of returning to the public house. He hadn't liked Alberton's questions, or the way he'd stared at Dalton's jaw, almost as if he had been searching for Trent's cut. With any luck Albertson wouldn't be there and they could be in and out with no fuss.

Thea sat in silence, obscured by the voluminous gray cloak, hidden behind Con's shoulders, her face covered by the brim of her bonnet.

Dalton sensed her disquiet as a fourth presence in the carriage, a looming reminder of the words he'd said to her only minutes ago. The lies fabricated to drive her away.

The ludicrous notion that he preferred the company of some dashing widow to Thea.

Badly done, that.

The moment the words had left his mouth he'd regretted them. And when the teasing light faded from her eyes and her smile faltered and disappeared, he'd felt like a coward and a criminal.

Confusion, betrayal . . . and finally resentment in the shifting seas of her eyes. How could he blame her? He'd abandoned control last night, binding her to him first with linen restraints and then with kisses, and today he'd pushed her away.

He couldn't tell her the truth of why he had to sever ties, but he hated the betrayal in her eyes. It seemed no matter what he did he wounded her.

The compulsion to fold her into his arms, stroke her silken hair, whisper that he hadn't meant what he said . . . that stopped *now*.

His next breath would be focused. Ruthless.

Thea-less.

This carriage ride changed nothing.

Thea and Molly would still travel safely in elegant chambers on a steam packet tomorrow while he and Con stole away on the merchant brigantine leaving for Ireland tonight.

No more confessions. Or kisses.

"Have you been to the Anchor before?" Thea asked Con.

"Just came from there, actually," Con said. "Rough place. Don't like Molly being there."

"It's broad daylight," Thea objected. "How nefarious can the place be at half four in the afternoon?"

Con shook his head. "No place for a young girl, the Anchor. Crawling with sailors from every port."

"Then it's a good thing I'm here," Thea said. "I have a calming effect on unpolished sorts. I soothed those beasts outside the inn last evening quite effectively."

She stole a glance at Dalton from under her bonnet, to see how he'd taken that pronouncement.

Calming effect, his arse.

There wasn't a calm, staid bone in that lithe body of hers.

He narrowed his eyes and she did smile then, a small, triumphant curving of her lips that clearly said she knew she'd vexed him and that tormenting him was her new purpose in life.

And damn him, despite all his resolutions, he

wanted to be tormented in every way her quick intellect could devise.

Before that precarious spool of thought spun too far, the carriage finally slowed outside of the soot-blackened bricks of the Anchor public house.

Dalton leaned over Con to address Thea. "You'll stay in the carriage this time, please. This won't take but a moment."

Delicate eyebrows arched disdainfully.

"Fine," Dalton sighed, even though she hadn't said anything, just shot him the *nobody, especially not a duke, is going to tell me what to do* glance that he was coming to know so well. "But please stay close beside me."

She nodded, tugging her gray bonnet ribbons tighter and squaring her small shoulders.

"Hurry now," Con urged, already heading for the entrance.

When the door opened, the raucous sound of sailors at play spilled into the street. The place had filled since Dalton had left. Not an empty seat in the room.

Lit by sputtering, odiferous tallow candles and hanging gas lamps, the dark, cavernous room brimmed with high-pitched laughter and slurred shouting.

Burly sailors in blue coats and red neck cloths swilled beer, joked with the barmaids, and gambled away their pay with cards and dice.

Some of them would no doubt wager the clothes off their backs before the night was through and slink home, half-naked and stumbling drunk, to wives gone prematurely old and gray with worry, and a room full of cold, sad-eyed children.

Thea's eyes widened as she watched a man with pockmarked cheeks and a threadbare coat grab the skirt of a woman with hard, jaded eyes and pull her over for a smacking public kiss.

It was disconcerting having Thea here in his world. Her sweet scent clashed with the rancid stink of spilled gin.

He'd been thinking of her as some larger-than-life temptation—a monumental peril that he must ward against at all costs—but here, in this restless crush of sailors, dockworkers, and costermongers, she was too slight and fragile, too easily lost.

He placed a hand on the small of her back because the inebriated ne'er-do-wells in the room needed to know she was under his protection.

Not because he'd been dying to touch her, he told himself.

She glanced at him from under long, sable lashes and he pulled her tighter, wrapping his hand around the curve of her waist.

Mine. All mine, his clasp proclaimed.

No sign of Albertson. Or Molly.

Con scanned the room, the wary angle of his shoulders betraying his tension.

"Back again so soon?"

Dalton met the bold gaze of Pearl, the barmaid with the bright red hair who'd propositioned him earlier.

She cocked her hip and winked. "Missed me, you rogue?" She squeezed his arm, as if testing his bicep for strength.

Thea's eyes narrowed dangerously.

"You brought *company*." Pearl looked Thea up and down, clearly sensing a potential rival.

"Humph." Thea tossed her head, which didn't have much effect since all her glorious curls were covered by her travel-wilted straw bonnet.

Dalton gently lifted Pearl's hand from his arm. "Missed your dark porter," he said heartily. "Two more pints of the stuff for my friend and me."

"What about you then?" She glanced hopefully at Con. "You're a seaworthy hull of a fellow, if ever I saw one. Need a passenger?"

Con shook his head distractedly, intent on searching for Molly in the crowded room.

"Only the pints," Dalton said.

Pearl flounced away, her faded red silk skirts swirling indignantly.

Con jerked his head toward the back of the room. "Over there."

The crowd gathered around a corner table parted slightly, allowing Dalton to see a dice contest in progress.

Molly stood against the far wall with her shoulders thrown back and a grin on her face, shaking the dice dramatically while the captivated onlookers watched each movement of her slender hands.

A tall, towheaded man in his twenties with polished brass buttons on his blue coat and his arm around a barmaid with saucy chestnut curls glared at Molly with a murderous expression from across the table.

He looked none too pleased about losing to such a young lad. If he hadn't known she was a girl, Dalton would have been fooled as well. With her braids tucked up under that floppy blue cap and the blue coat and vest, she could be a ragged scrap of a cabin boy who ran errands and served the captain and crew of a merchant vessel.

Dalton was intimately familiar with nearly every one of London's gaming hells and the usual games of chance played against the house, but he was not sure of the game the two played here.

The sailors in rapt attendance seemed to know what was going on, however, and shouted in unison after Molly rolled the dice onto a canvas mat.

Cocky, loud, and self-assured, Molly traded quips and bawdy jests with the sailors gathered around her. "Triple anchors, boys! I told you I stowed a large anchor, and I drop it deep as well!"

Dalton had to chuckle. She even sounded impressively like a sailor. She was so intent on the game, she never even glanced their way.

The tall man's already ruddy face grew visibly redder as he slowly counted out coins and slid them toward the center of the table. Molly laughed gleefully in the man's face as she raked in the coins.

"Must be Raney," Con said, tilting his chin at the tow-headed man.

Dalton nodded.

"I don't think he recognizes her," Thea said in an astonished whisper at Dalton's side.

"Aye," Con agreed. "I don't like it. Raney's been drinking and he's angry about losing."

Molly thumped her hand on the table until her stack of coins jumped merrily. Raney's eyes narrowed and his jaw jutted.

Con grew utterly still.

Dalton knew that expression well. He was sizing up the danger. Making swift decisions about the best way to mitigate the possibility of a brawl.

Best way would be to just walk up and retrieve her. Say the captain needed her and there'd be hell to pay if she didn't snap to immediately.

Raney had had a few pints, judging by the way he swayed on his feet. A situation like this could disintegrate swiftly. Losing money never made men feel charitable.

Con caught Dalton's eye. It was time.

"Stay back," Dalton whispered in Thea's ear. "Be ready to leave. Quickly."

"Isn't she winning?"

"Yes, but things could go wrong if anyone realizes she's female."

Thea's eyes narrowed slightly. "She doesn't require rescuing." She shifted until their bodies weren't touching anymore. "You don't need to interfere. Trust me, Dalton. Let Molly make her own choices. It's important for her to have this moment of power over Raney. After the way he treated her."

Con glanced at Dalton, his eyes asking what the delay was about. Dalton made the abrupt slashing motion with his index finger that was their signal to halt an operation.

To retreat.

Con frowned.

"Can you trust me, Dalton?" Thea's eyes sparked in the dim light.

She'd spoken the same words at the inn.

This wasn't all about Molly. It was important to Thea as well. She'd had only orders and coercion from her mother . . . never trust. She spoke of Molly taking control and taking the reins of her power, when Thea was the one who craved control.

She'd been testing her power the entire journey, assuming bold, sensual roles. She wanted to own her power. And she wanted to be free of her mother's rules.

Dalton watched Molly closely. If she were in any true danger, he and Con would act swiftly.

Thea saw the look pass between Dalton and Con. She rose on her tiptoes. "Thank you," she whispered in Dalton's ear.

He tightened his grip around her waist, loving the way her curves fit him so well.

She gave him a brilliant smile and suddenly the close, dark room shifted into vibrant color, as if he'd rounded a bend in a road and suddenly an ocean vista unfolded, sun sparkling on wide, blue ocean.

What he wouldn't do for that smile.

Now, to make her laugh. He loved the way she laughed. High and silvery like pealing bells.

Con wasn't happy about waiting but he didn't make any moves, standing with his head lowered, watching Molly intently.

It was Raney's turn to place his stake and throw the dice. He pushed a small stack of copper forward onto a portion of the mat marked with a crown. "All on crowns," he slurred.

The throng of spectators roared again. "The devil is smiling on you tonight, boy!"

"You're going to let that lad put your baubles in his pockets like that, Raney?"

The barmaid with the chestnut curls slipped out from under Raney's arm and sidled up to Molly and whispered something in her ear.

Molly gave her a coin and the barmaid threw her arms around Molly's neck and gave her a loud smack on the cheek. Molly kissed the barmaid's cheek in return and squeezed her waist.

The men around the table roared with laughter, pointing at Raney and thumping Molly on the back, obviously ribbing Raney about losing the affections of his fair-weather companion.

Raney glared at Molly and she grinned back at him, enjoying her triumph.

Dalton bent toward Thea. "Farm girls besting sailors and kissing barmaids," he whispered. "Now we've seen everything, eh?"

She stifled a laugh with her hand. "It's quite a sight."

"Swears and gambles like a sailor, your Molly," he whispered. "Wonder where she learned that?"

"She has ten brothers. I should think they were her tutors in those arts."

"Ten brothers." Dalton whistled softly and turned to Con. "Hear that, Con? She has ten brothers. Might know a thing or two about the male mind."

Con gave his usual noncommittal grunt, but his shoulders relaxed slightly.

Thea granted Dalton another approving smile, and he slid his hand along her back.

In a reckless move, Molly pushed her entire stack of coins onto the table. "I'm all in on spades. Time to bury you, knave. Prepare your coffin!" she called.

Raney's face darkened. "Your luck's bound to run out, my boy."

Molly lifted her pint glass and drained the contents in one long gulp, accompanied by the approving shouts of the small crowd. "Sure, and my luck ran out the day I met you, Jack Raney."

He glanced up sharply, searching her face, as if realization might dawn any second.

Con tensed.

Molly began her elaborate dice cup ritual again, the familiar rattling sound shaking loose too many memories in Dalton's mind. A cheer went up from the watching men as they started placing side bets.

"Five bob on the ship's boy!"

"Five on Raney!"

The crowd held its breath.

The dice hit the table and rolled.

Chapter 18

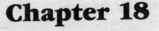

Thea couldn't bear to watch the outcome. She turned her head away from the table, watching Dalton's face instead.

The redheaded barmaid in the scarlet dress had called him a rogue. He did look the rogue with that cut across his jaw.

He hadn't shaved and there was dark brown stubble across his chin, obscuring the cleft, but Thea still knew it was there, just waiting for her to discover it again.

The barmaid had explored his body with her eyes as if he were a prize goose at Christmastime.

Well, who could blame her?

His was the dangerous beauty that made a woman stop and stare because she wondered if he'd fallen from the heavens, plummeted to earth, and might be ready to drag her with him down to hell.

His large hand clasped around her waist possessively. Claiming her.

Trusting her instincts.

A cheer rose up and Thea whipped her head back to the gaming table.

Molly snatched her cap off her head and her long braids tumbled out. "It's me, Jack Raney, you beef-witted gull. Molly Barton! Remember me?" She grabbed a fistful of coins and stuffed them into the basin of her blue cap. "I'll be taking these."

Jack's eyes screwed into mean slits. "You," he sputtered. "You . . . why, I'll—"

The crowd of sailors erupted into mirth, slapping their thighs and hooting with laughter.

"Gammoned by a girl!" one shouted.

Raney reached for his vest pocket with a deadly look in his eyes and Thea clutched Dalton's arm, but Con was already surging forward with long, powerful strides. He parted the crowd easily and thrust a menacing arm around Jack's shoulder, preventing him from drawing his hand out of his pocket.

"Met my niece, have you?" Con asked.

Molly gasped and stared at Con. Her head whipped around and she grew pale as she recognized Thea and Dalton as well.

"Leave off, old man," Jack gritted out, attempting to shake off Con, but the older man was far too strong.

"Seems to me she won fair and square," Con said. "Come along, Molly." Con dropped Jack and gestured to Molly. She grasped her cap in her hands and followed Con.

"Don't run," Dalton instructed Thea, taking her arm and steering her toward Con and Molly. "Walk with confidence. Like you own the place."

He threw some coins on the bar, more than

enough for their drinks, and the four of them sauntered toward the back exit through the jostling crowd.

The alleyway behind the public house was fetid with rotting refuse.

Thea glanced back, half expecting the door to burst open and an angry mob led by Raney to follow them outside, but the doorway remained empty.

The alley, however, quickly filled.

Three large implacable-looking men stood waiting for them, black-brimmed hats jammed low over brutish brows.

Dalton stiffened and stopped abruptly, shoving Thea behind him. Con did the same with Molly, the two men forming a bulwark of solid muscle between Thea and Molly and the three brutes.

Thea had to peer around Dalton's formidable back to see what happened next.

The men lumbered toward them menacingly. Guards hired by the tavern, no doubt. Prizefighters seeking a back-alley match.

Thea shivered and glanced at Molly.

"We'll be all right," Molly whispered. She squeezed her hands into fists. "We'll fight if we have to," she said with a fierce glare at the advancing men.

"Good evening, Albertson." Dalton's voice dropped to a deep and dangerous pitch. "You own this alleyway as well?"

"I'm about to own you," Albertson replied. Up close he had a crooked nose, mangled ears, and cruel blue eyes.

He stopped inches from Dalton and poked a finger into his chest. "There's a reward for your capture, Jones."

Thea's mind darted between the possibilities. Did Albertson think Dalton was Jones again? Should she speak up? Try to distract them?

She stole another glance at Albertson from around Dalton's shoulders and quickly decided against that plan of action. The man had shoulders even wider than the duke's and enormous fists with bruised knuckles. He was obviously a professional pugilist. Far more dangerous than the bumbling dolts at the inn yard.

"Mack," Albertson said. "The sheet."

Mack had a flat, wide brow and small, deep-set eyes. He fumbled in his breast pocket, drew out a sheet of wrinkled paper, and passed it to Albertson.

Paper rustled as Albertson held out the sheet. "Trent says be on the lookout for the Hellhound. Fled London two days ago disguised as a gentlemanly type. Got a drawing here of a bruiser of a fellow. Six foot. Twelve stone. With a scar." Albertson slashed a finger along his jaw. "Just here."

Thea gasped. Dalton had said the scar came from fighting a duel with a jealous husband. Or had he actually said those words? Maybe she'd only made an assumption.

Albertson crumpled the paper and threw it to the ground. "I'd say that matches the description of someone in this alleyway."

Dalton's entire body went still as a stone.

He didn't say a word, yet Thea heard his bass voice in her head.

If the Hellhound's real he's a dangerous criminal . . . he'll hang.

There's no champion who can cure society's ills and defend the powerless. He's only a myth.

And then . . . *You caught me. I have a secret reason for going to Ireland.*

All that denial and evasion.

Kissing her in the carriage when she'd mentioned the Hellhound.

He could have a bigger secret. He could be . . .

Dalton's laughter rumbled into the fading evening light, interrupting her churning thoughts.

"Curious way to turn a profit." He tugged off his gloves and handed them to Con. "Accosting paying customers in back alleys must not be very good for repeat business."

"Don't make another move." Albertson widened his stance and raised his fists. "Or I'll darken your daylights."

Following a sudden impulse, Thea darted out from behind Dalton. "You've the wrong man, Albertson. Mr. Jones flops more than he fights."

Dalton caught her skirts. "Thea. Get back!"

"Is that so?" Albertson chuckled, giving Thea an appreciative once-over. "Trent said nothing about *you*. Pretty thing, aren't you?" He reached for Thea's arm. "Spoils of war, as they say."

It happened like fire licking across a field of dry haystacks.

Dalton exploded forward in a blur of fists and a flash of bared teeth.

Every motion spare and perfectly calculated.

One powerful blow to the face and Albertson crumpled onto the dirty cobblestones like a rag doll.

The other two men rushed at Dalton but he evaded them easily, cracking their heads together.

Masterful. Precise.

And so swift Thea only had time to take one step backward before it was all over.

Men groaning on the ground, paralyzed by pain, stunned into submission.

Con hadn't even lifted a fist, just stood sentinel, with an expression of lethal intensity on his time-worn face.

Dalton rose to his full height, filling her view, his shadow looming across cobblestones slick with fresh blood.

His chest rose and fell rapidly, his fists still raised.

He lifted his head and stared at her.

Only a memory of blue in an obsidian sea.

Oh, Dalton, Thea thought. *It's you. The myth. The champion for the powerless.*

It's you they hunt.

She nearly flung herself into his arms, to tell him that he didn't need to push her away any-more because she knew his secret.

He broke the moment, stepping over the men and retrieving his hat.

Con handed him his gloves.

"Best be on our way then," Con said gruffly.

Molly stared at Dalton wide-eyed and curious. "Cor," she breathed. "That was magnificent."

"Back to the carriage now." Con took Molly's arm and led her around the still-unconscious men.

Dalton gestured for Thea to follow and began walking, his shoulder tilted at an awkward angle, as if it pained him.

So much pain he carried. In his bones . . . muscles. And his heart.

Thea snuck the crumpled sheet of paper Albertson had dropped into her reticule and hurried after Dalton.

They climbed into the waiting carriage, squeezing in tightly, Dalton's knees pressed against hers.

The door slammed and the carriage stuttered into motion.

"Never a dull moment," Con said, shaking his head.

Molly glanced at Con eagerly, and then at Dalton. "Teach me to fight like that! I may be small, but I'm fierce."

Con laughed. "Now isn't that the truth?"

Thea caught Dalton's eye. "We're coming to Cork with you."

He nodded. "I already informed the coachman to take us to the docks. Those men saw your faces."

Thea's breath caught. He wanted to keep her with him.

The clinking of coins sounded as Molly patted

her pocket. "Enough to replace Mam's savings, and then some. That's one sailor who'll think twice before betraying a girl's trust."

"The Dread Dark Baron strikes again," Thea said.

"I'm only glad you didn't bring the pistol," Con said.

Molly grinned. "Didn't need the pistol to make 'im quake in his boots." She sobered. "Did you pretend to be my uncle to scare Jack, or is it the Lord's truth?"

Con hesitated. Thea saw fear flit across his face. Then he nodded. "'Fraid you've got me for an uncle, Molly my love."

"Were you going to tell me?" Her lower lip trembled.

"Hadn't made up my mind yet," Con said truthfully. "You see, I knew your mam a long, long time ago. You look just like her." He tugged Molly's braid. "Except for the trousers, of course."

"Ha." Molly frowned. "If you're my uncle you'll probably make me put on a gown now and cane me if I don't wear it."

Con's whiskers bristled with emotion as he quickly shook his head. "Never, love. I'll never hit you. I'm nothing like Seamus."

Molly bit her lip. "You don't look like him, that's sure."

Thea's heart swelled with hope for these two lost souls. Molly desperately needed kindness, and Con deserved a second chance.

Everyone deserved a chance at happiness.

Thea stole a glance at Dalton from under her eyelashes.

She couldn't be this close to him and not want to wrap her arms around him. Did he feel it, too?

Their eyes met.

He felt it. She knew he did.

He reached for her hand and closed his fingers around hers.

It felt so right, touching him. Knowing he needed to touch her in return.

Her heart beat faster, thinking of tonight.

What drove a man to become a myth?

His brother's death. His mother's seclusion and fear.

His father's greed.

Everything began to slot into place, like the symbols in an allegorical painting combining to provide a deeper meaning.

The liaisons, the trysts, the widows and their rose trellises. The outrageous wagers, the duels, the scars . . . all were . . . diversions?

Dalton the consummate rake hid Dalton the force of justice.

She thought back to the evenings when she'd observed him ruling London's ballrooms. The golden rake the world revolved around, keeping the broadsheets in ink and the scandalous widows in breathless anticipation of his next exploit. She'd thought he was just like her father. Careening from woman to woman, leaving heartache in his wake.

Was he that man?

Or something entirely different?

Early-evening sun painted the sky amber as the carriage made its way to the quay. Obviously if he'd fooled so many people for so long he was skilled at lying, and if he was a skilled liar . . . did he truly want her, or were his kisses only a diversion as well?

She would convince him to open up to her and reveal his secret.

He trusted her. And he didn't have to carry the burden alone.

He could be himself with her.

And she could be herself as well. Formed from courage, not fear.

Seize life by the hand and travel the path of pleasure.

Thea pressed Dalton's hand and he looked at her, his eyes glittering in the gathering dusk.

Nothing had changed. She would choose to take a skilled, attentive lover tonight.

Everything had changed.

That lover would be both rake . . . and warrior.

Chapter 19

When they'd boarded the *Truth and Daylight*, Con had informed the shipmaster of the extra passengers. Of course he'd also informed the man that Thea was Dalton's wife, damn his scrubby gray whiskers.

Dalton hadn't been able to muster the strength to argue. The master had smiled and said his cabin would prove adequate.

They'd eaten a quick supper of cold meats, cheese, and bread in the galley. Thea had gone with Molly to settle her into her berth.

The master's cabin was surprisingly spacious, located at the stern of the upper deck and spanning the entire width of the ship. The beautiful woodworking of the built-in cabinets, table, and benches glowed in the evening light that streamed through the windows wrapping around the seaward walls.

Dalton's shoulder was killing him. Throbbing from the force of the cracking blow he'd given Albertson. Nearly jarred his bone out of the socket, that blow.

Dalton needed to rest. Preferably on a bed.

And if that bed had Thea in it, as most tended

to these days, Dalton would just have to be too tired to do anything about it.

He lowered himself to the bed. The ship's master evidently slept in comfort, and Dalton sighed as his aching muscles melted into the featherbed atop the well-made horsehair mattress.

Trent had probably spread word to every gaming hell and tavern across London to be on the lookout for a man with a cut across his jaw. But it didn't seem as though Trent had connected the Hellhound with Dalton. Albertson had called him Jones. But Albertson had seen his face. In daylight. With no soot in his hair and no kerchief to mask his features.

He'd have to be extremely careful now. Trent's men would be looking for the four of them. They couldn't be seen together again. They would have to separate, Con delivering Molly to Bronagh, and Dalton seeing Thea home to her aunt.

Then Dalton would have a day to find more details about O'Roarke before he confronted him. When forcing a confession it was best to be armed with vivid details of a man's life. Potential triggers for trapping a man to admit his sins.

He splayed across the large bed without bothering to draw the curtains, lulled by the rocking of the ship beneath his body, and allowed his eyes to close.

He heard Thea arrive. Listened as she scooped water from the washbasin and splashed it on her face.

Which meant she'd already shed her straw bonnet.

Which meant her hair was accessible and his fingers would want to twine in those curls.

He opened his eyes.

She stood in front of the circular mirror in its gilt frame, removing hairpins.

A slice of wary blue-gray eyes.

Fragment of lush, full lower lip.

The convex glass of the mirror gathered the last red caresses of the sun and painted them across her cheeks.

She removed the last of her pins and fluffed buttery curls over her shoulders, where they twisted to the small of her back.

Dalton squeezed his eyes shut.

"Is your shoulder troubling you again?" she asked softly.

He threw his left elbow over his eyes so she wouldn't see the pain. "I'm fine."

"No, you're not. Your mouth's all twisted."

The bed moved as she sat on the edge.

Her hands brushed a lock of hair from his brow. "What can I do?"

Hell, he'd been hurt before. Beaten to within an inch of his life. Injuries were nothing new. He threw his body around recklessly, feeling invincible even though he knew death lurked around every dark corner and in every footpad's knife.

"I'm fine," he repeated.

"What does Olofsson do for you, exactly?"

"Sometimes the shoulder freezes. Olofsson manipulates the muscles so I can move again. I've an old boxing injury I sustained when I was going a few rounds with my friend Hatherly."

"Oh yes. Boxing."

Dalton paused. There was a new note in her voice.

"That's right."

"Turn over," she commanded.

He thought about refusing for a moment, but the promise of her hands on his bruised and aching flesh was too enticing.

He rolled onto his stomach, lifting his arms and cradling his head on his forearm.

"I'll need to remove this shirt," she said briskly.

"That won't be necessary."

"Suit yourself."

She kneaded his right shoulder through the linen of his shirt.

Her small hands weren't doing much but it felt so incredibly good just to have her touching him. She pushed a little bit harder, digging into his shoulder blade, and he released a long sigh.

"Is that the place?" she asked.

"Aye."

"You flattened those three brutes in the blink of an eye. Impressive, I must say. A far cry from your performance . . . or lack thereof . . . in Bath."

"Albertson grabbed your arm. I saw red. I struck."

She spread something crinkling and flat onto the bed next to his face. He cracked an eye open. Trent's drawing of the Hellhound, with the scar in exactly the right place along the jaw.

He crumpled the paper in his fist.

She brushed a finger down his jaw. "Is there anything you want to tell me?"

So dangerous this impulse to share, to reveal himself. What would happen if he told her the truth?

"Dalton. Look at me."

He lifted his head.

Silken waves of hair fell around his face as she bent her head closer to his. "You trusted my instincts in the tavern. And you allowed Molly to make her own decisions. Now I'm asking you to trust me again. Tell me the truth. I'm strong enough to bear it."

He wanted to tell her . . . he wanted to unburden himself, but if he did, she would be in even more danger than she was now.

He buried his face back in his arm. "Nothing to tell. I defended you. Any man would have done the same."

"You're lying."

"Thea," he groaned. "Leave off. It's been a long day. Why don't you lie down."

"Tell me the truth," she persisted.

"I can't."

"Then at least admit that you want to."

The longing to bare his soul to Thea had built and built and now it was nearly unbearable.

"Thea . . . I . . ." *I'm out on the wide sea with no compass.*

She made him realize that he was completely and utterly lost. Her insistence on truth was a rope tossed into the stormy seas. He could grab hold of that rope and pull himself to safety.

Grab hold of her.

He reached for her hand and pulled her down

next to him on the bed. He buried his head in her neck.

She stroked his hair. "You don't have to bear this alone."

He folded his arms tighter, inhaling the sweet scent of her hair and the calm resolve in her voice.

He didn't want the waves to close over his head.

She lifted his head and held his jaw in both her hands. "I know the truth, Dalton."

He closed his eyes.

"You're honorable and noble," she whispered. "And I want you. Desperately. I need you."

She knew.

He hadn't been able to save Alec or stop his mother from descending into madness, but maybe Thea would be able to save him, and open his heart. Maybe he could be the man she needed him to be.

He was weak with the wanting of it.

So he reached for her and he held on tight.

And she twined her arms around him. "I want to know what my body is capable of experiencing." She climbed on top of him and settled her legs to either side of him. "I want to drown in pleasure."

She wound her hands around his neck and pressed her soft breasts into his chest. "I choose you, Dalton."

I choose you.

The words took his breath away. Oh, how he wanted it to be that simple.

"I may not be exactly the temptation you love the best." Her lips curved. "I'm not at all statuesque. And my figure is less than ample."

He cupped her breasts with his palms, squeezing gently. "You're perfect, Thea."

"I don't have flashing emerald eyes. My eyes can't decide if they want to be cloudy or blue." She leaned forward and pressed her soft lips to his cheek. "But if I had you, Duke, you'd change your preferences."

He kissed her then with all the pent-up longing he'd been denying. He kissed her because he wanted to believe life could be simple. All this pain and strife, the games men played to keep death from knocking too loudly.

Life could be the scent of roses when she drew near, and the lingering heat of her body on his palm.

Take her into his arms.

Build a bridge to another world.

A bright window, instead of a dark alley.

He could be a man. Not a force of vengeance.

Just a man.

A man who wanted to bed this woman. This complex, clever, beautiful woman.

He gave up fighting. She knew his secret. He didn't have to admit it aloud.

And he wasn't strong enough to push her away again.

She moved above him, supple and yielding. He filled his hands with her rounded breasts, her small waist, her flaring hips.

He kissed her.

And he grabbed hold of the rope.

Chapter 20

Thea pressed down, seeking relief from the sweet ache between her thighs.

When he moaned and settled her more firmly against him, guiding her hips with his large hands, a surge of triumph flooded her breast.

Forced into a mold by her mother. By society. By every single one of the people who'd laughed at her and whispered about her and christened her Disastrous Dorothea.

She brushed the tips of her breasts against his solid chest and the motion swayed down through her belly and to the hidden place she'd touched in the bath this morning.

The rule follower, the perfect duchess candidate . . . she was long gone.

Sloughed off like the skin of a molting snake.

Here she was, naked and real.

Simply here with him.

One night of pleasure to change her forever.

Propriety. Elegance. Refinement. *Drown it all!*

"Are you sure you want this?" he asked, his voice low and suffused with tenderness and need.

She arched her back and rubbed her thighs against him. "Yes," she moaned.

"God, Thea. You're so goddamned lovely."

Her heart pounded and her skin was so sensitive to touch that when he skimmed the tip of his finger down her cheek she jumped and shivered.

"Kiss me again," she whispered.

And he did. Firm, demanding lips claiming her, teasing her lips apart. His bold tongue filling her mouth.

He flipped her over, settling on top of her, pressing her into the featherbed.

Their bodies meshed, arms around waists, fingers in hair, thigh to thigh.

The hard length of him jutted into Thea's belly and she knew that soon he would be inside her and she would welcome him there, would wantonly spread her legs.

Lost at sea. Racing toward something new.

She wanted him. All of him. The rake and the rogue.

Man and myth.

Maybe she could make him believe that with her body, if not her words.

She'd do her best.

Her body knew what it wanted. It instructed her to rip his clothes off because her skin needed to be touching his skin.

She reached for the buttons on his shirt.

Too many buttons. Too difficult, her fingers too fumbling. She took his shirt in both her hands and tore the buttons off.

Well, only one button came off but it hit the floor with an impressive popping sound.

He lifted his shirt the rest of the way off his head.

That's what she wanted. All that smooth, scarred, bruised flesh above her.

He lifted her leg and unlaced one boot, then the other, sliding them off and placing them by the bed.

He tugged his boots off next.

He made short work of her gown and under-garments and, finally, her shift.

Suddenly shy, she crossed her arms over her chest, but he grasped them and brought them to her sides.

"Let me look at you." He made a noise low in his throat, a feral growl. "This is for me? All this beauty? These delicate, enticing curves . . ."

He ran his hands from her shoulders down the edges of her breasts, over her waist and hips.

Her entire body hummed with the awareness of what was to come. She held out her arms. "Kiss me more."

"Greedy," he chided. But he gathered her into his strong arms and kissed her until she couldn't breathe.

When he lifted over her, the fossil on the leather cord around his neck swung near and she caught it in her hand, the small jagged edges pressing into her palm.

A memento of his brother's death.

She could comfort him.

The only barrier between them now was his breeches.

Through a round window set high in the wall Thea could see the cold, gray ocean.

She threw her head back, moaning with pleasure as he covered her breasts in his hands and toyed with her nipples, teasing them to yearning points.

When his wet tongue flicked across her nipple she lifted her body into his mouth, shamelessly signaling her approval.

He spent a long time on her nipples, licking and sucking each one, and she felt the motion between her thighs, as if he were licking her there again. It was all connected somehow, a triangle of pleasure that stretched taut between her nipples and down between her thighs.

If her nipples were so very sensitive, were his? She lifted her head and swirled her tongue over one of his small, flat nipples.

He didn't push her away. She took that as a good sign. She kissed the other nipple and sucked, scraping her teeth just a little. He moaned and raised up on his arms, giving her more access.

That was an even better sign.

She kissed his chest and the hollow of his neck, the hillocks of his large, muscular shoulders.

His hands roamed down her sides and slid under her backside, he kneaded her bum cheeks, pressing her against his hardness.

The rough buckskin of his breeches rubbed her sensitive flesh, and she felt herself getting wet. He rubbed his thumb between her legs, sliding over her slippery flesh, setting her body trembling.

He pressed his fingers inside her. She rose to meet him, and when he pushed all the way, until he could go no further, his fingers rocked back and forth in slow, gentle motions.

He rocked harder, the heel of his palm rubbing her sensitive flesh while his fingers beckoned her toward pleasure.

Something in her belly unwound. She clenched around his fingers, and then the pleasure broke, so instant and acute that she cried out. A high sound like a distant seagull wheeling over the ocean. Flying in the wide, limitless sky.

Already this release with his fingers. What would it be like with the hard, straining organ she'd clasped last night?

He fumbled with his breeches' buttons and his shaft burst free, looking extremely pleased to see her.

As he slid his breeches and smallclothes down and off, she did a little exploring of her own, sliding her fingers around his shaft in greeting.

He groaned. "Thea, I promised I wouldn't ruin you."

"Stop. Don't speak. Look at me, Dalton. I'm here. I don't want anything from you except this moment."

He pressed between her thighs, asking for entrance, and she opened wider. A stretching feeling, larger than his fingers.

Much larger.

With his weight supported by his solid, muscled arms on either side of her body, he dipped his head to suckle her breasts while the hard weight of him nudged her thighs further apart.

The next motion of his hips had her gasping as he entered more, stretching her around his girth, shaping her body in a new way.

"You're so wet, Thea. I need to be inside you now."

Instinct told her that the only answer she needed to give was to lift her legs and wrap them around his back, holding him in place.

"God," he breathed and then he reared back and entered her with a slow, implacable thrust.

He stopped moving, breathing heavily, staring down into her eyes.

"I'll wait for you. Until it feels good," he said, his voice rough and strained.

That might be a while.

The intrusion had her stretched to the limit and it was more than uncomfortable. She bit her lip. "Will it feel good?"

"I promise it will. Breathe with me. Match my breathing." He took a deep breath above her and she sucked in a deep breath as well.

The gentle rocking of the ship lulled her mind. He wasn't moving, just staying there, inside her, giving her the time and space she needed to accommodate the newness of it.

Then he began to move, only slightly, matching the motion of the waves cradling the ship. While he moved he smoothed the hair off her brow with tender fingers.

He suckled her nipples, sliding a thumb between their bodies and rubbing the swollen flesh there, the sensitive place that craved his touch.

Suddenly it began to feel more than good. "Oh," she moaned. "I like that."

"I thought you might." He smiled, the wavering light from the oil lamp mounted on the wall casting blue shadows across the sharply angled planes of his face.

Probably she should be feeling self-conscious about the fact that her legs were spread wide and that he was halfway inside her, gently rocking and sliding in more.

How much more of him was there?

She could see the hair around his shaft pressed against her curls. He was almost all the way inside now. She pressed with her heels against the dense muscles of his backside, drawing him closer.

He groaned and sank the last inch until their bodies pressed together with not even space for his thumb anymore. She moved tentatively. What would it feel like if she pressed her body up against his and found something to rub against?

Like she'd just discovered a doorway into heaven.

The pain receded swiftly as she experimented. Her heels on his backside helped her press up with just the right pressure.

"Yes," he said. "Find your rhythm. Listen to your breathing."

There it was.

Like the ocean waves, the perfect slow tempo. She rubbed against him and then he filled her.

Back and forth they slid. Waltzing with the waves.

Now the tremors started again, deep inside, squeezing her inner muscles around him. "That's right," he urged.

He kissed her long and deep as he thrust into her body, finding the same delicious place his fingers had found. The place that had her clenching around him and poised on the brink of more pleasure.

It was so sweet she felt like crying.

He rode faster, shifting the angle so he could go even deeper. She loved the way he grimaced in the wavering light.

The way his eyes were so dark and blue, like the bottom of the ocean. He needed her in this moment. They needed each other to find satisfaction.

Harder and faster, rocking the bed, riding with the ship.

Pleasure calling. Just over that horizon. Flying faster as the wind picked up and the sails of her pleasure filled and stretched taut.

"You feel so good. It's so damn good." He framed her face with hands. "Oh, God." His whole body tensed and quivered.

"Now, Thea," he moaned. "I won't spend inside you. But you must come for me *now*."

She sped into the wind, letting the pleasure take her.

Body singing.

Singing a Bach chorale in four-part harmony in an echoing cathedral.

Oh, God, hear my song.

He groaned and slid free of her body, sliding his hardness against her belly, and she felt his seed spilling against her skin, warm and thick and vital.

He collapsed on top of her, breathing heavily, his head cushioned by her breasts.

She stroked his damp hair and sweat-slick shoulders.

"The best, Thea." He kissed the tip of her breast and pleasure billowed again. "I knew you would be the best."

She basked in the sweetness of those words. "Do you say that to all your lovers?" she asked, keeping her voice light.

"Never. I've never said that before."

"Surely that can't be true." She ruffled his hair. "When you've had so many lovely women."

He lifted his head. "Sometimes it's not about experience." He traced a lazy circle around the outer edge of her nipple with his tongue. The teasing motion made the wanting return.

"We happen to be made for each other," he whispered, blowing on the tip of her nipple until she begged for his mouth to take her.

Did he know what those words did to her heart?

In this unguarded moment with his seed still pooled in the valley of her belly, she was vulnerable.

And she wanted to believe that when he said they were made for each other, it meant more than just their bodies fitting together.

For now, she'd take his firm lips closing over

her mouth, the roughness of his cheek against her sensitive flesh.

The pledge of more pleasure to come.

Sated. Thoroughly pleasured. Shoulder pain forgotten in a sea of euphoria.

Selfish to hold her in the darkness, take the comfort she gave with her sweet kisses and her perfect body, knowing he had so little to give in return.

Quiet on the boat now. Only the creaking of ropes. Gentle splashing of waves against wood.

They'd fallen asleep intertwined.

She had this effect on him. The reveling in warm, soft arms around him, forget-all-his-troubles effect.

So seductive, the woman curled in his arms.

Contentment. That's probably what it was called, this feeling.

But of course it was only a brief forestalling of the inevitable. Back to the darkness, back to the hunt.

What could he give her? What promises could he make?

He was uncertain what awaited him in Ireland. A formidable foe or yet another chimera; an answer, an end to his mother's suffering, or only more questions.

What he wanted to give her was safety, security, and belief in the power and strength he saw in her.

She snuggled into his chest and that was good and right in an elemental way.

Like taking that first gulp of night air after being inside a gambling hell for hours, inhaling cigar smoke and desperation.

Dalton had laughed at his friend James for falling blindly in love with his wife, Thea's half sister, with a heated intensity that Dalton had been sure would fade with time. Now, with his arms wrapped around Thea, he wasn't so sure.

The woman sleeping against his chest, inside the knot of his arms, knew his deepest secrets and it hadn't made her run away.

He could be himself with her. He didn't have to play a role.

"Are you awake, Thea?"

"Yes," she whispered, not lifting her head. She spread her fingers over his chest. "I'm here."

She was still and quiet in his arms. He hugged her closer.

Did he dare?

He breathed slowly, deeply, and took the plunge. "The first time I tied a kerchief around my mouth and slipped into the night searching for vengeance I was twenty years old."

He paused. If she said the wrong words he could stop. He wouldn't have to tell her.

She said nothing. But her hand remained spread across his chest, pressing down slightly, as if anchoring him to the story.

"My brother, Alec, didn't drown accidentally," he continued. "He was murdered. I seek revenge on the man who stole his life. I've been searching for ten years now."

A slight rustling movement was the only betrayal of surprise.

"The murderer left behind a note. 'You stole what was mine, so I stole something of yours.' And my father had stolen so many things he had no idea where to begin searching. His list of enemies was too long."

The words welled up in his throat like some biblical flood waiting to be unleashed.

"I didn't know any of this until I turned eighteen. I thought . . . I thought it had been my fault. Alec was five years younger than me. He followed me everywhere. Followed me onto the cliffs that day. He reached for my hand and I drew away. Told him to go back to the house. And when I came back . . . he had drowned."

Still she remained silent. Didn't tell him it wasn't his fault. That he'd only been a young boy of ten and couldn't be held responsible.

She listened with a quiet intensity that acted as a balm, numbing the edge of his anger and allowing him to speak of things he never spoke of, not to anyone, not even Con.

"When I turned eighteen my father told me the truth. Alec was murdered in retribution for my father's sins. That's why my mother hated him. And then I hated him. At first I went out to the hells and lost his money, to spite him. Then I began searching for the murderer in my own way."

He wanted her to know why he couldn't love her. Why he had no heart to give.

"I didn't set out to become some mythical avenger. I only wanted to find my brother's killer. And then it became something more."

A finger tracing the scar along his jaw. Comforting silence.

He inhaled the sweet scent of her warm skin. If he held her tightly enough, maybe he'd never have to leave.

"My mother went mad with grief. My father wanted more children but she refused. She said her son had died for his sins and she wouldn't bear another martyr."

Dalton had felt her pain more keenly than his own. His own pain was buried too far below the surface.

"This need for vengeance has driven my life for so long, I can't conceive of living for anything else."

She shuddered against his chest and he quieted her, stroking her hair. "I'm not going to Ireland to find a wife. I'm going to find my brother's murderer. There's a man named O'Roarke . . . he could be the one."

She stilled.

His chest ached with emotion. "I'm sorry I lied to you. Thea, I'm so sorry."

Silence.

The muffled sound of a sniffle.

"Thea, say something. You're not . . . are you crying?"

She lifted her head and wiped her eyes with her

hands. "I'm crying for ten-year-old Dalton. What a cross to bear all these years. Thinking it was your fault, and then learning your brother was murdered. It's too much for a young child to endure."

"I'm not asking for sympathy."

"Of course not. You would never need sympathy, or understanding, or . . . love." She whispered the word and his chest ached.

"Revenge is my life's companion, Thea. When I wake in the morning it's the first thing I think about and when I go to sleep at night it's the last."

"Revenge won't bring your brother back."

"I know that. But it could help my mother. If she knew retribution had been served, maybe she'd feel brave enough to leave the house."

"I understand now, Dalton," she whispered. "I know why you push me away."

"Being here with me puts you in danger. As Con is in constant peril as well. If my secret came to light he would be implicated. He could hang. And I will never let that happen."

He fisted his hand in her satiny curls. "And I will never let anyone hurt you because of your association with me, Thea."

"I know you would never do that."

"Those men outside the Anchor were searching for me tonight. And they could have harmed you. I'm a danger to you."

Empathy surged in Thea's heart. She'd heard the words he didn't say. That finding his brother's killer was a chance to make his mother love him. He'd had no love. Not from his mother or his father and he'd borne the heavy weight of guilt.

With her ear pressed against his chest, and his arm forming a cocoon for her other ear, she felt that there was no other world but the warm, silent one that was only his heartbeat, her breathing, and the perfectness of that moment.

It was an intimacy she'd never experienced.

Her cheeks burned from the scratch of his whiskers, and that rawness translated to her heart as well. There were still tremors running through her body. She felt satisfied and mellow and there was sadness for him but also gratitude for this new awareness.

"What if I told you that you've given me a rare gift, Dalton?" she asked.

"I've compromised you. How is that a gift?" he said bluntly, twisting away from her.

"I'm not speaking of what we've done tonight, although it was amazing, and . . . I want to do it again."

"You do?"

She lifted her head and smiled. "Oh, yes," she purred. "But I'm not talking about pleasure. I'm talking about trust. In the tavern you trusted my instincts and it was a wonderful, soaring feeling. I honestly don't think anyone's believed in me like that before."

"You should trust your instincts, Thea. You're brilliant. Your instincts are excellent."

She buried her face in his neck. "All my life

I've second-guessed myself." She searched for the right way to make him understand what being with him meant to her. "We females are taught to doubt our worth, to apologize for our strengths. My mother taught me that skill. I was never good enough for her and so I thought I'd never be good enough for anything." She touched his cheek. "So . . . thank you."

He kissed the top of her head. "Thea, after what we've done, there should be an arrangement."

She stilled. "I don't want anything from you except tonight."

Liar. You know you want more.

She brought his head down to her lips and kissed him. He moaned into her mouth and deepened the kiss, using his hand on the back of her neck to pull her closer.

He drove her to distraction. That was a phrase she'd never understood until now. He drove her, as waves bore a ship against cliffs, shattering her calm.

He broke the embrace and trailed kisses down her body until his head was buried between her legs, until she moaned her pleasure.

All she had was right here and right now.

This moment.

She reached for him and brought him back up her body.

Her head fell off the side of the bed and her hair brushed the floor.

One of his strong arms wound around her waist.

"On second thought"—Thea raised her head—"I will make a demand."

The solid muscles of his abdomen clenched above her.

He closed his eyes.

"I demand"—she reached between them, guiding his shaft where she needed him to be—"satisfaction."

Chapter 21

Slumbering on the featherbed with Dalton while the ship gently rocked on the calm waters wasn't exactly as pleasurable as she'd imagined.

His leg pinned her thighs to the bed and one of his large arms rested on her chest, weighing her down like an anchor.

His other arm hung off the edge of the bed. He managed to occupy every inch of a more than adequately sized bed for two.

What had last night meant to him? Would she ever know? He wasn't adept at expressing his emotions, or admitting to weakness. And he seemed to view his connection with her as a weakness.

She knew what their union had meant to her. An unraveling of fear, a reckless leap into a new life, free from familial and societal expectations and strictures.

A welling of love in her heart, flooding her chest and threatening to bring tears to her eyes.

Maybe she could have separated her emotions from her body's response to a callous, careless rake. But knowing his true nature had overpowered her defenses and left her raw and filled with yearning as inevitable as the tide and as sturdy as stone cliffs rising from the sea.

She didn't want sunshine to warm her face, because that meant they'd arrived in Ireland and their journey would end.

With his arm pinning her to the bed and his chest pressed against her breasts, just for the space of a few heartbeats, Thea allowed herself to picture not an end . . . but a beginning.

She saw them descending the stone steps to the terraced Italian gardens of Balfry House. Saw Dalton help her remove the linen from gilt painting frames.

They'd sneeze in the dust as they wiped away years of grime and cobwebs.

There'd be an awed hush when they discovered Artemisia's self-portrait—so much buried beauty and uncompromising truth.

And if she imagined him there with her at Balfry House, she could also imagine him confronting O'Roarke, his brother's murderer, dredging words from the depths of his soul to vanquish the anger and hurt he'd borne for so long.

Impossible to shoulder his burden for him, or absorb his anguish.

But perhaps she could accompany him to a deeper understanding. He'd escorted her on this journey reluctantly at first, witnessing her transformation, allowing her to safely experiment with new identities, and then, when she needed him most, he'd simply been there—rock solid and sharpened to a single purpose—the relentless warrior and the consummate lover.

She wanted to be there for him, by his side, to protect him when he tested the boundaries of his new existence. When he was freed from the stranglehold of this fixation with revenge.

She turned and rested her forehead against his. Brushed a finger lightly against the cleft in his chin.

He'd have to allow her to be there.

And he'd have to be the one to pry open his rusted heart and believe himself worthy of love and understanding.

Gently, she lifted his arm and slid out from under him. He rolled over but didn't wake.

She drew on her stockings and her petticoats, and threw her dress over her head, wrestling with the hooks up the back. Twisting her hair into a simple knot and securing it with pins, she slapped her one bedraggled bonnet on her head.

Donning her satin pelisse for warmth, she opened the door from the master's cabin and walked out onto the deck, the sea air bringing a salt sting to her eyes.

The helmsman standing above her on the deck caught her eye and tipped his cap. "Morning, madam."

Thea waved before continuing toward the bow.

The *Truth and Daylight* had a high-railed forecastle deck that she had noted earlier while boarding the vessel. Thea carefully made her way up the ladder to the forecastle. Molly stood at the prow of the ship, leaning out over the railing.

Thea joined her, soaking in the shimmer of the sun as it danced over silver waves and dipped into lines of white, frothing wake.

After a time, Molly tilted her head toward Thea. "I'm a bit scared to go home," she admitted, her brown eyes vulnerable.

Thea looped an arm around Molly's thin shoulders, holding on to the railing with her free hand. "That's understandable."

"My mam will be so angry with me for stealing her savings. And then I went and cast my pearl to a swine, as Mam would say. Bollocks. What's wrong with me?" Molly lifted her head, blinking her eyes to stave off tears. "Da always said I had the devil in me."

Thea gave her shoulders a squeeze. "And you won that money back with interest, taught that swine a lesson he won't soon forget, and you're bringing an uncle home with you. That ought to soften the blow, don't you think?"

"Could help, at that." Molly wiped a sleeve across her eyes. "Though she'll be angry with him, too. The both of us. It'll be stale bread and scalded milk for supper tonight."

Thea smiled. "Give her time. Con's a good man."

At first she'd thought him rough and rude, but now she knew he was just as soft inside as Dalton. Strong and stoic. Honorable and kind.

"You'll always land on your feet," Thea continued. "You're meant for great things, Molly Barton. Mark my words."

Molly grinned. "Will you allow me to raid the library when you live at Balfry House?"

"Pardon?"

"When you're married to the duke and live at Balfry. Or maybe you two will live in London?"

Thea dropped her hand from Molly's shoulders. "That will never happen."

"Dunno 'bout that. You smile so much more than when I first met you, and your eyes get all shiny like when you look at him. And the way he stares at you . . ." She gave a low whistle and scrunched up her freckled nose. "It's kind of disgusting."

Thea smiled.

"See?" Molly said, poking her arm. "You're smiling."

She couldn't help smiling. It was all that lingering bliss still humming through her body. The bracing breeze on her cheeks. Her heart couldn't help but lift with the wind.

The day was gray and the fog thick, but somewhere the sky was blue.

The deck teemed with activity. Sailors in dark flannel and wool trousers, peacoats and caps, seemed to be conducting a strange dance, *one-two-three*, coil this rope, pull on that rope, climb this mast, *one-two-three*.

"Stand by to set sail," a booming voice called out from the stern of the ship.

"Fore manned and ready," yelled back a sailor standing near the foremast.

"Lay aloft and loose haul sail!"

At the command, four sailors leapt onto the shrouds that secured the foremast to the sides of the vessel and began racing up toward the rigging.

"Oh, look." Molly pointed. "They're going to set the sails!"

The sailors went hand over hand up the rope latticework at an unbelievably fast pace. More sailors jumped onto the shrouds and began climbing up after the first group, swarming up and out like ants, they were so high.

Thea caught her breath as the first sailor released his hold on the mast and began sidling out sideways on a precarious perch.

In a matter of minutes the men had spread out and released the ropes that had held the sails up in bunches. The sails dropped down halfway, staying partially furled at the bottom, and instantly filled with the strong wind that had blown in overnight.

"Imagine doing that in the pitch dark during a storm!" Molly said excitedly. "I'm going to go get a closer look." She strode away, hat in hand.

Thea smiled as she watched her hurry away. The seamen didn't seem to mind Molly wore the same trousers as they did. They'd surely seen stranger sights on their travels.

Compared to the shackles of the poverty Molly had been born into, the restraints of Thea's strict upbringing and the weight of her family's expectations seemed trivial.

But words and rules sometimes formed barriers as strong as the thickest dungeon walls.

She was free now.

She'd study Dalton's art collection and write to the governors of the British Institution when she'd finished the catalogue.

Perhaps she could even hire Molly as her assistant.

The ship flew across the ocean, white sails billowing over her head.

Endless waves stretched before her and seagulls swooped overhead.

"It's a pleasing sight, isn't it, my lady?" Con joined her at the railing. "Soon we'll be seeing the green, green shores of Ireland."

He doffed his cap and placed it across his chest. "'When Erin first rose from the dark-swelling flood, God blessed the green island, He saw it was good. The Emerald of Europe, it sparkled, it shone, in the ring of this world the most precious stone.'"

He set his cap back on his head. "Dr. Drennan captured it, don't you think?"

Thea nodded. "Will you stay in Ireland, Con?"

Con gripped the railing with rough and worn fingers. "My home's in London now. I'm set in my ways. I've steady employment and other . . . activities."

"I know."

Con nodded absently.

"No. Con." Thea held his gaze. "I *know*."

He blinked, searching her face. "Well now. Sure and you've truly cracked him, my lady. Never thought I'd see the day. Maybe there's hope for that sinner after all."

"I know about your past with Molly's mother. Is there hope for . . . ?" Thea didn't want to say something to scare Con away from the idea of reconciling with Mrs. Barton, but surely he had to be thinking along those lines?

He squinted his eyes. "Probably no chance of rekindling something that died nearly twenty years ago."

Thea fingered the raised embroidery on her cuff. "There's always hope. Even for you. Even for the duke."

The ship plowed through the waves too quickly. Drawing them to Ireland. She planned to stay there forever. Aunt Emma needed someone to help her with the beekeeping. And Thea would be free there. "The duke will go back to London after . . . after he seeks answers."

"He may find more than he bargained for in Ireland. I believe he . . ." He raised his voice. "Well, speak of the devil."

Thea's heart wheeled like the seagulls above her as Dalton rose from the stairwell and walked toward them.

Really, a girl didn't stand a chance. He was only a fraction duke and mostly rogue this morning. The curving brim of his black hat cocked at a rakish angle over deep blue eyes that matched his coat. He wasn't wearing a cravat, and the top buttons of his shirt were undone, displaying a tantalizing hint of flesh.

What did he wear when he stalked the streets of London by moonlight, searching for evil?

A shiver chased between her shoulder blades.

"Speaking of me, were you?" Dalton asked, a secret, teasing smile that was just for her playing across his lips. "Only praise, I trust."

Con raised both of his eyebrows and gave him a scathing look. "What do you think now?"

Molly came barreling across the deck. "Have you a ship?" she asked Dalton, remembering her instructions not to address him by his title.

He gave her an amused smile. "I've several docked in London."

"Do you need a ship's boy? I want to see a volcano erupt on the Sandwich Islands!"

Dalton's lips quirked. "Ship's *boy*?"

"That's right." Molly gave a determined nod. "I'm not for staying in boggy old Cork and marrying some sod of a farmer."

Thea's heart flip-flopped when Dalton didn't laugh at Molly's outrageous ideas. He merely nodded with admirable gravity. "I'll make some enquiries, shall I?"

"Oh yes, please do," Molly said eagerly.

"Want to see how the ship's wheel works?" Con asked, giving Thea a quick wink that clearly communicated he plotted to leave her alone with Dalton.

Her heartbeat sped even faster at the prospect.

"Do I!" Molly grabbed his hand and they set off across the deck, stepping over coiled ropes and stopping to speak with the crewmen.

Dalton stood beside Thea, nearly touching her. The heat and strength of his nearness had the same effect on her every time, turning her knees wobbly and setting her cheeks aflame.

"Slept well, my lady?" The suggestiveness of the simple words and the knowing glint in his eyes made her hands tighten around the railing.

"Not enough, I'm afraid." She gave him an arch smile.

"And whose fault was that?" He reached over on the pretext of tucking a curl into her bonnet and murmured in her ear. "*Someone* demanded satisfying."

She tilted her cheek into his hand. "And someone *stood* and delivered."

His laughter rumbled low and delicious along her spine. "And someone stole my breath away."

And your heart? she wanted to ask. *Was it stolen as well? Because mine's lost forever.*

He rubbed his thumb across her cheek and over her lower lip.

Her skin was still sensitive from the roughness of the stubble along his jaw where he'd pressed against her as they kissed. Her cheeks had been ruddy and scrubbed-looking in the glass this morning.

Her heart sensitive and scrubbed raw as well.

He dropped his hand from her cheek and pointed into the distance. "Cork Harbor."

A solitary lighthouse perched on a rock promontory cast a baleful red eye out to sea, and rising in the distance were the cliffs of Ireland, blanketed in green, misty with fog.

His shoulders stiffened and his eyes lost their wicked glint. He stood with his legs braced against the movement of the sea and his hooded eyes searching the horizon.

He must be thinking about the last time he saw those cliffs.

So many years ago.

She covered his hand with hers. "Tell me what you see, Dalton."

What do you see when you're ten?

Not darkness. Not revenge.

Simply life. Sailors heaving ropes and hoisting sails, singing interestingly bawdy songs about mermaids.

The rocking of the waves and a swelling of pride. *I'm not seasick, Papa. Alec's heaving in a bucket but I'm strong like you.*

Ten years old and desperate for his father's approval.

Mama doesn't love me best, but who cares? I'm not a mewling mama's boy like Alec. I'm already a man.

Delicate touch along his knuckles.

Soft fingers interlacing with his.

His body tall. Substantial. Not ten years old.

Thea's hand clasping his on top of the ship's railing.

His chest tightened. He wasn't alone. She was here with him.

Brisk breeze ribboning marmalade curls away from her bonnet and into the sunshine.

In the distance, jagged cliffs over the ocean.

"What is it?" she asked softly, the concern flooding her eyes jolting him back to the present.

"I was ten the last time I saw those cliffs," he admitted. "Thought I'd invented the world. Thought it was mine for the taking."

"Maybe someday if . . . if all goes well, you might bring your mother to Ireland." The wind whipped curls against her cheeks. "Home is a powerful cure."

"The physicians never offered much hope that she'd ever leave Osborne Court," Dalton said gently. "It's the only home she has now."

"She can learn to conquer her fear with your love and support."

Looking into her eyes, banded with pure steely determination, he could almost believe she was right. He wanted to believe O'Roarke was the shadow he'd hunted for so long, and confronting him would end this obsession for revenge.

"I want you to be right, Thea. Truly I do." He tightened his grip on her hand. "But I don't know what will happen tomorrow."

"Forget tomorrow, then." A smile tilted up her lips. "We have this moment. And it's more than enough."

The desire to kiss her was so strong he nearly cast caution to the breeze. He needed to untie that bonnet and chuck it over the railing as well. It hid her too much.

He needed her free and unobstructed by wire and straw.

Lower the sails. Calm the wind.

Stay rocking here on the ocean long enough to make love with Thea one more time.

A few more hours of sweet, explosive pleasure and whispered secrets.

"Thea." The word wrenched from his lips like a prayer.

"I'm here, Dalton." Unwavering gaze. Bold invitation in her eyes.

"Hate to interrupt, but we're nearly there." Con's gruff voice shattered the moment.

So they were.

They'd sailed through the deepwater harbor proper, passing the large ocean-going vessels that anchored there while ships with shallower drafts like the *Truth and Daylight* continued up the river Lee toward Cork.

The Great Island loomed large to the starboard, the town of Cobh sprinkled with pinpricks of lamplight. The fog was beginning to stack and thicken as the wind weakened. Rows of cannons could barely be seen across the harbor, slumbering sentinels keeping silent watch from the fortifications on Haulbowline Island.

"We can't be seen together. Not after yesterday. Trent's spread the word. Maybe even to Ireland," Con said.

"Of course." Dalton drew away from Thea. "I wasn't thinking." And that's why he couldn't succumb to these longings. Because he had to protect her from the men who sought to expose his secret. And the dangerous man he sought.

"I'll stay below with Thea while we dock," he told Con. "You leave first with Molly."

"I'll send word when all's clear," Con said

tersely. "There'll be a carriage waiting to take you and Thea."

Dalton nodded. He owed Thea safe passage to the door of her aunt's house, at least.

"I'll join you later in town," Con said.

Dalton laid a hand on his arm. "No. Stay with Molly and Bronagh. I can find O'Roarke alone."

Con searched his face for a few tense moments. "All right, then. But if you need me you know where to find me." Con struck Dalton lightly on the shoulder. "Be careful, you ungrateful gob-shite."

"And you, you grizzled bastard. Try not to muck things up too badly with brown-eyed Bronagh."

Chapter 22

"The carriage will be waiting farther down the quay," Dalton told Thea as they descended the gangplank, she shrouded in her voluminous gray cloak, and he in the sober black coat, a blue kerchief around his neck, and his scuffed old boots.

He never had polished them.

She'd seen through his act so easily. The face he showed the world, the blasé charm and careless laughter.

He'd lowered his guard with her and she knew him better than anyone in the world now. And the wonder of it was that she still clasped his hand as they walked along the wooden pier of the Cork harbor.

"Your aunt's cottage is near Balfry House?" he asked her.

"Very near. Along the coast road."

"I've heard about this marmalade your aunt makes." Dalton wanted to bring back her smile. "Do you think she'd be willing to part with a jar for a hungry traveler?"

"She never lets anyone leave Ballybrack without a jar. Dear Aunt Emma. I've missed her. I'd like you to meet her."

"I'd like that," he admitted.

He couldn't force himself to push her away anymore. He was tired of it. He wanted to be with her. And every second he spent with her was going to be as good and perfect as he could make it.

"Perhaps before we go to Ballybrack we could . . . visit Balfry House first?" she asked. The words slipped out in a nonchalant tone, but he knew what they meant to her.

He squeezed her hand lightly. He wasn't afraid of crushing her delicate bones anymore. He knew she was made of fire and steel.

He didn't have to search for O'Roarke until tomorrow.

One more day with Thea. Unmasked and free from the weight of secrets and lies.

Visiting Balfry would force him to face those awful memories, but she'd be there by his side, holding his hand as she did now.

"Why not?" he said with a smile. "You can show me the *Sleeping Venus.* Point out all her hidden symbolism."

Her answering smile lit the misty spring afternoon like a glimpse of July sunshine. "I'd love to show you! The afternoon is the perfect time of day for illuminating the play of light and shadow along her limbs. Artemisia was very skilled at the technique of chiaroscuro."

Chiaroscuro. The contrasting of light and dark.

Passionate, full-of-light Thea by his side. And dark, secret twisting of vengeance in his gut.

Dalton knew exactly what would happen when

she showed him that painting. She'd hook her hand through the tassel on the drapes and slide the curtains open, and something would open inside Dalton as well.

Something would shift inside his chest as sunlight pierced the gloom and settled directly upon a rich, beautiful painting, not half as beautiful as the woman by his side.

And maybe he was ready for that now.

"Goddesses," Dalton said with a knowing glance. "I like goddesses. Especially when they're in my bed."

"I thought you said no more beds." Her lids lowered seductively over blue eyes misted with gray.

"And I think you want more scandalizing."

Hang it all, he needed to kiss her when she smiled at him in that fully wicked way. He caught her waist in his hands and pulled her against his chest.

"Oh!" she exclaimed. "We're on a public pier, darling."

"Darling?"

Her cheeks flushed. "Er . . . that is—"

"No, don't retract it. I like *darling* far better than *arrogant arse* . . . and I don't care who sees me kiss you. We'll scandalize every quay worker from here to Dublin." He'd kiss her and claim his patch of sunshine in this gray, uncertain world, if she'd have a sinner like him.

He cupped her cheeks in his hands and brought her lips to his mouth.

She tasted of the butter and marmalade she'd slathered on the hard, stale bread this morning to make it more palatable. He kissed her hungrily, reveling in the silken smoothness of her plump lower lip, worrying it between his teeth before plunging inside her mouth with his tongue.

She rose on tiptoes and knotted her arms around his neck, demanding more.

He forgot where they were, forgot everything except the crashing wave of need. He ripped the bow of her bonnet ribbons apart and flung the ragged, obstructionist bit of straw and silk away.

She gasped as a cart promptly squashed her millinery beneath its wheels.

"Never mind," he growled. "I'll buy you another. I'll buy you a new gown, too. And silk garters. Blue ones." That was a lot of shopping. He'd never taken a woman shopping before. But who cared? He'd never felt this way about a woman before.

"Garters," she said breathily, flashing him a smile. "I like silk garters."

He claimed her soft lips again, picturing her in blue silk garters, white stockings, and a smile.

He'd pose her on the ducal bed at Balfry House in exactly the same position as the Venus. And then he'd pleasure her so thoroughly the walls of that crumbling ancient house would shake and moan and all the bad memories would flee.

She broke free for a moment. "Dalton," she breathed.

"Mmm." He kissed her soft neck. The stubborn

point of her chin. The tip of her slightly upturned nose.

He'd known her such a short time. How had she woven herself so completely into his thoughts . . . and his life? It was difficult to imagine being alone again.

He wanted to believe that he could change with her. Become the man she thought he was.

Noble and good.

A thought struck him then. A memory. His hand clasping a pen and scratching words across a page. He lifted his head.

He'd written the letter to her mother. Her parents could be on their way from London right now, hoping to salvage their daughter's reputation.

The reputation he'd thoroughly ruined. Christ. What had he done? He had to warn her.

"Thea, I—"

"Didn't you say O'Roarke's ship is called the *Rambler?*" she interrupted, staring beyond his shoulder. "You'd better turn around."

Something in her voice made him glance up sharply and twist to look behind him.

His heart stopped beating.

Right there beside them.

A well-appointed brig with dark wood gleaming in the morning sun and the name *Rambler* in gold lettering on the side, plain as day.

How had he missed it? How had Con missed it?

Numb with shock, Dalton's mind registered that the ship was preparing to leave. The sails billowed.

"Well?" Thea pushed curls out of her eyes and cast him a challenging look. "What are you waiting for? Let's go find him!"

She gave him a shove on the chest and ran past him.

Stunned, Dalton's blood froze.

Thea. Running toward God knew what danger. He chased after her but she was already running up the gangplank, lifting her skirts to run faster, her hair streaming behind her as she ran.

Everything a blur now.

He vaulted up the gangplank, catching hold of Thea's arm.

A man in a blue officer's coat with shiny brass buttons sped toward them. "Here now, what're you doing? This ship's about to sail. No visitors."

And then Dalton saw the man standing at the prow of the ship with an expensive spyglass held in his hand, sighting the horizon. He was garbed unmistakably as a gentleman among the sailors and officers.

O'Roarke.

Dalton grabbed hold of the officer's sleeve. "Is that the owner of this vessel? Mr. O'Roarke?"

The officer's eyes narrowed. "Who wants to know?"

That was all the answer Dalton needed.

"Keep this woman safe," he said urgently, thrusting Thea gently into the officer's arms.

Struggling to ignore her indignant cries of protest, he sprang across the deck. Force of habit jerked the kerchief over his lips, whipped the ivory-handled knife from the special sheath inside the top edge of his boot.

"O'Roarke," he bellowed. "Turn around."

He didn't turn, but Dalton could tell by the guilty hunch of the man's shoulders, the tensing of his knees, that O'Roarke wanted to spring over the railing and plunge into the ocean to make his escape.

This was the man he'd been hunting.

Sailors climbing down from the riggings now, hurtling toward Dalton. Any second he'd be mobbed by men, unable to move.

But he couldn't knife a man in the back.

"O'Roarke," he bellowed.

The man straightened his knees and turned.

Slash of dark auburn hair under the top hat, and slitted green eyes.

Young. So young. *Too young.* Mid-twenties at most.

A weight crushing his chest, not enough air to breathe. Knife still gripped in hand.

Thea by his side, somehow, eyes stormy and intense.

The world stopped tilting and slid back into place.

Two huge sailors and the officer nearly upon them. Dalton thrust Thea behind him, keeping his hands on her arms so she wouldn't spring forward as she had with Albertson in the alley.

He braced for the impact.

"Stand down," the man with the green eyes shouted, and the sailors skidded to a halt.

Thea's fingers scrabbled at Dalton's hands where he still held her imprisoned behind his back. He loosened his grip and she shifted to his side.

Dalton's hand flew to the piece of calcified rock hanging against his chest. His fingers closed around the familiar jagged edges.

Ghost footsteps echoed behind him.

Wait for me, Dalton. I want to come, too.

Go back to the house, Alec.

Memory jarring with reality. Stomach-churning leap of hope.

Dalton pulled the kerchief off his mouth, needing to shatter the silence. "But you're dead."

Leaf green eyes hardened to flint. "Not dead, as you can see."

Not dead. *Not dead.*

Dalton's mind spun.

If not dead . . . then . . . "You're my brother, Alec."

Chapter 23

"What were you going to do?" Alec asked tersely, anger mottling his face with red. "Knife a feeble, elderly man in the back like a damned coward?"

It was Alec. Something in Dalton knew without the shadow of a doubt.

Alec was American?

A jag of hysterical laughter caught in Dalton's chest. It was laugh or weep.

"Father was right," Alec spat. "You're an animal."

"I thought you were . . ." Dalton couldn't finish the sentence. His mind had reached some insurmountable wall.

He wanted to reach out, touch this phantom brother, take his hand. And all he saw in Alec's eyes was disgust.

"Leave us," Alec said, waving the sailors and the officer away.

"Sir, I think I should stay," the officer said. "For protection—"

"No." Alec shook his head. "Go."

The men walked away, leaving them alone in the prow of the ship.

Thea drew closer to Dalton's side until her shoulders collided with his arms. "You're Dalton's brother?" she asked, her brow furrowing.

"Who's this, then? Your doxy?" Alec asked with arched eyebrows, surveying Thea's wind-swept curls and travel-worn cloak.

Dalton took a menacing step forward. "You'll speak to her with proper respect. She's a lady."

"Doesn't look it." Alec snorted. "Decadent aristocracy, living for pleasure, squandering your wealth on gambling and fancy ladies while your tenants starve. You sicken me."

The loathing in Alec's voice was palpable. He may as well have spat on the deck.

"You're one of the aristocracy, Alec, I hate to tell you," Dalton said.

"Don't call me Alec. My name's Patrick. Patrick O'Roarke. I was raised in the proud city of New York and I'm an American."

"We thought you were dead," Dalton said. "Murdered. Your clothes washed up on the shores of Balfry. The note the killer left . . ."

"He's not a killer," Alec said coldly. "He's my father."

"But he stole you."

"For good reason."

"Didn't you have memories of that day? You followed me outside onto the cliffs. I let go of your hand . . ." The memory was so strong for him.

"I had hazy memories but they faded. They were replaced with my new life. I'll never be like you. Never accept wealth I didn't earn. Riches steeped in the blood of others." His green eyes narrowed to slits. "Oh yes, I know all about our sire, the old duke."

Dalton's breath rattled in his chest.

What lies had O'Roarke fed to Alec? What truths?

Thea placed a hand on his arm. "Why don't we begin again? Where's your father, Mr. O'Roarke? Still in New York?"

"Gone and buried." Pain flickered through Alec's eyes. "Six months ago. On his deathbed he begged me to come back here, to the old country, to settle his remaining affairs. I found a letter. A confession."

Dalton tensed. "He confessed to stealing you."

"He confessed to rescuing me from our criminal of a father, the Duke of Osborne. That's you now, isn't it? The heartless duke. Corrupt as the bilgewater on a ship."

Thea's fingers massaged his forearm. "Dalton," she whispered. "You're still holding your knife."

Here he stood in his scuffed boots and ragged kerchief, knife blade glinting in his hand, and he'd been named as the duke.

A quick darting glance told him there was no one within earshot, but the words had been said. The secret uncovered.

He flipped his knife back inside his boot and scrubbed a fist across his eyes. "How long have you known?" he asked, his voice sounding wooden and hollow.

"Two weeks." Alec searched the deck and lowered his voice. "The secret stays with us," he said urgently. "I'm a Counsellor at Law in New York. I don't want to disrupt the life I've built for myself there."

"That's just plain *selfish!*" Thea wheeled on Alec like a lioness protecting her den. "You say the duke is heartless but what about you, Mr. O'Roarke? Can you think of what your brother is feeling right now? He loves you. He's been grieving for you this entire time. His whole life he's been atoning for the imagined sin of letting go of your hand, that day on the beach. Believing he was responsible for your death."

Alec's gaze faltered for a moment. "Twenty years have passed. Please. Just leave and pretend this never happened."

"You truly want us to leave?" Dalton asked. Pain clenched his chest.

Go back to the house.

I don't want you following me.

This was what he deserved.

He gripped the leather cord around his neck so hard it broke off in his hand. He ripped it off and threw it on the deck.

Thea glanced down at the bloodred fossil and then shook her head. "We're not leaving."

She took a step toward Alec. "Not until you two talk to each other like men instead of snarling beasts."

Alec closed his eyes briefly. "Please, my lady. I don't want any trouble."

Thea's eyes flashed bluer than Dalton had ever

seen them. "Your brother has gone searching for trouble in every gaming hell across London. Avenging your father's sins and protecting the helpless victims of the gambling world."

Dalton's chest swelled with pride at the way she leapt to his defense, but clearly Alec was set on keeping the past buried. "Thea." He clasped her hand. "We should leave now."

The sharp point of her chin raised defiantly. "No. Not yet." She widened her stance and addressed Alec. "Did O'Roarke also tell you about your mother?" she demanded. "How he broke her heart by stealing you? How she hasn't left her house in ten years and is only a shell of a woman?"

Before Alec could answer, a small figure darted across the deck and flung his arms around Alec's legs.

"Father?" The child was about six years of age with reddish-brown hair and wide, hazel eyes. He gazed up at Alec. "Why are you angry? Who are these visitors? Aren't we setting sail now?"

Alec ruffled the boy's hair. "I'm not angry, Van. And these visitors are leaving. Go below and find Ned, there's a good boy."

Was Van his nephew? Did that mean Alec had a wife? The boy's small face tugged at Dalton's heart, dredging up memories of Alec when he was that age.

The boy stared at Dalton. "How did you come by that cut across your jaw? Did you fight a duel?"

He drew himself up tall and straight. "I'm a great swordsman." He made a slashing motion as if he held a fencing sword. "No one escapes my blade."

Dalton dropped to his knees so he was on eye level with the lad. "You'll have to work on that forehand stroke. You need a good fencing master."

Van pulled on his father's hand. "May I have a fencing master?"

Alec unclasped his son's hands and took him by the shoulders. "Go below, Donovan."

So Van was short for Donovan. Dalton had a nephew.

This was so much to absorb.

Thea smiled and bent toward Van. "The duke could be your fencing master."

Alec tensed.

Van turned to Dalton, his eyes wide and shining. "You're a *duke?* I've never met a duke before!"

"Go below," Alec said firmly. "Now."

"But I want to talk to the duke," the boy protested.

Alec pointed to the doorway. "Now."

Van left reluctantly, shuffling his feet and casting lingering glances back at Dalton.

Alec waited until the boy was gone before rounding on Dalton and Thea, his entire body shaking. "I won't have my son corrupted. He'll never know the taint in his blood."

Dalton nodded. "We're leaving."

"Dalton, please," Thea urged. "If your mother was able to see her son, and met her grandson, it would help her so. I know it would. You have to explain, you have to fight—"

"I'm through with fighting," Dalton said, bowing his shoulders.

Alec nodded tersely. "Thank you."

Dalton forced himself to turn his back on his brother and lead Thea off the deck.

Alec.

Not dead.

His mind still reeled with shock and there was still that churning of hope in his gut . . . but he knew one thing.

Alec didn't want him there. And so he had to leave.

Thea couldn't believe they were just leaving. She glared at Dalton but he avoided her eyes, using his strength to hustle her along the dock toward the waiting carriage.

She tried to dig her boots into the planks but he was too powerful. He easily kept her walking, fairly lifting her off the ground.

"I'll carry you to that carriage if I have to," he muttered, his face dark and closed.

Ominous dark clouds had overtaken the sky during their conversation.

There would be a downpour soon.

No sunshine for viewing paintings today.

"But," Thea sputtered. "You need to go back there, find a way to convince him to go to London. You can't just let his ship leave, Dalton. You can't do that."

He kept marching, his arm an implacable force

around her waist. "Not my choice. He told me to leave. I left."

"That child can't be more than six years old. He's resilient. Adaptable. He'd adjust to the idea of having a new identity. Should it be your brother's choice to deny his son a grandmother?"

Dalton set his jaw. "He doesn't want the boy to know he's half-British and a descendant of a corrupt, evil aristocrat."

"But that's cowardly!"

"It's his choice."

"He doesn't know you like I know you." Thea curled her fingers around his forearm in a vain attempt to slow their forward motion. "You must go back there and speak to him. Before the ship leaves. Convince him he's wrong. If he got to know you he would want his son to have an uncle. A strong, kind uncle to guide him."

Why were his eyes so cold? Why did he shake his big, stubborn head like that?

"I don't know what to think, Thea. All this time I thought he was dead. Maybe it's better this way. Better for the truth to stay buried."

"No! I don't accept that." Thea clutched his hand, trying to make him understand. "I don't accept that our fates are written in stone. As long as we draw breath we can change. Until we're only bones resting in a crypt we have the power to shape our own destinies."

Dalton didn't even answer her impassioned speech. He merely opened the carriage door, lifted her by the waist, and set her inside.

He climbed in after her, cutting off all escape.

As the carriage wheels began to spin, carrying them over the uneven planks of the pier, Thea clenched her fists in her lap.

Obviously she wasn't going to be able to talk sense into him. It was so maddening.

The man was too stubborn.

He was letting his chance at happiness and wholeness slip away on the tide. It made her want to cry.

He sat beside her, heavily cloaked in silence, and she could almost believe that he was heartless and cruel and everything his brother had accused him of being.

Except she knew better.

She knew he had a heart. And right now that heart was grieving for the brother he'd lost once and was in danger of losing again.

She wanted to comfort him, help him make sense of the turmoil of emotion he must be feeling. But he was grieving in the only way he knew how—by shutting away his feelings and keeping her out.

The carriage kept an easy pace along South King Road. The green fields and estates of Lough Mahon that she'd used to delight in leaving her cold now.

"Turn the carriage around, Dalton." She took his hand. "You'll regret this the rest of your life."

A muscle tensed beneath the jagged scar across his jaw. "It's better this way," he finally said.

"How is it better?"

"It's too complicated. Alec is right to leave the past buried."

"You stubborn arse," she choked out.

"You don't know the half of it," he replied cryptically, retracting his hand.

What did that mean?

"It's twenty minutes to Ballybrack," he said in an emotionless voice.

"We're not going to Balfry?"

He shook his head and turned away, staring out the window.

The rain started then.

A sudden spring downpour; the sky turned dark, just like her thoughts.

Relentless needles of water. Rain running in rivulets down the carriage windows.

Two can play the silence game, thought Thea.

She wrapped her cloak tightly around her arms and shifted to the far side of the carriage.

It was all going so wrong. Finding his brother should have freed Dalton. Instead he'd only put up more barriers.

Finally they arrived and the dear, familiar whitewashed walls and trailing rose vines of Ballybrack Cottage filled the carriage windows.

Her heart couldn't help but lift at the sight. Aunt Emma wouldn't be outside in this rain. She'd be sitting by the parlor fire, reading a book about beekeeping methods, or knitting socks for neighboring tenant families.

She'd bustle into the kitchen to put on the kettle.

And the duke would have some of her home-
made apricot and honey preserves.

Maybe their sweetness would improve the
beast's temperament.

One could always hope.

He helped her down from the carriage, still
avoiding her eyes, and walked with her to the
front door.

The door opened abruptly, as if someone had
been at a window, watching for them.

Thea lifted her head and pale blue eyes skew-
ered her to the front steps.

"Mother?" she asked, disbelief coursing
through her mind.

"What took you so long?" the countess asked.
"We've been waiting, the dowager and I."

The dowager countess was here?

As if in a nightmare, Thea drifted into the
parlor, small details exploding in her mind.

Four teacups on the table. Scent of the dowager's expensive French lily eau de toilette.

The dowager stiff-backed in the horsehair chair
by the fireplace.

Aunt Hen here as well. She waved to Thea.
"Hello, dear. Pleasant journey?"

Thea was too stunned to reply.

Aunt Emma rose. "I'll fetch another teacup." She
stopped as the duke entered the room, stooping
a little to make it through the low doorway. "Oh!
Your Grace." She dropped into a deep, flustered
curtsy.

He nodded curtly, his eyes dark and flat.

The dowager countess's gaze swept disdain-fully over Thea's mussed curls and Dalton's scuffed boots. "My, my, my. You two must have a tale to tell."

Thea finally located her voice. "What . . . what are all of you doing here?"

The countess flashed her a triumphant smile. "Why don't you ask His Grace? He's the one who invited us."

Chapter 24

"**W**hat did you do?" Thea asked Dalton, advancing on him and backing him out of the parlor doorway. "What did you *do?*"

His face turned blank and emotionless. "I was going to tell you."

She backed him out of the room until they were near the front door. "When? When were you going to tell me that you invited my family to come fetch me like some sheep who broke loose from its pen?"

"Today. I was going to tell you but then . . . everything with O'Roarke. It fled my mind."

"When did you do this?" Her mind felt numb and frozen and her words came from far away. She wanted the facts. The exact sequence of events.

The anatomy of a betrayal.

He flinched. "I wrote another letter and posted it with yours. I couldn't let you throw away your future like that."

His back hit the doorjamb.

He thought he'd done this to protect her. *Arrogant, controlling arse.*

"It's better this way," he said.

The same words he'd said in the carriage.

"Better for whom?" She was nearly shouting now but she didn't care. Let them hear. Let them know how she'd changed. How she'd found her voice and it would never be soft and diffident again. "For you? So I won't be your burden anymore?"

His eyes darkened to coal. "I'm not any of those things you said I was, Thea. I warned you not to trust me. I betrayed you. My own brother hates me. I've lived my life based on a lie. I have no answers."

"What did your letter say?"

"What difference does it make? I sent it. They're here."

"I want to know what it said."

"I told your mother you were lying. You hadn't been ruined. I told her you still had a choice and a chance for happiness." His head fell against the wall with a thud. "Now what *I* wrote is the lie. I ruined you. I limited your options."

"I heard that," came the dowager's sharp, reedy voice.

Dalton started, his gaze darting to the parlor doorway.

"You didn't trust me enough to let me make my own decisions," Thea accused.

"And that's the man you'll marry, Lady Dorothea," he said, raising his voice. "You'll marry a heartless rake. You're saddled with me now."

Emotionless. Flat. No love for her in his words . . . or his voice.

Only duty. Stupid honor and duty.

"We'll go back to London. You'll live at Osborne Court," he announced.

Excited gasps from the parlor.

No, no, no.

She clenched her hands. This wasn't what she wanted.

She opened the door and pushed him outside, fighting desperately to keep from crying.

Outside, slashing rain pounding her bare head, sliding down the hood of her cloak and seeking out the opening to trickle down the middle of her back.

Thea slammed the door behind them. "I can't believe you'd do something like this." Hurt and anger raced through her mind, galloping for the finish line. The end of this journey and the end of the dream she'd had of a future with Dalton.

She'd never imagined it ending like this. Never thought he would betray her. Seek to force her back into the cage of her family's expectations.

"I warned you not to trust me," he repeated.

He'd tried to warn her, but she'd deluded herself into believing . . . what exactly? That she yearned for the same outcome her mother and grandmother wanted for her? To marry a duke?

Ha. That's the last thing she wanted. Marry a duke who didn't love her. *Never.*

"I won't marry you, Dalton. You're precisely what I ran away from. I'd rather be alone here in Ireland than be shackled in a loveless match. I will only marry if there is love and trust and—"

"You have no choice."

And that was the proverbial last straw.

"I do have a choice," she shouted, glaring at his arrogant, cold face. "And I choose not to marry you. You don't love me. You don't even know me." She kicked the muddy path, splattering dirt across her red boots. "I thought you were listening to me, truly hearing me. I thought you understood my need for this hard-won independence. I was wrong."

"You're right." He squared his chest, standing erect, taking the abuse she leveled at him with infuriating calm. "I'm not worthy of you."

"You," she sputtered. She'd never been this angry. She was wet, and tired, and the events of the past few days had left her so raw.

The passion they'd shared. The intimate conversations.

All lies.

"You're an expert at building walls between yourself and your emotions," she said. "A wall to keep me out. A wall to distance your brother. Barriers like the ones hemming in your mother. Walls around your heart."

"You're right," he said again, bowing his head slightly.

"See? There you go again." She stamped her foot, even though it spattered more mud on her hem. "Admitting I'm right is just another wall." She wiped her wet hair out of her eyes. "Our journey meant nothing to you?" she asked, needing to hear him say the words. "You never began to believe that life could hold more. The possibility for trust . . . and love?"

She whispered the last word, knowing what his answer would be, knowing it would only be another wall between them.

"Love's only an illusion. And so is the person you thought I was. I'm not good or noble. You were falling in love with a fantasy. A person you created out of your own needs. I told you I'm nobody's answer." He spread his hands wide. "My own brother, who I thought was lost forever, hates me enough to deny our mother comfort and peace in her old age."

Thea shivered.

His eyes softened and he half raised one of his hands, as if he wanted to touch her. "You're right to refuse me. I can never give you what you need. You don't need me to believe in you. You're strong enough on your own."

"You're right. I don't need you." She wrapped her cloak tighter, even though it was already a sodden mess. "Leave now, Dalton."

Of course that's what he wanted her to say. Just as Alec had said the same words an hour past.

"Leave me and never come back," she commanded.

"Thea." He touched her, the ghost of a caress along her cheek. "I wish I had a heart to give you. It would be yours, Thea. All yours."

He left her then.

Tall and strong, walking away in the rain.

Back to the carriage. He'd go to Balfry House, maybe.

Or he'd go to the devil.

The barricades he'd erected were too high and

too thick. And she had walls of her own to blast apart. They waited for her back in the parlor.

She was not going to cry.

She had her own battles to fight and she needed to be strong and uncompromising to withstand the maelstrom of censure that would attempt to bend her back into obedience.

She'd stand firm. She wasn't going anywhere. No one was going to control her anymore.

The dowager's steely tones met her at the door. "Well? What happened, child? Did you accept the duke—"

"Stop!" Thea walked into the center of the room, planted her muddy boots on the blue-and-white carpet, and clenched her fists. "Not one more word."

"Lady Dorothea," hissed the countess. "You forget—"

"You can't speak," Thea interrupted. "For once in your lives, you're both going to sit there and listen!"

"Well!" The dowager fell back in her chair.

"I've refused the duke," Thea announced.

"Pardon me? Did I hear that correctly? Refused—"

She raised her voice, nearly shouting to be heard over the dowager. "I choose to live the rest of my days as a spinster here in Ireland rather than marry someone who doesn't love me."

She whirled on her mother. "I don't want a loveless sham of a union such as yours."

"You ungrateful little fool," the dowager spat. "You don't know what you're speaking about."

"This is what I will say, whether you hear me or not," Thea said, struggling to keep calm. "I'm a woman. Not a marionette dancing to your whims. I have needs and thoughts of my own. You'll never control me again." She glared first at the dowager and then at her mother, daring them to disagree.

The room filled with a charged silence.

Aunt Hen and Aunt Emma stared at her with the exact same befuddled expression, the lace on their caps wobbling, plump hands folded in their laps.

The dowager thumped her cane on the floor. "What a world! Young ladies speaking so to their elders. This is insubordination. Mutiny. It will not be tolerated."

"Oh, hush, you domineering tyrant," said the countess. "This isn't mutiny. It's truth."

Thea swung to face her mother. "Why, thank you, Mother." How unexpected that her mother would rise to her defense.

The countess rose from her chair and advanced on her mother-in-law. "You raised an egotistical, profligate son, indulging his every whim as if he were Julius Caesar. I don't think Lady Dorothea needs your guidance. If she doesn't want to marry the duke, then she shan't. And that's the end of it."

Thea felt like cheering.

"But you heard what he said," the dowager said coldly. "She's ruined. Damaged goods."

Thea lifted her chin. "By my own choice."

"You little fool," hissed the dowager.

"I understand why she doesn't want a marriage like mine." Thea's mother slashed an elegant hand through the air. "Desmond neglects me. He makes a fool of me. He takes a new mistress every month and flaunts her around town. I'm sick of it, I tell you. I've had enough."

Thea experienced the strangest feeling of admiration for her mother. For the first time she saw the vulnerability beneath the cold, hard surface.

"He doesn't deserve you," Aunt Emma agreed, with a decisive nod.

The dowager's nostrils flared and her mouth snapped shut with an audible click. "I've never been so mistreated in my life. I advised Desmond not to marry you, you . . . *harpy*." She grasped her cane and jerked to her feet. "Come along, Henrietta, we're leaving this very moment."

Aunt Hen glanced up from where she and Aunt Emma had been watching the exchange from their armchairs by the fire.

"You know?" She cocked her head. "I think I'll stay here with Emma, Mother." She lifted her soft, round chin. "She needs help tending her bees. I should be inured to *stings* by now."

The dowager blinked. "That's completely absurd. You can't stay here. Who will prepare my tinctures?"

"Why, I don't know." Aunt Hen's lips curved in a half-guilty, half-gleeful smile. "And to be completely honest, I don't much care." She half jumped out of her chair, as if she couldn't believe she'd said the words.

Thea gave her an encouraging smile. She'd always felt sorry for poor, cowed Aunt Hen.

"We'll travel back together," the countess said to the dowager.

The dowager narrowed her pale eyes. "I won't travel with you."

"You've no choice." The countess gave Thea a brief flicker of a smile. "You're saddled with me now."

Instead of continuing to Balfry House, Dalton had the carriage drive back to the quay. He didn't want to visit Balfry yet. Maybe he wouldn't visit at all.

Everything there would remind of Alec . . . and Thea.

The quay crawled with merchants disgorging their cargo and fishmongers loading carts in the gray, misty afternoon.

Not even a hint of roses here. Fish guts and salt brine. Hot tar and seagull droppings.

The *Rambler* was gone, of course. Alec had sailed back to New York, taking young Van with him, keeping him safe from the dark legacy of the Osborne family.

Couldn't blame him, really.

Thea thought he should have fought harder, but if Alec didn't want to be his brother, he couldn't force him.

He should go find Con, tell him the news.

There was no killer to find. No killer at all.

Alec was alive and well. And the man who stole him dead and gone.

Nothing to wreak revenge upon. No more searching and plotting and running.

There was an odd feeling in his chest. An emptiness, as if there had been a heart there and it had been wrenched out, leaving him concave and hollow.

All the emotion leached from his mind.

Only observations now.

I'm walking along a quay.

Thea's with her family and she's angry and hurt:

I hurt her. Just as I knew I would.

But what else could he have done? It was wrong to mail that letter, probably, but he hadn't known her very well at that stage and he'd thought he was doing the right thing.

He hadn't wanted to limit her options. Give her regrets.

Christ, you really made a mess of things, didn't you?

No woman wanted a forced proposal flung at her like that. Of course she'd refused him. And the suffering in those wide, stormy eyes.

She'd wanted him to beg her forgiveness, give her all the pretty words she needed to hear and he'd been . . . empty. Reeling from the knowledge that he'd built his life around a lie.

As long as we draw breath we can change. Until we're only bones resting in a crypt we have the power to shape our own destinies.

Something about her words struck him then, and he stopped walking, staring out over the bristling masts and choppy gray ocean.

She thought he could change.

Could he? With time, could he become the man she needed him to be?

Mitigate the threat of Trent somehow. Find other ways to fight for justice.

Less dangerous ways. So that she would never be a target.

And if he changed . . . then would she have him?

"Hello!" a small voice shouted.

Dalton turned his head.

Alec walked toward him along the pier, holding Van by the hand. The boy waved and called to him again. "Hello!"

Tentatively, Dalton raised his hand. Then, when his brain began to process what his eyes saw, he waved his hand harder.

"Hello," he shouted, striding toward them. "I thought your ship sailed," he said, when he reached them.

Alec grunted. "There'll be other ships."

"Hello Van," Dalton said.

Van tugged on his father's hand. "What do I call a duke?" he whispered.

Dalton glanced at Alec.

"You can call him uncle," Alec said in a tight voice.

The empty place in Dalton's chest began to fill.

What did that mean? Was Alec willing to hear his side of the story?

He didn't dare hope too much.

Alec's eyes softened a fraction. "Is it true what the lady said about our mother?"

Dalton nodded. "Losing you fair killed her. She's afraid to leave the house."

"Why's she afraid?" asked Van. "Is there a bad man outside the house?"

"She thought there was," Dalton said.

Alec met his eye. Dalton saw a tentative understanding there.

"O'Roarke was an orphan," Alec said. "We've no family in New York." He straightened. "My wife died in childbirth and her parents are gone."

Poor Van. "You have a mother," Dalton said. "And Van has a grandmother. Her name is Abigail. She lives at Osborne Court in London."

Van cocked his head. "Do I truly have a grandmother?"

"You do." Dalton dropped to his knees on the muddy quay. "She has your father's same green eyes. And she owns at least five fluffy cats. Ten maybe. I dunno." He scratched his head and made a face. "All look the same, those fat orange tabbies."

Van laughed delightedly. "That's a lot of cats. Does she have sweets to eat?"

"Cupboards full."

He nodded decisively. "I'd like to meet this grandmother."

"Well, I don't know. That's up to your father." Dalton stood.

"I think it could be arranged," Alec said gruffly. "And what did the lady mean about you avenging our father's sins?"

"Now that's a *very* long story," Dalton said. "One that involves sword fighting. And dark alleyways."

Van's eyes lit. "Like Rob Roy?"

"Something like."

"Sounds interesting," Alec said, a tentative smile playing across his lips. "Care for a pint?"

Dalton nodded. "I might at that." He glanced down at Van. "May I?" he asked Alec, holding out his hand.

Alec grunted. Dalton clasped Van's hand.

They walked along the pier, two men and a boy.

Thea had been right again about Alec being able to give Dalton a chance.

She was always right, damn her marmalade curls.

But she was wrong about one thing.

The instant he took Van's hand, he'd had a sudden, blinding realization.

He loved Thea. Deeply.

Irrevocably.

He'd leave her for a time, as she'd commanded, but damned if he wouldn't fight to have her back in his arms.

With his brother striding next to him, and his nephew's hand in his, anything seemed possible.

And the world agreed. The driving rain had been chased away by brave sunshine and the world was sharp-edged and saturated with light.

And damn if there weren't faint, shimmering bands of color across the sky like the memory of Thea's smile chasing away the darkness in his heart.

His heart.

The one beating wildly inside his chest, pumping hope through his body.

If his brother could begin to forgive him . . . if they could talk about the reasons O'Roarke stole him, maybe Dalton could convince Thea to give him another chance.

He wasn't going to let this be the end.

"Look," said Van, pointing at the sky. "A rainbow."

Chapter 25

"Wake up, dearie. Wake up now." Aunt Emma bustled into Thea's bedchamber, followed by Aunt Hen, the two of them rustling about, drawing drapes and poking grates.

A shaft of sunlight flitted across the cheerful red-and-yellow quilt.

Thea rubbed her eyes. "What time is it?"

"Half ten, you lazy thing. And you've a visitor. Hurry now," Aunt Emma urged.

"A visitor?" Thea sat bolt upright, her mind racing ahead to the duke in the parlor, pacing back and forth, very much the handsome rogue in that dark blue coat that matched his eyes.

"Oh yes, sweetheart," said Aunt Hen. "A big brute of a fellow carrying the most enormous parcel."

Thea thrust off her covers and jumped out of bed.

Aunt Hen smiled indulgently. "Only he's not the duke, dearie."

"Oh no, not the duke. Says he's the duke's manservant," Aunt Emma said. "Though he doesn't much look like any manservant I've seen."

Thea strove to hide her disappointment. Why was Con here? Had Dalton sent him to talk to her? Her heart sped again as she quickly ran a soft-bristled brush through her curls.

She scrubbed her teeth at the washbasin as Aunt Emma and Aunt Hen fussed about, laying her gown out on the bed and fetching her stays.

"No time to waste, dearie," Aunt Hen said, clucking her tongue against her teeth when Thea was dressed. "Lace up those smart red boots now."

"Did you clean them? Oh, how kind of you." Thea gulped back a jag of emotion when she saw those brave boots, all the mud gone, glowing strong and red yet again.

Thea flew down the stairs. "Con!" Dear old Con, ducking his head and tugging on his gray beard, hiding his pleasure behind a gruff façade.

"Grand day, isn't it, my lady? I brought you something from the duke." He hoisted a large, flat package in his hands. "He said you've been look-ing for this."

It couldn't be . . . was it the self-portrait? It was wrapped in white linen. Tears pricked her eyes. Thea was fairly certain what lay beneath that linen and twine.

Con set it against the wall. "I told him he should come himself but he was that set on leaving for London today."

Her heart fell. "He's gone?"

"Afraid so, my lady. He left with Alec . . . Mr. O'Roarke . . . and his young nephew only an hour ago."

"With his brother? And his nephew? Are you sure?"

Con grinned. "Sure, and I'm sure. I don't know what you said to that duke, but he told me he turned right back around after he left Ballybrack and returned to the docks. Convinced that brother of his to go with him to London and meet their mother."

"Oh, Con, that's wonderful!"

Thea just knew that discovering her son was alive, and meeting her grandson, would heal the dowager duchess of her ailment and free her from her self-imposed prison.

"But . . . you didn't go with him, Con? Does that mean . . . Mrs. Barton . . ."

His whiskers retreated into his collar as he smiled shyly. "Well now, Bronagh didn't try to kill me with her bare hands. It's a start. And she did allow me to sleep on the sofa instead of putting me out to pasture with the cattle. A very hopeful sign, if you know Bronagh and her ways."

"And Molly? Is her mother very angry with her?"

"She came round. Even ate some mussels after I steamed them in beer the way she used to love."

Thea clasped her hands together. "I'm happy for you, Con."

He cleared his throat. "There's something else. Nearly unbelievable 'tis. The duke's appointed me landlord at Balfry House. Going to see about leaving it to me, permanent like. We're to restore the tenancy. And ensure rich lands for the farmers to till." He blinked rapidly. "And Molly's the proud owner of a library-full of books. She'll never read them all."

"Won't she love that?" It was Thea's turn to blink back tears.

"And this isn't the only gift for you, my lady. He said the entire contents of the attic were to come here, to Ballybrack." He glanced around the small room doubtfully. "But the Lord only knows where you'll put them."

"How magnanimous of the duke." A small voice in Thea's head couldn't help but wonder . . . were the paintings a parting gift?

Thea turned away from the concern in Con's kindly blue eyes.

"He only pushes you away because he cares for you," Con said. "Think back on your childhood. Did you ever have a lad pull on your plaits? He only did it because he fancied you."

Thea shook her head. "I never had any playmates."

Con frowned. "Well, trust me when I say we men are a heathen lot. Undeserving of your sweet smiles. And the duke more heathen than most. Don't give up on him, my lady."

"I told him to leave and never come back."

Con tugged at his beard. "And did you mean it?"

"I . . ." Thea closed her eyes. "No," she finally whispered.

"Well then, it'll all work out, I've no doubt. Just remember, my lady, sometimes the good Lord reveals his plan in his own time. To make life more interesting like."

"Will you stay for tea, Con?"

"Nah, I've got to get back to Bronagh before she changes her mind." He set his cap back on his head. "I'll be seeing you soon, my lady."

"Goodbye, Con."

Watching him leave, Thea realized the journey was truly over. Dalton had gone back to London and she was here, where she'd wanted to be, with Aunt Emma in Ireland. She should be happy.

Aunt Hen and Aunt Emma hurried into the room.

"What did he want?"

"Did he give you a message from the duke?"

They fluttered around Thea, fluffing her hair and guiding her toward the package.

"Unwrap it, dearie!" Aunt Hen said.

"It's a love token." Aunt Emma sighed. "Oh, this is all so romantic."

A love token . . . or a parting gift, to assuage his conscience. Thea hesitated in front of the package, reluctant to unwrap it.

"Where's my mother?" she asked her aunts.

"Abed with a headache. I still can't believe what she said to the dowager," Aunt Emma breathed.

"I know," Aunt Hen agreed. "It was magnificent."

"Wasn't it, though?" Thea had been very proud of her mother for taking a stand . . . and for defending Thea.

"I've scissors for that twine somewhere," said Aunt Emma, eyeing the linen-wrapped parcel. She searched through the sewing basket that perched on a table near her favorite armchair by the fire. "Ah-ha!"

With a swiftly pounding heart, Thea cut the twine and Aunt Hen helped her remove the linen.

"Careful now," Thea breathed when her suspicions were confirmed by the sight of a gold frame and cracked oil paint. "She's two hundred years old."

"Oh my," her aunts exclaimed in unison.

Oh my, indeed.

A shaft of sunlight from the mullioned windows illuminated the emerald green of full sleeves and the rich brown of an artist's smock.

Artemisia stood, black hair glowing, her head tilted at an angle, one arm poised, brush in hand, the other arm braced on a stone surface, holding her palette.

From her letters, Thea knew that in its day the painting had sparked an outcry of controversy.

A woman portraying herself as the epitome of the arts.

A bold, fierce statement to make.

"Why, she's lovely," Aunt Hen exclaimed. "So full of . . . *strength,* somehow. As if she might leap off that canvas and cross the span of time to be with us here in this room."

A fall of soft light, deftly portrayed, illuminated half of Artemisia's face, the contrast of light and dark imparting a sense of pathos . . . as if she were waiting to be fully lit.

Like Thea. Waiting for her day to shine.

That day had come. An idea occurred to Thea and she nodded her head. "I'm going to hold an exhibition of all female works of art. And if I can find enough, the paintings will all be self-portraits." It was perfect. A fitting way to reintroduce Artemisia to the world.

"What a wonderful idea, dearie," murmured Aunt Hen. "And so you must go back to London, mustn't you? For you can't have such a grand event here in Cork."

Go back to London. She'd only just run away from there.

"What does this mean?" Aunt Emma asked, peering closely at Artemisia's neck. "This pendant she's wearing."

The gold pendant around her neck shimmered in the sunlight.

Thea bent closer. "It appears to be a mask. Which would symbolize the arts."

"A mask. How clever," Aunt Emma said.

The mask symbolized art, but it held another meaning for Thea.

Artemisia was trying to tell her something. The mask Dalton wore had slipped and shattered. She knew the real man now.

And her own mask wasn't needed anymore. The timidity. The nervous giggle.

The fear of failure.

In such a short space of time she'd become something wholly different.

And by giving her this gift, Dalton was trying to tell her something as well.

He believed in her dreams and her goals . . . and he wanted to be part of them.

"Oh, my dear." Aunt Emma reached behind the painting. "There's a letter here! It was nearly lost behind the painting." She handed a folded sheet of paper to Thea.

With suddenly trembling fingers, Thea unfolded the paper. She recognized the sprawling, confident hand immediately.

"I think I'll take a walk down to the shore," she said abruptly.

Aunt Emma smiled warmly. "Of course, sweetheart. I'll fetch your cloak."

Balfry House, County Cork, Ireland

Dear Self-Portrait,

I see now why Thea wanted to unveil you. You are, quite simply, breathtaking. Gloriously female. Uncompromisingly powerful.

You don't suffer any nonsense from difficult beasts who don't know how to speak the things they truly wish to say.

Can you forgive me for allowing you to molder in my attic so long?

You see I have no heart.

But that's only because I left it with you.

> *Sincerely,*
> *Your unerringly foolish . . .*
> *Duke*

A tear splotched across the page. Followed by another.

Thea folded up the letter before the ink became too blurred to read again.

Was he saying he loved her?

If so, it was a roundabout way of expressing the sentiment. But at least he'd admitted that he wasn't very good with words.

And he'd done all of those wonderful, kind things. Given Balfry to Con and Bronagh. Gifted all the books in his library to Molly.

Aunt Emma had Hen now to stay with her and keep her company at Ballybrack and help with the beekeeping.

Con had Molly, and Bronagh, and her sons to fill that enormous house with laughter and love.

She knew in her heart that Dalton had sent the letter to her family because he'd thought he was protecting her from regrets. He'd gone about it in a completely crackbrained way . . . but it had come from a place of caring.

Maybe he just didn't know how to tell her he loved her.

She hugged the letter to her chest, staring out over the misty green hills and foggy cliffs of Balfry Bay.

As much as she loved it here, perhaps Ireland wasn't her home any more than London.

Maybe home was more than a location. It could be . . .

Dark, midnight eyes that took no prisoners, yet transported her to a place of freedom.

An intriguing indentation softening an uncompromisingly angular jaw.

Strong, powerful arms around her, bordering the world with heat . . . and desire.

The wind whipped her curls into her face and she pushed them away impatiently as she climbed back up the steps to the cottage.

She had a letter of her own to write.

And another journey to begin.

Chapter 26

Two long weeks later

"**V**an and I are walking to the square," Abigail announced. "His toy soldiers wish to launch a campaign next to the fountain."

"It's not a fountain, it's the Berezina River," Van amended. "Napoleon's forces must cross . . . or die horrible deaths."

"Ah yes." Abigail nodded soberly. "Silly me, I forgot."

"That sounds nice," Dalton said nonchalantly. He'd been waiting for this moment since Patrick and Van arrived.

He nodded at Baum, his mother's German lady's maid, who stood by Abigail's armchair with near-excitement in her normally staid and stolid brown eyes.

Baum curtsied. "I'll fetch your bonnet and cloak, Your Grace." She practically ran from the room.

Osborne Court, silent and shrouded for so long, now echoed with Van's laughter and incessant chattering. The boy couldn't seem to sit still or stop talking for more than five minutes at a time. And he terrorized the poor cats, which were accustomed to ruling the house, capturing them and subjecting the plump peach beauties to the indignity of a six-year-old's kisses.

When the cloak was wrapped and the bonnet tied, and a dancingly impatient Van had been chided by his father for pulling on the dowager's hand, the entire party—Abigail, Van, Dalton, Patrick, and a phalanx of footmen—walked to the front door, and the dowager set her foot outside the doorway for the first time in ten years.

She took a tentative step out the door and her green eyes clouded over.

Dalton held his breath, prepared to bundle her inside, but then Van grabbed her hand.

"Well, come *on*, then," Van said, tugging on her hand. "Don't be a slowpoke."

"And what on earth is a poke?" the dowager asked. "My, how American you are." She stroked Van's head. "I hope your soldiers are proper British subjects at least?"

Van cocked his head. "I'm not sure. They're all made of tin. And they can't talk, you know. Wouldn't that be something? A talking toy. Why can't they invent one of those?"

"Because you chatter enough for everyone," Patrick said affectionately.

And they were down the front steps and walking across to St. James's Square, Van chattering the whole way, a steady stream of boyish enthusiasm that carried along the dowager duchess.

Abigail walked with short, trembling steps over the lawn of the square . . . but she walked.

And Dalton's heart soared.

There had been moments of joy since he'd left Thea in Ireland, and moments of pain. But the need to have her by his side never flagged.

She should be here to see this triumphant moment. It was all because of her.

Dalton had written her another letter but he hadn't posted it. He'd said what he wanted to say in the letter he'd left with Artemisia's portrait.

He knew Thea had to make the choice to contact him.

That he couldn't push her into anything. She had to be ready to forgive him.

He'd been such an ass. *Could* she forgive him?

"Well, would you look at that," Patrick said, shaking his head. He refused to be called Alec, but that was all right. The most important thing was that he was here.

Dalton cleared his throat as an answer.

The two brothers understood each other perfectly now.

They didn't have to speak much. They communicated in other ways. By helping each other, and taking care of Abigail and Van.

They'd had one long conversation in Dalton's library at his bachelor apartments that had involved some exceptionally potent Irish whiskey.

Dalton had told him all about being the Hellhound. And how Trent was hunting him. And Patrick had spoken of his law practice. And the impoverished clients he assisted with suits against powerful, corrupt men.

When they opened that second bottle, the ideas began to flow.

It had been Patrick's idea to dig into Trent's past even harder, using the information Dalton had gathered in his nights at the gaming hells, and combining it with his brother's status as a counsellor to uncover more secrets they could use against him.

And what he'd found—Dalton hadn't even been able to believe his ears. Flat-out treason.

It had been Dalton who'd cornered Trent late one night, outside his own house, and laid out the evidence to him in a manner he hadn't been able to refute.

Because he was unconscious on the cobblestones. With a note pinned to his vest enumerating his crimes.

Trent had left England the next day. Back in Paris, most like. But he'd never dare show his face in England again.

Which had led to further brotherly collaboration.

Foxford retreated to a hiding hole next.

And then Marwood developed a sudden desire to journey to an alpine village in Switzerland.

Admittedly, those two were grudge targets, but they deserved exactly what they received.

Dalton had packed up his bachelor apartments and moved in to Osborne Court with Patrick and Van.

He wasn't going to hang up his mask forever,

but, little by little, he began to focus more on the legal possibilities of prosecuting evil without the use of fists.

Getting a bit old for the beatings.

Shoulder still creaky from the cracking blow he'd dealt Albertson in Bristol.

Patrick still maintained he wouldn't stay in England long, that his practice was in New York, but Dalton had high hopes of finding a way to convince him to stay.

All Dalton had to do was find Patrick a British second wife.

He was passably handsome, Dalton supposed—he *was* his brother, after all—and in line to a dukedom. That ought to help. Even though he spoke with an American accent and preferred inferior cigars.

Maybe Thea would be able to help find his brother a suitable bride when she arrived.

If she arrived.

If she could find it in that strong, loving heart of hers to forgive him for pushing her away.

He missed her every second of every day.

During the long, lonely nights, he missed her most of all.

Every day he had to wrestle with himself not to saddle his horse and start riding for Ireland.

He'd had several letters from Con, the hoary old bastard, informing Dalton that he'd delivered the painting, and that Molly had read half the books in his library, but still asked about a position as a cabin boy on one of Dalton's ships.

The last line of Con's latest missive, slipped in

there as if it were of little import, informed Dalton that Bronagh had agreed to be Con's wife.

Dalton still couldn't picture Con as a family man.

But then he'd never pictured himself pining for a petite lady with an inconvenient habit of not listening to a damn word he said.

He'd even taken to writing her truly terrible verses. Even worse than the ones he used to compose at Cambridge.

When he visited his friend James, Duke of Harland, at his town house, he performed dramatic readings of his poetry between glasses of Harland's excellent brandy, to his oldest friend's everlasting amusement.

Roses are fine. Violets are well. For Thea I pine. Without her it's hell . . . and if she doesn't come soon I'll tie her up, hoist her over my shoulder, carry her back to London, and throw her across my bed.

Well, not *quite* a classic quatrain.

But James completely understood, because he was so thoroughly besotted with Thea's half sister Charlene.

Dalton had been running from the fact that he needed love his whole life.

Now he knew love didn't make people weak. It drew them together, bonded them into something so much stronger. So much more powerful.

Now he had a house full of loving family, but he needed *Thea's* love and her belief in him more than anything.

He was a hair's breadth away from storming to

Ireland and fetching her when the letter finally arrived.

County Cork, Ireland

Dear Unerringly Foolish Duke:
   After decades moldering in your attic I can finally feel light on my face again! I am very much fussed over, of course. And they tell me I am to travel to London, to meet the governors of the British Institution.
   How grand that will be!
   Throngs of admirers. Mounds of roses at my feet.
   It's only my due, after all.

Waiting to be adored,
The Self-Portrait of Artemisia Gentileschi

Coming to London, was she? Waiting to be adored? Surely that all boded well.

Though it had been written as the damned painting, not as Thea.

And she'd told him quite unequivocally that she didn't wish for adulation. She wanted freedom.

Could she be happy with him?

He wouldn't have to wait long now to sweep her off her feet and kiss her so masterfully that she would say yes to anything at all he might propose.

It was fine spring weather. No rainy delays. She should be here within two days at the most.

So he waited.

And waited.

Rehearsing the right words to say.

Dreaming of what he'd do with her in his great big lonely ducal bed.

Because a bed wasn't welcoming at all without a demanding, delectable Thea in it.

And when he had her in his bed . . . he'd never let her go.

Chapter 27

One even longer week later . . .

"I'm late," Thea announced.

The extremely correct and proper-looking butler who'd answered the door at Osborne Court stared at her blankly. "Pardon me, madam?"

"I told the duke I would arrive a week ago."

"I see." The butler stared disdainfully down his long nose, obviously considering the best way to eject her without dirtying his spotless white gloves or scuffing his polished shoes.

Well, who could blame him? She was dressed like a trollop. A *Swedish* trollop.

"Please inform His Grace that Olofsson is here to see him."

He looked her up and down. "Just . . . Olofsson?"

"That's right." Thea shook her head and her un-bound hair swished over her shoulders.

The butler's eyebrows raised in an impeccably butlerish manner. "Please wait here, *madam.*"

It didn't take long for him to return.

"Just as I thought." The butler sniffed. "His

Grace did not order any . . . *services*. And so I must bid you adieu, madam."

He shooed her back out the door.

Thea refused to be shooed.

She planted her red boots on the marble tile. "Tell him Olofsson refuses to take no for an answer. Tell him she demands satisfaction."

"Does she now?" a deep voice asked.

Thea's heart thumped.

Dalton stood at the top of the stairs, staring down at her forbiddingly, so handsome it rendered her momentarily speechless.

How she'd missed the bold, powerful lines of his jaw and the enticement of the deep cleft in the center of his chin.

Thea raised her own chin. "She does."

The duke strode down the stairs.

"What is the meaning of this?" he asked with mock sternness.

Thea cocked her hip. "Didn't you receive my note, Your Grace? Why are you so surprised to see me?"

He gave her a devilish grin and hoisted her into his arms.

"Oh," she cried. "You'll crush my gown. And there's a jar of orange marmalade in my cloak pocket."

"I'll teach you a lesson," he growled. "About why it's not wise to keep a duke waiting for weeks."

The butler, clearly scandalized but struggling to maintain the indomitable composure of his profession, edged out of the way as Dalton carried her across the entrance hall and up the stairs.

She wrapped her arms tightly around his neck, thrilling to his nearness and the possessive look on his face.

"What are you wearing under that dress?" he whispered in her ear.

"Blue silk garters," she replied saucily.

"God, Thea," he groaned. "How I've missed you. Can you ever forgive me? I've been such an unmitigated ass."

"You forgot *puffed-up bastard*. Or how about *pompous tyrant?*"

"All of those," he whispered fiercely, clasping her to his chest. "And more besides."

He kicked open the door to his chambers and then kicked it shut again.

"You belong in my bed, Thea."

He tossed her gently into the center of his bed and stared at her with dark intent.

Like any rake worth his salt.

"I'll tie you to the posts if you think of leaving me again," he said sternly.

"I didn't leave you, you crackbrain," she laughed. "You left me."

"Did I? Now why would I ever do anything as stupid as that?" His eyes turned serious. The bed sank as he lowered his huge frame beside her. "Will you . . . can you forgive me?"

Her heart beat so swiftly she thought it might sprint away and leave a gaping hole in her chest.

He wrapped her hands in his fists. "I was so

focused on revenge I couldn't imagine any other future. The possibility of a long, contented life with someone to love by my side."

Bringing her hands flat against his chest, he stared into her eyes. "I love you, Thea. I think I fell in love with you the moment you climbed atop me, stomped on my shoulder, and left an imprint across my heart."

She smiled through sudden tears. "Someone had to teach you a lesson."

Dalton wiped her tears away with his thumbs, stroking her cheek, eyes darker than a rookery alleyway.

"That's not all you've taught me. I've been running away from the fact that I needed love my entire life. Like a bloody fool. Having Patrick and Van here is so very wonderful. But nothing's complete without you. I've missed you, Thea. Desperately."

He brushed a rough thumb across her lower lip and she shivered. "I'm nothing without you. Please say you'll stay here with me. Say you love me."

"Yes," she said simply. "Oh, Dalton, yes. I love you. Quite irrevocably."

He gathered her into his arms and kissed her with firm, strong lips, setting her blood on fire and her body melting.

And that, Thea thought as he kissed her until she was half-mad with pleasure, *was exactly how to topple a monumental duke.*

Epilogue

Two months later

*The Duchess of Osborne's Painting Exhibition
    & Art Auction
Grand Gallery, Osborne Court*

"She's quite remarkable, isn't she?" Lord Haselby, the learned gentleman from the British Institution for Promoting the Fine Arts in the United Kingdom, remarked to his equally erudite companion, Lord Kingsford.

Thea stood behind them, watching as they peered at Artemisia's self-portrait, stroking their learned, barbed beards.

"See here, Haselby." Lord Kingsford hoisted a magnifying glass at the painting. "To follow Ripa's *Iconologia*, the mask on the chain around her neck should have the word *imitation* inscribed upon it."

"By George, you're right, Kingsford. What do you make of that?"

Thea drew closer. "The mask has no inscription because Artemisia was imitating no man. She was a true original."

Lord Haselby turned his magnifying glass on Thea. "Not much is known about her, Your Grace."

"No." Thea smiled. "But this portrait allows us to fill in some gaps. Do you know, gentlemen, that I have a theory? After studying this painting, I believe it was she, and not her father, who painted the allegory of *Peace Reigning over the Arts* on the ceiling of the Queen's House in Greenwich."

"You don't say," Lord Kingsford exclaimed. "Would you care to attend one of our meetings to elucidate on your theories, Your Grace?"

Thea inclined her head. "I would be honored."

"Now that ceiling, if I recall, was painted in 1636 and features Peace with olive branch and staff presiding over the twelve muses, who are each . . ." Lord Haselby launched into a long and dry description of the entire ceiling.

A possessive touch on Thea's elbow. Dalton beside her, a lock of burnished hair curved stubbornly over his brow, above midnight eyes.

"You must excuse Her Grace, gentlemen. She's wanted," Dalton said.

"Of course, Your Grace." The gentlemen made their bows.

"You looked as though you might need rescuing," Dalton whispered in her ear.

"I did, rather," Thea laughed. "I'm *wanted*, am I?" she whispered as they made their way through the milling crowd, who attempted to appear to be studying paintings but were mostly searching for gossip.

"Desperately," he growled.

"Not yet, my wolf." She smoothed her hands over the heavy satin of a new gown that shimmered with gold and green like the wings of a scarab beetle. Familiar red leather glowed merrily beneath the green. She'd had to wear the half boots tonight. Because the path through polite society was probably going to be muddy.

This was her first public appearance as the Duchess of Osborne.

In the gathering of humanity mingled every person who'd ever laughed at her. Who'd gleefully recounted her transgressions, crowned her Disastrous Dorothea, and borne witness to her humiliations.

But the whispers of the crowd no longer held the power to wound her.

She had too many people here tonight whom she loved. And trusted. And who loved and trusted her.

Dalton, of course. She squeezed his strong arm.

Her mother. She glanced around, finding the countess, regal as ever in a cool silver silk gown that mirrored the shining streaks of gray in her hair, talking to Dalton's mother, the dowager duchess, who was frail and thin, but still lovely with silver-streaked auburn hair and leaf-green eyes.

"Your mother looks well tonight," Thea said to Dalton.

"Doesn't she?" His eyes shone with love.

And then there was Thea's half sister Charlene,

the Duchess of Harland. They'd become the best of friends in the past months.

Where *was* Charlene? Thea scanned the crowded room but didn't find her.

Charlene's younger sister Lulu had a piece in the exhibition: *Self-portrait with Ruined Castle.* A delightful work, full of promise.

As they approached the grand staircase, Patrick's young son, Van, and Charlene's stepdaughter Flor, came whooping down the grand staircase.

Laughing, Dalton caught both of them in his arms before they could tumble into the crowd. "And just what do you two think you're doing?" he growled.

"Fighting a duel." Flor narrowed her green eyes at Donovan. "And I'm winning!"

"No, you're not." Van jutted out his jaw. "You're a girl. You can't win a duel."

Flor placed her hands on her hips. "Ha! That's the most ridiculous thing I've ever heard."

Dalton ruffled Van's red-tinged brown hair and set both the children down on the stairs.

"Up you go," Thea said. "Back upstairs. And try not to set the drapes on fire like last time."

They were always getting into trouble, those two.

Thea and Dalton reentered the crowd, stopping to nod and chat with their guests.

Thea overheard two matrons discussing their somewhat hasty union.

"They say the duke swept her off her feet at the conclusion of the ceremony and kissed her so thoroughly one of her aunts actually fainted dead away," one of the women said, her ostrich plumes quivering.

That rumor was entirely true.

A shiver chased down her spine as she remembered that epic kiss.

Which led to thoughts of the wedding night that followed.

And then her knees were too weak to support her.

"Ready for more?" Dalton whispered, propping her against him with a solid arm at her waist.

More what? Kisses?

Thea blushed.

"What are you thinking about, wicked wife of mine?" Dalton whispered, low and hot in her ear. "You're turning the most delectable shade of pink. I thought I'd cured you of that. I think you want more scandalizing."

"Later," Thea remonstrated. "Look," she said, to distract him. ". . . Isn't that your friend Lord Hatherly talking to Miss Alice Tombs by the Vigée Le Brun portrait? You don't see him venture from his den often."

"Why, so it is, poor Nick. Shall we rescue him?"

"I like Miss Tombs. She's terribly clever." Alice Tombs was one of Charlene's best friends, and the three ladies had spent many enjoyable afternoons together discussing new plans for Charlene's charitable ventures. The sale of several art works tonight would benefit her women's refuge.

Dalton raised his eyebrows. "And terribly odd."

Thea smiled. "She has her reasons."

As they passed, Thea caught a snatch of Lord Hatherly and Alice's conversation.

"But the lady's only wearing a thin drapery. She looks awfully chilly," Alice said, pursing her lips so her dimples deepened.

"It displays her . . . *attributes* . . . to the best advantage." That from the always-scandalous Lord Hatherly.

"But she's apt to catch the grippe and die of a bilious fever."

"It's only a *painting*," Thea heard Lord Hatherly say, with a dazed expression in his gray eyes.

As Dalton steered her toward the balcony, Thea noted with pleasure that the Duke and Duchess of Harland stood just beyond the glass balcony doors, leaning over the railing, their shoulders touching.

The air was warm outside, and scented with the jasmine that twined over the balcony railing.

"There you are," Thea said when she and Dalton joined them. "Are you hiding?"

"We were kissing," Harland announced, his green eyes sparking.

Charlene swatted his arm. "James."

"Well, it's true, my love."

Thea surveyed the crowded gallery through the glass doors. "Really, one medium-sized scandal would have been enough to lure them here. And we've provided at least four large ones."

"Four?" Dalton asked. "That many?"

"Exhibits A and B," Thea said. "The Scandalous Duchesses."

Charlene smiled, her blue-gray eyes, so similar to Thea's own, sparking with laughter. "The courtesan's daughter and her runaway half sister."

"Exhibit C." Thea swept a hand toward the glass doors. "The Dowager Recluse making her first appearance in society in over a decade."

"Exhibit D," James proclaimed. "The Prodigal Spare, returned from the dead."

Thea found Patrick in the crowd. He stood, tall and commanding and nearly as sinfully handsome as his brother, talking to a pretty girl in a pale pink gown.

"You see?" Thea crowed. "Four large-sized scandals. They hardly know which one to gawk at first."

"Speaking of scandal, there's Alice and Hatherly," Charlene said. "We'll go and fetch them. James has a flask in his pocket."

She and James reentered the room, leaving Thea and Dalton alone.

"I think you forgot one of the scandals, little lamb," Dalton said.

"Did I?"

He backed her against the French glass doors.

"You forgot this one." He laced his arms around her and claimed her mouth with his strong, sensual lips.

She sighed, leaning in to the kiss, thrilling to the danger. She didn't even care that the *ton* might see her green satin-covered arse pressed against the glass panes.

Because every single time they kissed, she tumbled deeper in love with her husband.

The green hills of Ireland would always wait for her.

And London had become far more welcoming.

But Dalton's arms around her?

That was *home*.

And don't miss the first sparkling romance in Lenora Bell's Disgraceful Dukes series,

HOW THE DUKE WAS WON

The pleasure of your company is requested at Warbury Park. Four lovely ladies will arrive . . . but only one can become a duchess.

James, the scandalously uncivilized Duke of Harland, requires a bride with a spotless reputation for a strictly business arrangement. Lust is prohibited and love is out of the question.

Four ladies. Three days.
What could go wrong?

She is not like the others . . .

Charlene Beckett, the unacknowledged daughter of an earl and a courtesan, has just been offered a life-altering fortune to pose as her half sister Lady Dorothea and win the duke's proposal. All she must do is:

- Be the perfect English rose [Ha!]

- Breathe, smile, and curtsy in impossibly tight gowns [blast Lady Dorothea's sylphlike figure]

- Charm and seduce a wild duke [without appearing to try]

- Keep said duke far, far from her heart [no matter how tempting]

When secrets are revealed and passion overwhelms, James must decide if the last lady he should want is really everything he needs. And Charlene must decide if the promise of a new life is worth risking everything . . . including her heart.